Laurel Velarde

It was fifteen years since she'd held her baby in her arms. It seemed like forever. Now she was being given a second chance, a chance to meet her teenage child for the first time. She packed up and headed for Cortez, Colorado, without a second thought.

Joe Buck

A tribal policeman on the Ute reservation in Colorado, Joe was suspended for reckless endangerment. That shouldn't have surprised him; he'd always been a maverick, too proud to ask for help. Then he met Laurel. When he found out her life was in danger, his pride didn't matter anymore....

ABOUT THE AUTHOR

The Lynn Erickson writing team has almost as much fun researching their stories as writing them. Both Carla Peltonen and Molly Swanton are now in the "empty nest" stage of life—and loving it! "We have so much more time to travel and research now," they say. Research for *Laurel & the Lawman* was particularly interesting, as they investigated recent events on the little-known Ute Mountain Ute Reservation in southwestern Colorado.

Carla and Molly live in Aspen, Colorado, and have been writing as a team for more than fifteen years.

Books by Lynn Erickson

Don't miss any of our special offers. Write to us at the following address for information on our newest releases.

Harlequin Reader Service
U.S.: 3010 Walden Ave., P.O. Box 1325, Buffalo, NY 14269
Canadian: P.O. Box 609, Fort Erie, Ont. L2A 5X3

Lynn Erickson

Laurel & the Lawman

Harlequin Books

TORONTO • NEW YORK • LONDON
AMSTERDAM • PARIS • SYDNEY • HAMBURG
STOCKHOLM • ATHENS • TOKYO • MILAN
MADRID • WARSAW • BUDAPEST • AUCKLAND

ISBN 0-373-70614-6

LAUREL & THE LAWMAN

Printed in U.S.A.

Laurel & the Lawman

PROLOGUE

GRADUATION DAY. Laurel Velarde couldn't believe it. Four years of high school had come and gone, and now it was June and she was graduating. Yes, there it was, right on the program she clutched: Berkeley School for Girls, Class of 1978.

Laurel looked down at the program, then up at the audience, the proud parents, sisters, brothers, aunts, uncles. She spotted her mother in the back of the crowd, very smartly dressed, her expression neutral. But Laurel's stepfather hadn't come, it seemed. Typical. Probably had a golf game. As for her real father... Well, she hadn't seen *him* in two years.

She took a deep breath as the principal droned on at the podium. She was aware of her friends sitting close by, looking nervous, anxious, happy. There was Sandra Garcia on her left, actually taking notes about the ceremony. And Meg Delgado sitting directly in front of Laurel—Meg who wanted to become a crime reporter. Oh, and there was Kim, Kim Tanaka, standing in front of the platform taking pictures for the summer edition of the school newsletter. God, they'd all worked so hard on the paper this year, put out super editions and become so very close. Laurel sat there and wondered what she would have done without these friends.

The truth was that everyone else in her life seemed to let her down. Her own mother cared only about her second marriage and barely knew Laurel was alive, except, that was, to control her, to make sure Laurel didn't do anything to embarrass her. Her stepfather... What a self-centered jerk! Never once had he asked what Laurel wanted. As long as she stayed out from underfoot, that was fine with him. In fact, as long as Laurel did what everyone else wanted her to do, they were happy. Maybe that's why she kicked up her heels too often and rebelled. She was just trying to be her own person. And then there was her real father. Was he even still living in Berkeley?

Well, there was a lesson to be learned from these adults: don't put too much trust in them, because they'd sure as heck disappoint you.

But she had her friends. *They* understood. And, of course, there was Gray. Gray Baxter, a college man, who not only understood Laurel but loved her.

None of them knew her secret, though, and she couldn't tell them, not yet, not until she was sure of what was going to happen. Oh, she wanted to let the cat out of the bag so desperately that it was tearing her up inside, but she was afraid. It had only just happened, after all, and she wasn't even sure yet how she really felt, what course of action was open to her. God it was scary!

"... Class of '78 is going to make its mark on the world," the valedictorian was saying at the podium now, but Laurel wasn't hearing a word. Instead, she was thinking about her secret, the immense responsibility that was now on her shoulders. There was no hiding from this behind her usual defenses, rebellion, quick retorts, her so-called free-spirited nature. No.

What she had to do now was to trust. Her friends, yes, but most important, she had to put her faith in Gray, who saw so clearly past all her defense systems and treated her as an intelligent, mature adult. Together, she and Gray would work this out.

"...My honor and privilege to have been asked to speak at this ceremony" came the voice of the guest speaker, someone's very important father, and Laurel tried to concentrate. This was, after all, her graduation day. But it wasn't long before her mind wandered again. After the graduation dinner party tonight, she and Gray had a date. She'd tell him then. When they were alone. Sure. And she'd just say it straight out: *Gray, I'm pregnant.*

CHAPTER ONE

JOE BUCK WALKED the desolate land of his ancestors. It was night, and he was alone except for his dog, an odd-looking, mottled mutt of indeterminate heritage. Joe was a Ute Indian of the Ute Mountain Ute tribe, and he had some thinking to do, some problems to sort out, as he strode across the desiccated, broken mesa-land of the reservation in southwestern Colorado.

The land around him was warm and dark; the moon was rising, a faint glow on the eastern horizon, and the stars were out in splendid array, spilled like fistfuls of diamonds on black velvet. Joe thought of the stories his grandfather had told him about the constellations, not named for an alien race called the Greeks, but named for Ute heroes and heroines and the all-powerful bear, the puma, the coyote. And then Joe had to tear his mind away from the comforting old tales and focus on his problem. He got angry all over again and tried to still the reaction, walking, listening, calming himself.

"Okay," he said aloud, and Dog perked up his tattered ears, wagged his stump of a tail. Joe ignored him. "Okay," he said again, "so maybe Charlie Redmoon's right, maybe I blew it big time. Or maybe he's just getting too old, too set in his ways."

Unfortunately, Charlie Redmoon was his direct superior, captain in the Bureau of Indian Affairs Law

Enforcement Services, the federal police force on the reservation, and Charlie had just that day put Joe on suspension for what Charlie had termed reckless endangerment—of Joe himself.

Reckless endangerment. Joe walked the broken land and felt humiliation churning in his gut. He was thirty-four years old, and Redmoon had treated him like a wet-behind-the-ears rookie. And the worst part was, he'd probably deserved it.

Ahead of Joe the land rose, twisted and cracked in the passing of the ages, an unforgiving land that held no water and baked, day after day, year after year, beneath a merciless desert sun. Land that no one wanted. How generous of the whites to have given it to the Utes, he thought derisively, the Utes who'd freely roamed the Rocky Mountains from Wyoming to New Mexico, from Denver to Salt Lake City, who'd stepped so lightly on the earth that no footprint had been left. What a bargain, this land.

Joe Buck walked, breathing deeply and evenly, never stumbling in the dark, as if he possessed a sixth sense that told his sinews and muscles where each rock lay, where the land was split before him. He moved silently and tried to reason with himself as he came to the top of the rise; ahead, in the distance, the mesas beckoned, their sharp lines delineated even in the soft moonlight. He walked miles, and breathed in the pure, sage-scented night air, and tried to release the tension, tried to figure out how he'd gone wrong.

An owl hooted somewhere off to the west, as if in answer to Joe's thoughts. Sure, Joe had almost gotten his butt shot off yesterday by Neil Dawes. Hell, the guy had been having a good spat with his wife, and the neighbors had called the police. Joe really didn't blame

Neil for being so damn mad he'd leveled his shotgun on Joe. It'd been tense there for a bit, but he'd handled it, hadn't he? He'd known Neil Dawes since they'd been boys together, and he hadn't been about to call in reinforcement for a simple domestic dispute.

But Charlie Redmoon had worked himself into a fit, accusing Sergeant Joe Buck of pulling one too many Lone Ranger routines. "You can't go off half-cocked like that!" his boss had stormed. "We're a team. We're professionals. We follow procedure. Can't you get that through your thick skull? Joe, damn it, this is the last straw!"

Joe had stood there, tall and tight-lipped, stiff with embarrassment and indignation. He'd thought of throwing his badge and gun on Charlie's desk and quitting the force right then and there, but something held him back, some indefinable realization that he wasn't a quitter, that he wouldn't turn tail and run. He'd gotten himself into this mess; somehow he'd get through it.

Joe was a modern native American, well-educated, immensely proud and often troubled by the direction some of his fellow tribesmen took. There was too much alcoholism, suicides, disease and poverty, and too few of the reservation children sought a higher education. It was a battle within Joe—tradition versus the realities of the modern world. He knew that in order for his people to survive they had to plant their feet more firmly in this century, and yet the world the white man had created was plagued with greed and violence, and it lacked respect for the land, for Mother Earth.

But the whites, at least, were beginning to see the light and take steps to correct their past disrespect for the land.

His own people, however, needed to search a whole lot harder for that balance. As yet, Joe Buck knew, the native Americans of the western United States had not melted into that immense pot of humanity that was America. There had to be a balance, and men like Joe were struggling to attain it.

He moved on into the night and thought a lot about these things and realized that, despite the esteem Joe had for him, his boss Captain Charlie Redmoon was getting to be a part of the problem on the Ute reservation. Certainly Charlie was a good medicine man. Certainly he was highly respected in the tribe for that, but Joe had to deal with him in a different setting, and at headquarters it was starting to show up—Charlie was definitely stranded in a vanishing past, becoming unable to cope with the enormous influx of tourists who visited the reservation now that gambling had been legalized and casinos were popping up like mushrooms after a spring rain. Times were changing fast, but Redmoon wasn't, and his inability to handle the rise in crime due to the number of visitors was becoming painfully obvious.

Okay, he thought, so Redmoon's days were numbered. That was true. But old Charlie—and Superintendent Thomas, Joe reminded himself—hadn't been entirely wrong when they'd suspended him. He *should* have called for backup; Neil Dawes was no angel and had pulled a shotgun on intruders more than once. Maybe, just maybe, Joe should have put aside his damn pride and asked for help.

"Reckless endangerment," he muttered aloud. Joe stepped lightly on the dry, stony soil, his arms swinging easily, his midnight-black hair pulled back into a ponytail, his faded blue shirtsleeves rolled up, his jeans

well-worn, fitting snugly over a flat belly and lean hips.
He felt absolutely safe, as at home walking this vast
dark land as a city dweller turning a neighborhood
corner. He automatically registered the night sounds,
checked them for potential danger, wrote them off—
the crack of a twig under a deer's foot, the far-off
warbling cry of a coyote and the haunting answer. Tonight was singularly quiet, though, yes, very quiet, and
Joe and his dog added no more to the silence than a
faint whisper as they passed the clumps of rabbit brush
and sage, the ledges of crumbling red rock, the gully
that this late in the summer season held only dust.

He walked and he tried to come to terms with his
immediate problem: Should he simply throw in the
towel and quit? Maybe even kiss the reservation goodbye?

He mulled that over and found that the very notion
of leaving this land left a foul taste in his mouth. This
was his home; these were his people. He'd gone out
into the world—to college and then a stint in the U.S.
Army—and, in his opinion, the reservation, even with
all of its problems, still offered a better, cleaner life.
Hell, he was a pure-blooded Ute Indian and he could
deal with whatever problems arose. He could swallow
his pride and try to learn from this experience. Sure he
could. He'd deal with it by looking inward, the way
Orientals have always done, and not looking outward
to a confessor or a psychologist or a self-help group,
the way Europeans might. His mind craved privacy, the
security of the natural world around him and maybe,
later, a sweat bath for purification. Sure, he could
cope. He was coping when he'd driven his old Scout up
to the cabin he used for hunting in the fall, left it there
and set out walking hours ago. He was far from any

people, far from towns or outlying ranches or even scattered herds of cattle or sheep. There was nothing where he strode but what had been there when the white man came over a century ago—spiders and snakes, coyotes, birds, rodents, tough grass and stunted, dryland brush, rocks. He liked it that way. It gave Joe a feeling of peace to be alone in this vastness. Not that it belonged to him, for it didn't: he belonged to it.

Charlie Redmoon, he thought again, but his mood had finally changed and he could no longer conjure up the anger that had fueled his abrupt departure from headquarters that afternoon. Hey, things would work out. They always did one way or the other. And then he smiled to himself. He sounded like an old Chinese philosopher—either that or a whacked-out teenager.

Dog growled then and stopped short. The rising moon glinted off a long white canine tooth as he raised his lip. Joe halted and watched him for a time; Dog did not believe in false alarms. What was out there? Joe stood absolutely still and tested the air with his ears and his skin and his nose.

Yes, he heard something when the faint hot breeze touched his face, carrying far-off vibrations. A mechanical grinding, as out of place here as an ice cube in hell. And a faint, cloying smell—diesel fuel.

"Come on," he said softly to Dog, and they went toward the sound, gliding as silently as two dim ghosts among the bunch grass and hillocks, displacing only the air of their passage.

The sounds got louder, a definite noise now, engines, vehicles. What in God's name was going on out here in the middle of nowhere? This area was still on the reservation, and Joe would know if a project were going on, but he knew nothing of this.

Louder. An insistent, gear-clashing civilized noise, like a construction project. And now the stronger whiff of diesel exhaust reached his nose. Trucks?

He slowed his pace and held a warning hand out to Dog. He saw the white flash of headlights sweep the land; dust rose in clouds in the beams of light. He heard a man's voice, then more engine noise. A low ridge of rock lay between him and the activity. Silently Joe moved behind the ridge, lay flat near the top and looked over.

He had to let his eyes adjust for a few seconds, then he could see clearly. There were trucks, a caravan of heavy eighteen-wheeler flatbeds, all parked now. A bulldozer worked feverishly, and a kind of backhoe with a long arm that was unloading and laying down something on the ground, its arm like a dinosaur's neck, swinging slowly, methodically.

Joe climbed over the ridge, closer, trying to see what the machine was unloading. Garbage? He couldn't think, could barely comprehend what these behemoths were doing out here in the middle of the night. Laying a pipeline? Digging a new oil well? No, the equipment was wrong.

Lights swung wildly across the landscape, crisscrossing, just like in the old World War II movies when the antiaircraft searchlights came on. Joe crouched, watching, fascinated, curious.

Abruptly one of the lights brushed him, went on, stopped, reversed, impaled him on its beam. He heard a man shout something. Dog growled. He stood, suddenly feeling naked, and wished he had his badge and gun, some token of his office.

"Hey," he called, "What the . . ." A sound whistled by his ear and he threw himself flat before his mind comprehended what it was. A shot. A shot from a rifle.

He scrabbled backward on the ground, scraped by gravel, the light stabbing at the darkness, trying to find him, then he was up and over the ridge, his heart pounding drumbeats in his ears. "Goddamn," he whispered, "guess they don't want company."

Crouching, he ran, and then there were twin beams sweeping the high desert, searching for him, and he heard an engine and the bumping of an empty pickup over the rough ground.

More shots. Dust kicked up in the headlights. Joe ran, zigzagging, using the scant cover, his breath hoarse in his throat. Nowhere to hide, just rolling mesaland, sparse grass and brush. Damn! And everywhere he dodged, the truck kept after him, losing him, finding him, its lights twin demons cleaving the darkness.

For a time he thought he'd lost it in a dry wash and stopped to catch his breath, kneeling, a hand on Dog's head, and then he'd felt the vibrations as the truck hurtled around a corner of the wash, its lights right on him, and he'd had to go on, shots thudding into the ground, whining by his ear like a pesky insect.

The moon was fully up now, grinning down on him, lighting him up for his pursuer. Bad luck. Dog panted, racing alongside him, his tongue hanging out like a pennant.

Joe knew there was a road ahead, not far now. Not a main road, but there'd be someone on it, someone to flag down and get him the hell out of there, away from the manic killer in the pickup. He must have run for miles. He was hot, covered with dust, feeling like a damn fool. A damn fool in a real bad position.

Someone better be on that road!

He ran, the truck's gears ground and its headlights swung toward him, bumping too fast across the uneven terrain. Maybe it'd drop an axle, Joe thought, serve him right!

The moon glared down on the strip of road, gleaming on its dark surface, casting shadows on either side where there were shallow ditches.

No cover, damn it! No cars! Too late! The pickup was behind him, closing. A bullet whined by. He ducked, dodged, ran into the sagebrush next to the road.

He felt the pain in his arm before the crack of the rifle sounded. He swore, grabbed Dog and threw himself into the ditch as the pickup roared toward him, in its element now. He lay there, breathing hard, his arm burning like the fires of hell, and whispered up a prayer to the old gods.

SHE WASN'T TIRED. It was late—or depending upon how you looked at it, it was very early in the morning—and she should have been beat, but Laurel Velarde was wide awake.

Most people would have felt lonely out here in this country, in the middle of nowhere, really, and at this hour, but Laurel had been on her own too long, and worked in some pretty remote regions. She was used to going it alone, and tonight she was feeling just fine, enjoying the utter solitude of the black ribbon of road stretching endlessly before her. Plenty of time for thinking.

She drove and listened to the radio, amazed that she could so clearly pick up stations from such vast distances: Oklahoma, Los Angeles, even Nogales, way to the south and across the Mexican border. Her favorite, though, was the Navaho language station from the huge Navaho reservation to the south in New Mexico and Arizona. The tribe there had 200,000 members, unlike the small Ute tribe, whose reservation she was on now.

Every so often, every ten or fifteen miles, a big eighteen-wheeler would come screaming along the arrow-straight road behind her at ninety miles an hour or better and pass her white Honda, rocking it, the semi's red taillights fast disappearing into the inky blackness ahead.

Laurel drove and tapped her fingers on the steering wheel to some Spanish music—salsa—playing on the radio. She thought about the day, a productive day, and switched her thoughts to the lead for the article she'd write on the rock-climbing expedition.

"If blood-tingling adventure is what you're seeking, Citadel Rock in the Ute Tribal Park near Mesa Verde National Park is not to be missed. The climb is not for the faint-of-heart or the weekend..."

No, Laurel thought, too many negatives. Her editor at *Travel Adventure* magazine would red-pencil it to death. The idea of the magazine was to encourage adventure-seekers to try the unusual, to take that next step, not to discourage the reader.

"Okay," she said, still tapping her fingers, she'd begin the article on a positive note. "Citadel Rock in the Four Corners region will provide hair-raising thrills for even the most seasoned rock climber."

That's better, she thought as she recalled that afternoon with the group of four climbers—three men and a woman from Boulder, Colorado, who'd urged her to try the first hundred feet of the perilous wall of rock on the Ute Mountain Indian Reservation. She'd made it up thirty or so feet and then chickened out, her heavy, braided hair wringing wet from the tension. Whitewater rafting, Laurel could handle that okay. Hiking dizzying twelve-thousand-foot trails was a cinch. Helicopter skiing in British Columbia was manageable, and trekking the banks of the Amazon could be...well, exciting. But hanging on to a rope on a precipitous mountainside was just a little too much, even for the cocky thirty-three-year-old Californian.

The team of climbers had laughed at her, all in good humor, of course. And she'd scribbled her notes and shot four rolls of film and teased them right back, saying, "Maybe you have a death wish, but not me, guys, thank you very much," all the while aware that rock climbing wasn't her primary reason for being in Colorado. Maybe her whole life-style was an attempt to fill that aching, empty place where she had once, oh so briefly, held her daughter.

Laurel checked her watch as the road made a long, graceful sweep around a mesa and then straightened again. It was late. And she still had fifty or sixty miles to go before arriving back in Cortez. She could sleep in tomorrow, though. And the next day, too, if she wanted. But after that life was going to get real busy.

The trip to Cortez and the Four Corners region was no spur-of-the-moment notion for a magazine article. Laurel had, in fact, been planning this for months. No, she thought, correcting herself, she'd actually been planning this move for more than three years now, though she hadn't known her exact destination. That had been determined by a California private detective and a whole lot of money. It was worth it, though. Worth every last dime the creep had milked out of her and all those months of hellish frustration to find out that a particular fifteen-year-old girl was living on a ranch in Cortez, Colorado, with her parents, Earl and Fran Schultz.

A deer was caught in her headlights and standing stock-still in the middle of the road. She jammed on her brakes and swerved while the blood pounded through her heart, and then the doe leapt away, disappearing into the clumps of sage.

Laurel let out a breath and felt the tremors in her fingers. That was close. She'd been sailing along, paying no attention whatsoever to her speed or the road, and it didn't take a rocket scientist to know that deer abounded out here in no man's land. If you hit one— at this hour of the night—you'd be lucky to get help before morning, if you lived through it, that was.

Laurel checked the speedometer, then fixed her eyes on the road ahead, straining to see into the darkness. She wouldn't think about the girl, best to concentrate on the road. It was pointless to fantasize about meeting her at last or to wonder if her scheme was going to be too transparent. The girl, whose name was Holly, would arrive at the little rental cottage, put in a few hours' gardening, mowing the lawn, and no one would be the wiser. Laurel was just another renter in Cortez for the summer who'd needed some part-time help and called the high school and got a list of names of willing students. No big deal.

Except it was a big deal. The biggest of Laurel's life. And in a few short days this teenager was going to walk up the weedy drive and knock on the door.. . .

Forget it, Laurel told herself. What was going to be was going to be. And things were seldom what you'd expected, anyway. In reality, this might not work out at all.

She switched the radio to a station out of Phoenix, Arizona, that was playing oldies, lively stuff, and she forced herself to pay attention to the road. She thought about the reservation and the sparsely populated country of the Four Corners. It was sure a different place to be raised. It was all so open, so incredibly big. To the north the majestic San Juan Mountains of the Rockies stretched away, still snow-capped in the middle of summer. To the east the land rolled greenly until it reached the flatlands of the Great Plains. To the south and west was mesa country, fantastically formed, endless and empty except for the huge stone monolith called Shiprock that floated on the undulating desert, visible for hundreds of empty miles. It was almost chilling, this immensity, and yet the Indians called it home—the Pueblo Indians, the Navaho and Hopi, the Apache, the Ute and the gone-into-the-mists-of-time Anasazi.

"Twist and Shout" played on the radio, and Laurel sang along, reminding herself that soon she'd see the lights of Towaoc, the town that acted as headquarters for the Ute Mountain reservation and was pronounced "Toy-ak"—a Ute word meaning "all right." Cortez was just beyond Towaoc. She sang and drove, still watching for game on the road, and thought about the beauty of this land, the boundlessness of it—a land that few people ventured into. Indian country.

CHAPTER TWO

THE HEADLIGHTS CAME UP behind Laurel so fast she was startled, and when they kept coming, too bright in her rearview mirror, she slowed down and pulled over to let the madman pass. That was when he came out of nowhere, an apparition lurching onto the road in front of her right into the glare of her headlights. She slammed on her brakes as a cold-hot spurt of adrenaline shot through her, and screeched to a rattling halt, plowing onto the shoulder and raising a cloud of dust that obscured everything.

Gripping the steering wheel, Laurel gulped in a lungful of air, her blood rocketing in her veins. She hadn't hit . . . ? But there was no time to even finish the thought, because suddenly the passenger door flew open, and a big man, an Indian, jumped into the seat. A dog slid in beside him like a shadow.

"What?" Laurel gasped.

"Drive," he said harshly.

She sat there staring at him, dumbfounded. There was blood on his shirt and dust all over him.

"Drive!"

"But . . ."

"Goddamn it, lady, get the hell out of here!"

She jammed her foot on the accelerator and the wheels spun as her car careened crazily back onto the road. The vehicle that had been coming up behind her was gone now, and there was only the long black ribbon of road. She thought for a split second that she should be scared to death of this strange man in her car, but she was still too shocked to muster up fear.

She drove, foot down, as fast as she could. He didn't say another word, but she noticed he kept looking around, in front, behind them, out over the dark landscape. He didn't have a gun or a weapon of any sort, not that she could see, and he wasn't threatening her. He just seemed to want to get away from there—fast. She thought about that and checked the rearview mirror. No lights. Nothing. But there *had* been a vehicle back there, and it had sure disappeared quickly, as if it wanted out of the area fast.

She gave the Indian a quick sidelong glance. She should jam on the brakes, order him out. She really *should*. But somehow Laurel knew he wasn't going to budge. He'd probably just leave her by the side of the road and take her car if she stopped. And she sure as heck couldn't throw him out herself.

"There's blood on your shirt," she finally said, looking straight ahead now at the road and the twin tunnels of light her high beams made. She noticed only then that her limbs were shaking.

"Yeah," he said.

"Somebody's after you," she tried, feeling braver.

"Brilliant deduction."

"You almost got yourself killed. You jumped right in front of my car," she began.

"Sorry. I didn't have a lot of choices."

She drove faster, eighty miles an hour, eighty-five. She liked driving fast. Maybe she'd scare him into begging to get out if she went fast enough. Silence hung between them like a heavy weight. He could be dangerous, a criminal, a murderer. He could be running from the law, and she'd be arrested as an accessory because he didn't have a gun on her. She shot another glance at him and saw his profile, high-bridged nose, strong chin, bronzed skin where the moonlight caressed it for a moment.

"Where you going?" she asked eventually.

No answer.

"Did your car break down?"

He shot her a look but kept his silence.

"Well, where do I go?" she asked, exasperated.

"Straight ahead, lady. This car go any faster?"

"Maybe, but I don't," she said coolly. Nevertheless, she pressed on the accelerator a little.

The miles flashed by. There still hadn't been another vehicle on the road when the lights of Towaoc appeared ahead. Not many lights—Towaoc was the governing seat of the Ute Mountain reservation, but it was only a small roadside village, really.

"Do you live there?" she asked.

No answer. She was getting mad and curious, too. Okay, she'd given the guy a ride, gotten him out of a tight spot, but he could be polite, at least. And he could get out of her car as soon as possible.

"You know," she said, "I think you owe me some sort of an explanation, buster. I don't have a clue what's going on with you, but there is one thing I'd like to know: are you the good guy or the bad guy in this lousy movie?"

He said nothing for a minute, as if deciding, then finally, grudgingly, he spoke. "I'm a sergeant in the Bureau of Indian Affairs Law Enforcement Services. Someone back there was trying to kill me."

Laurel let his words sink in as her pulse once again quickened. Someone was trying to kill him? "How do I know you're telling the truth? I want to see your ID. Maybe you're a mad rapist, for all I know." She applied the brakes, slowing as Towaoc got closer.

"I'm off duty. I don't have any ID on me."

"Uh-huh."

"Lady, it's true."

"My name is Laurel."

"Okay, Laurel."

They were passing through the town now, but there wasn't a soul on the road. It was too late.

"Okay, say I believe you. Where do I drop you?" She slowed even more. "Well?"

"I'm thinking."

She was passing one of the few lighted buildings in town, the police station. In black letters over the door were the words Department of the Interior, Bureau of Indian Affairs, Law Enforcement Services, Towaoc, Colorado. She stepped on the brakes.

"Not here," he said.

"But you're a . . ."

"Go on, keep going."

"Some policeman," she muttered.

"Where do you live?" he asked.

She almost said Berkeley out of habit. "Cortez."

"Okay, go there."

"Sure, mister, whatever you say."

"My name is Joe Buck, Sergeant Joe Buck."

"Okay, Joe," she said, stepping on the gas, passing the lighted casino now and the sign that read Cortez— Eleven Miles. After they'd left behind the brightly lit casino, the moon slid behind a cloud and it was utterly dark out. And late. And here she was all alone with this big Indian and his dog in her car, but she wasn't exactly frightened anymore. After all, if he'd wanted to hurt her he'd have done it already, back when he'd first jumped in her car, back where the only witnesses were the creatures of the black, empty night.

"Are you really a cop?" she asked then.

"You talk a lot."

"You don't talk enough."

"I don't have anything to say right now."

"Why were you out there in the middle of nowhere?"

"Walking my dog."

She snorted. "Come on."

"You don't want to know."

"Sure I do. I'm curious. It isn't every day I get my car commandeered."

He gave a kind of laugh and turned his head to look out of his window. His neck was strong and brown. He had a hand on his misbegotten mutt's head, as if to reassure it. His fingers were long with big joints, his forearms strong and sinewy.

"How's your arm?" she asked, continuing on the highway toward Cortez.

"Sore."

"You need to see a doctor."

"You order everyone around like this?" He turned and leveled black eyes on her.

"If they need it."

"My arm's okay. It's only a graze. I'm not going to a doctor."

"That's right. Doctors have to report gunshot wounds."

"That's not why. The bullet only nicked me and I don't need a doctor. I need to lie low for a while."

"What're you hiding from?"

"Whoever tried to kill me back there."

"Okay, I forgot for a minute."

"You sure have a smart mouth on you."

"Want to get out?"

"Just drive," he said.

Cortez was ahead now, quiet and mostly dark. The moon was high, casting a silvery light on the landscape. Laurel should have been exhausted, but she wasn't.

"Where do you live?" he asked.

"Four blocks from downtown. On Cottonwood Street. A little house."

"Take me there."

"Hey, wait a minute...."

"I need a place to lie low, I told you. Just for tonight."

"You're not invited."

"I didn't ask for permission. I need a place."

"I'll take you to a motel."

"Like this?" he asked, gesturing to his bloody, dusty clothes.

"Well, you can't stay with me. I don't have room."

"I don't need room."

Laurel stopped the car at a dark residential intersection. "This is ridiculous. I don't know you. You cannot stay at my house."

"Do you have a garage?"

"What?"

"A garage."

"Yes, but..."

"Put your car in it. They might have seen me get in your car back there. They might have your license plate number. They might be looking for you."

"Hey," she said, "whoever it was had his chance back on that road. I don't really think..."

"*Whoever* it was," he said, "was taken by surprise. By now he's probably kicking himself in the butt for letting us get away."

"Great."

"Sorry." Then he gestured with a hand. "Go on."

She drove. Crazy, she thought. This whole thing is crazy. Why did she always run into these insane situations? Other people didn't. But she attracted risk like some women attracted men.

Laurel stopped at the base of her drive and stared straight ahead. This was her chance. She could leap out and start screaming bloody murder. She could. But what if he really was a cop and someone was after him—and now maybe after her, too? He sure didn't seem as if he was going to hurt her, or anyone else, for that matter. All he'd asked for was a place to lie low till tomorrow. And she couldn't quite imagine him just walking out of her life, not now. She just couldn't resist her own curiosity.

"Well?" he was saying.

"Well, what?" she said, deciding.

"Are you going to put the car in the garage or sit here all night?"

Laurel let out a breath. "You're being straight with me?"

"A hundred percent, lady. Now can we get off this street?"

"Uh-huh," she finally said and, wondering if this wasn't the biggest mistake of her life—or next to the biggest—Laurel drove into the blackness of the garage.

She unlocked the door and flipped the lights on inside the kitchen, then closed the door to the garage behind them. Joe Buck took a quick look around, then seemed to relax, feeling safer inside. It was still very hard for Laurel to believe all this was really happening. But there he stood, this big Indian, in the middle of her cozy kitchen, with blood on his shirt, his dog crouched at his feet.

"Why was that truck after you, anyway?" she asked.

But all he said was, "That's something I'd give a helluva lot to know myself." And then he turned his back on her and began rummaging around in her cupboards until he found a bowl, which he filled with water and set on the floor for his dog, who lapped at it greedily.

"That's an ugly dog," Laurel said.

"Yeah, he is. But he's smart."

"What's his name?"

"Dog."

Joe Buck moved around her kitchen with a lithe grace, as if he owned it. He wet a towel, gingerly patted at his arm where the fabric of his shirt was torn and bloody. He grimaced and Laurel flinched.

"Is it bad?" she asked, still standing there uncertainly.

He shook his head, then unbuttoned the blue shirt and stripped it off, favoring his left arm. He sat down on one of her cheap stainless-steel-and-plastic chairs and leaned his elbow on the table, twisting to see the wound, pressing the wet towel to it.

Laurel swallowed. He was a big man, broad and muscular with a permanent, coppery tan. He seemed to dwarf her kitchen. A thought flashed through her brain: here she was alone in her house with a half-naked Indian and she had absolutely no reason to trust him!

"You need soap or antiseptic or something," she said.

"Do you have any?"

"I'll look."

Relieved to have something to do, she went down the hall to the bathroom and opened the medicine cabinet. Everything she did had an unreal quality, as if she were watching a film of herself. Her mother would have called this another of her "wild and crazy" acts. But suddenly, Laurel was overwhelmed with the effects of a long day. Perhaps her judgment wasn't the best. She pulled a tube of antiseptic cream off the shelf and a box of Band-Aids. She couldn't let him bleed to death, now, could she?

The house Laurel had rented was set up much like a small, one-bedroom apartment. The living room and kitchen faced the street, and behind them off a short hall was a bedroom and a bath. She'd had to pass through the living room to fetch the antiseptic, and on her way back through she paused and stared at the telephone. All she had to do was snatch it up and dial 911....

"Forget it," came his voice, and she felt her blood freeze as she moved toward the kitchen again and drew a bowl of warm water from the tap.

"Sorry," he said to her from where he still sat cleaning his wound, "but I mean it, no calls."

"Right," she said, and she set the water on the table and stared at him. "Here, let me," she said.

He gave her a look, then handed her the towel. She dabbed at the nasty furrow on his brown arm, at the crusted blood. "Does it hurt?"

"Yeah, it hurts."

She tried to clean away the clotted blood, dipping the towel in the water again, and she had to rub at it harder. She could feel him flinch. "Sorry," she said.

He only grunted.

The bullet had not penetrated but had torn his skin and left an ugly gash that had bled a lot. She wiped carefully at his skin around the wound, her stomach tightening a little. It looked as if it had stopped bleeding, at least, but she was sure a doctor would want to put some stitches in it. "It's not pretty," she said.

"Are you going to be sick?" he asked in an exasperated tone.

She straightened abruptly. "No, of course not."

"Get on with it, then."

She wet the towel again and went back to work. His hair was glossy black and straight and heavy, the tendons in his neck taut. She could smell the faint odor that rose from him: sagebrush, desert dust and dried sweat. A heady aroma. His skin was singularly smooth, satiny and cool. She breathed shallowly, as if to avoid inhaling his scent. But still it made her faintly dizzy, and the melting in her belly made her feel weak. It was the blood.

"You okay?" he asked.

"Uh, fine," she said, realizing her hand had trailed away from his arm. She drew in a deep breath and took hold of his arm to steady it, rubbing, dabbing. He never moved again, not once, but her fingers on his skin burned, and she had to fight the urge to snatch them away.

"You really should go to the hospital. This could get infected," she finally said.

"We already discussed that option."

"Well, you can't stay here forever," she said. "You do realize that, don't you?" She kept dabbing, rubbing harder now, almost wanting to see him flinch.

"I need some time to think," he said finally. "I need to sleep."

"I'm beginning to think this whole thing's a bad mistake. You can go to a motel. I'd be nuts to let you sleep here."

"Why?" he asked, oh-so-innocently.

She dropped the towel in the now-pink water. "Because I don't want you here. How do I know what kind of person you are?"

He looked at her, a faint smile pulling up the corner of his mouth. "Yeah, that's right, I could be that mad rapist, couldn't I?"

"A girl can't be too careful."

"Don't flatter yourself, lady."

"Laurel."

"Okay, don't flatter yourself, Laurel."

Tight-lipped, she put some of the antiseptic cream on his arm, then picked up the box of bandages. He quirked a dark brow at her.

"What," she said, irritated. "They're all I've got."

He raised his good arm, untied the red bandanna from around his head and held it out to her.

"God, this *is* a lousy western," she said, taking it and tying it around his arm. "You'll probably get gangrene from this rag." Then, when she was done, she sat down and sighed. "You should have an antibiotic."

"Are you a nurse?"

"No, a magazine writer, but everyone knows about antibiotics."

"What magazine?"

"Travel Adventure."

"Never heard of it."

"I don't suppose you would have." She got up and put the kettle on. "You want some coffee?"

"God, no. I told you, I need to sleep."

"Decaf?"

"Okay."

"Then you'll really have to go. It's almost morning, anyway."

"What'll you do if I don't leave?"

"Don't push me, Sergeant Buck. I'm capable of almost anything."

In answer he got up and let his dog out the back door. He hadn't put his shirt on yet, and suddenly Laurel found that terribly disturbing in the small kitchen with its cheerful wallpaper and yellow countertops. His black ponytail hung down his neck like an exclamation point, dissecting the brown expanse of his body.

The teakettle whistled, and Laurel busied herself making coffee. She was beginning to feel a weary heaviness. She yawned. God, she'd love to get rid of Joe Buck and go to sleep herself.

They sat at the bright yellow Formica-topped table and sipped at the coffee. He took his black, she noticed. He'd also put his shirt on carefully over the wounded arm and let it hang unbuttoned over his jeans. His chest was tanned and smooth.

"So you really are a policeman," she said.

"Yeah, I really am. Eight years now."

"Then why won't you call the police if you really think someone was trying to kill you? Why won't you call them now?"

"The Cortez police?" He laughed. "The incident happened on the reservation. It's Indian business." With a quirk of his mouth, he said, "Bad blood between the white-eyes and the injuns," and she couldn't tell if he was joking.

"Then for God's sake call your own police. Why didn't you want to stop in Towaoc? I don't get it."

"What is this, the third degree?"

"I think I have a right to know."

He sat there considering that for a time, his dark brows drawn.

"It's a long story," he finally said.

"I've got time."

"Let's just say that my boss wouldn't take real kindly to hearing I got shot."

"It wasn't your fault, though."

"Yeah, well . . ." he said. "Redmoon, my boss, that is, wouldn't quite see it that way."

"I don't get it."

"Like I said, it's a long story. And besides, I don't even know why I got shot, not yet, anyway."

"So what're you going to do? And what *was* going on out there?"

"I'm not sure. Something illegal, and I sure wasn't supposed to see it."

"The plot thickens," Laurel said in her best stage voice.

"I've got to get some sleep." He stood, went to the back door and opened it to let Dog in, patting the animal on his head.

"Not here," Laurel said staunchly.

But Joe Buck didn't respond to her in any way. He just stood there staring at her, as if deciding something. "Okay," he finally said, and she knew he'd made a decision.

"Okay, what?" she asked warily.

"I can't figure out any other way," he replied, but it was almost as if he were talking to himself. "Come on."

"Where to?" she asked, and backed off a step.

"To your bedroom, to sleep," he said, then he took her arm in a surprisingly gentle grip, but there was steel under the velvet. His face was close to hers, his eyes dark.

"Wait a minute," she said, shrinking away from him. Her voice sounded oddly weak to her own ears.

"We both need sleep. It's the only way," he repeated, and steered her down the hall toward her bedroom.

She dug her heels in and stopped. "No," she said.

"No, what? I won't hurt you. I just need some sleep."

She jerked her arm out of his grasp. "No one manhandles me, buster."

He gave a short laugh. "I'm too damn tired to touch you. I want some sleep, and I need to make sure you don't stir things up while I get it. Come on." And he took her arm again, propelling her into the bedroom, flicking on the light switch.

"You wouldn't dare!" she said.

"Get into bed. I'm too tired to argue."

She sat down stiffly on the bed, on the foot of it, because the other side was shoved against the wall in the small room. She twisted, turning her back to him, thinking frantically.

"Want to take your shoes off?" he asked, and she heard his boots thump to the floor.

She wouldn't answer, she wouldn't respond in any way. She wouldn't turn around. This is what she got for picking up strange men in the middle of the night! God, what would her mother say to *this?*

"Look," he said, and she could hear him stripping out of his shirt, a small grunt of pain escaping him—his arm. *Good,* she thought. "Just lie down, next to the wall. I won't hurt you."

She refused to move.

"You don't want me to force you, lady, so please, just do it. We both need to sleep."

Force her? Reluctantly, her whole body rigid with indignation, Laurel eased herself onto the bed, as close to the wall as she could get. Damn him.

"If you move, try to get up, I'll hear you," he warned, and she bit back a reply.

Finally he turned the lights off, and then she felt the bed sag as he lay down. She inched even farther away, practically flattening herself against the wall, but she felt the bed move as he shifted.

"Want some covers?" she heard him say, but she refused to respond, lying there as stiff as a cadaver and, she hoped, as inviting.

"Suit yourself," he said, then he sighed, a long exhalation, and she could imagine his body relaxing.

She waited. *The bastard,* she thought, her body quivering with tension. He wanted her in his control, and she hated him for that. She couldn't bear anyone, especially a man, making her do something she didn't want to. It had become her credo. She'd learned the hard way, but she'd learned the lesson well.

God, this galled her! She lay there waiting, listening, too aware, totally awake, her muscles tense as coiled springs. She couldn't sleep, she'd never sleep. What did he think she was? Crazy, this whole thing was crazy.

After a time she heard the rhythm of his breathing change, heard it slow and deepen. He was asleep. Damn him. She thought of moving then, inching off the bottom of the bed, but something told her he'd wake up, and the mad situation would start all over again.

Laurel listened to his breathing and felt the bed move subtly with it. She tried to relax. She'd never sleep, though. Not with this renegade stranger next to her, so close she could hear his breath, smell the male scent of him. If she stirred an inch she'd touch him, touch his bare torso or arm or maybe his back.

She willed herself to relax. He wasn't worth all these mental gymnastics she was going through. Sure, it was a crazy situation, but she'd been in tight spots before. It was sort of her MO, wasn't it?

Damn. She moved ever so slightly, trying to get comfortable. The worst of her tension had abated somewhat, but she was sure she'd never sleep, despite her exhaustion. It was going to be a dreadful, endless night.

CHAPTER THREE

THE ELEVATOR DOORS HISSED closed; the crowded car began its ascent to the lofty heights of Denver's downtown Petroleum Building, and Jack Tolliver felt claustrophobic. For most of his forty-five years he'd worked outdoors, a trailer for an office, heavy machinery the tools of his trade.

He stood in the rear of the car and was aware of the smartly dressed executives keeping their distance. His khaki workshirt and trousers were dusty and sweat-stained, and damp lines of salt marked his baseball cap.

"Excuse me," a woman said, carefully shouldering by him when the elevator reached her floor.

Jack didn't move to make way; instead he sneered behind her back.

He was tired. He hadn't slept at all last night, but then he hadn't planned on making the eight-hour drive from Cortez to Denver, either. But what he had to say to the CEO of Blackwell International couldn't be communicated by fax or phone.

Jack stepped off the elevator at the penthouse level. Above was one last floor, housing the executive gym and restaurant—he'd never been invited up there, never would be. Hell, he was just a lowly geologist.

He stopped at the reception desk, telling the girl that he was there to see Mr. Tyler Grant IV. When she took in his sweat-stained attire and looked doubtful, he said,

"Just ring him, honey, he'll want to see me." And then he tried to prepare himself for what promised to be an ugly encounter.

When the girl buzzed his desk, Tyler Grant IV, CEO of the giant aerospace conglomerate Blackwell International, was sitting at his immaculate smoked-glass desk and staring out the tinted windows of the penthouse office south to the sixty-mile-distant colossus of Pikes Peak. He was contemplating neither the spectacular scenery nor the bludgeoning heat outside the windows of the skyscraper; he was thinking about his golf opponent's score that morning. The chairman of Denver's Commerce Bank, an old Yale roommate of Tyler's, had been cheating at golf since their college days. Everyone suspected it; but only Tyler knew it for certain. This morning at the elite Cherry Hills Country Club Harold had lost his ball in the woods on the fourteenth fairway, and what a stroke of luck he'd had, finding his ball like that right on the fringe of the fairway. Tyler and his partner had had to pay up in the locker room, Harold's team beating them by a single stroke.

Someday, the handsome, sixty-year-old Tyler thought, someday he was going to pay back that asshole Harold.

The buzzer sounded and shook Tyler from his reverie. When he heard that Tolliver was there he frowned, the perfectly tanned skin on his face crinkling. *What in hell... ?* "Show him in," Tyler said, a sense of foreboding scratching under his skin.

A minute later, Tolliver was sitting down across from him, eyeing the spacious, ultramodern office with a look of disgust on his weathered face, and Tyler Grant remembered how much he disliked the man—but then

Tyler had little use for anyone with a potbelly and a chip on his shoulder. Tolliver worked for Blackwell for one reason only: money. More money than the ex-Army Corps of Engineers geologist could make at any other job.

"I expected a call from Cortez," Tyler said evenly, his long fingers steepled beneath his chin as he fixed Jack with cool blue eyes.

"Yeah, well," Jack said, "I thought I'd be calling you from there myself."

"Has there been a snag, Jack?"

"Not with the unloading, Mr. Grant. That went like clockwork. The trucks all ran fine, the site I picked is still ideal, and..."

"Still? I think you better just get to the point, Jack."

Tolliver shifted in his chair. "There was a man out there last night, Mr. Grant."

"Out there?"

Tolliver nodded. "An Indian."

"And?"

"Well, I chased him down with the truck..."

"He was on foot?"

"Yeah. On foot. And I think I wounded him...."

"There was gunplay?"

Jack Tolliver swallowed. "No one heard a thing, Mr. Grant. I mean, this site is isolated."

"So what happened?"

"He got away. Someone came along and picked him up on the old road that..."

"Did this someone see you? The truck?"

"No, no. It was too dark. The whole thing was just a fluke and..."

"But this Indian saw our trucks? The site?"

"I don't know how much he actually saw. It couldn't have been much. And like I said, I wounded him. He might even be..."

"Goddamn it!" Tyler came to his feet and walked to the windows, a muscle working furiously in his jaw.

Tolliver squirmed. "I got a line on him, though," he said quickly. "I sent the trucks off safely and then scoured the entire area, and I found an old Scout, you know, one of those four-wheel drive..."

"Yes, yes, go on."

"...up at this old cabin. I got the license number, Mr. Grant, and this pal of mine works over at the Colorado Department of Vehicles and..."

"How in hell can you be sure the vehicle belongs to the Indian?"

"Well, it only makes sense, sir. The area's so isolated, and the car was there and the cabin was empty. Plus there was a dog with the Indian..."

"A dog," Tyler scoffed.

"What I mean is, there was a water bowl for a dog in the cabin. Anyway, sir, Mr. Grant, I plan on heading right on back to Cortez and finding that Indian. I'll take care of it."

Tyler whirled on him, furious. "Don't you think he's gone to the goddamn cops by now!"

"No, Mr. Grant. He's an Indian, like I said. He'd never go to outside police, not in a million years. I've worked around a lot of reservations in my day, and I'm telling you, the Indians distrust the white police."

"How about tribal authorities?"

"That's a possibility, Mr. Grant. But I don't see a problem there, either."

"Oh, really?"

"No, sir. See, they can't even keep up as it is with the workload they have, you know, what with all the new gambling and tourists and stuff on the reservation. And besides, when I was working near this other reservation, you remember, back in '85, well, the Indian cops are pretty damn lax. I mean, what's a gunshot on the reservation? They all have guns and hunt there. Even if this guy did go to the authorities, well, nothing'll come of it. They all seem pretty incompetent to me."

Tyler thought about that for a time. Hands jammed in his trouser pockets, he considered Jack Tolliver's words. "Okay," he said, trying to calm himself, "do what you have to do, Tolliver. Just make sure that Indian is silenced."

"I will," Tolliver said. "I just wasn't sure if you'd go along with that kind of...solution...you know."

"I don't give a damn what you have to do or who you have to do it to, just get the job done," he barked.

"I promise, sir, no problem."

But Tyler shrugged off his confidence. "Just you keep in mind that there're millions at stake here, Tolliver, billions if Blackwell keeps getting these government contracts. This is the sweetest deal to have come down the pike since the aerospace industry took a beating when the Cold War ended. We can't lose this contract, we can't let one single Indian screw this up."

"I understand."

"It's your neck, Tolliver," Grant added. "You want to see those kids of yours get a college education, you just keep in mind that the ball's in your court. Find that Indian."

"I said I would."

"Then for God's sake get to it!"

Jack left the office and rode the elevator back down to street level. Outside, the late-afternoon heat smote him and he swore under his breath. He was exhausted, too, and badly needed a night's sleep. Maybe he'd stop at his house in Lakewood, catch a few hours' rest before making that long drive again. Hell, he still had to get the name of the Scout's owner from motor vehicle registration. What if his buddy over at the department was on summer vacation?

He climbed into the pickup truck and switched on the air-conditioning, which was barely working. Sweat streamed down his neck. He had to get some goddamned rest.

Driving west toward the Denver suburb of Lakewood, Jack thought about what he'd just told that pompous ass Tyler Grant. Okay, so he'd informed him about the Indian, but there was another problem, the person who'd picked the Indian up on the road. Whoever it was had been driving a late-model white Honda. And the tags were from California. But Jack hadn't gotten the license plate number. If the Indian told the driver the whole story, if the driver was one of these do-gooder, get-involved types, there could be a problem there, too. Well, Grant had given him the go-ahead now. Jack's only hope was that the driver was staying in Cortez and he could find that white car. After all, it was a small town. Actually, if the driver wasn't from around Cortez, well, all the better. In fact, maybe the car had headed straight on toward California, in a hurry to get clear of the wounded Indian and problems that didn't involve him. Sure.

Caught in the heavy rush-hour traffic on the Sixth Avenue Freeway, Jack clung to that hope. The only trouble was he'd still have to try to find that car. But first, the Indian, that damn redskin who'd fled across the desert like a jackrabbit.

LAUREL OPENED HER EYES and stretched, and the first thing she wondered was why she was dressed. And then she remembered. . . .

Oh, my God, the Indian!

She smelled it then, bacon frying, and she had to fit her mind around the reality that someone—it had to be him—was in her kitchen cooking. Cooking!

Swinging her legs off the bed, Laurel headed for the bathroom. She had to go like mad, but more important she needed to think. In the light of day, well, the light of late afternoon, everything seemed too real—or unreal—she decided, locking the bathroom door and turning on the shower.

Laurel wasn't into hair blowers and makeup. Her life-style didn't allow for it. For years she'd worn her thick honey-colored hair in a French braid, and why wear makeup when those freckles on her nose couldn't be covered up with cement? Who would care? Who would she *want* to care? She had put Gray and his ilk behind her, but never her baby, the girl she was determined to find, if only to reassure herself that she'd done the right thing. Her daughter. The one chink in her armor.

Ten minutes later, the public Laurel emerged feeling fresh and halfway alive, clad in a clean white T-shirt and functional khaki shorts. She could hear Joe rattling around her kitchen, and it occurred to her to slip out the bedroom window and call the police, but no way—in a house this tiny she'd be caught in a flash, and, besides, he really hadn't harmed her. She could kill him for that stunt he'd pulled last night—but he hadn't hurt her.

She threw her dirty clothes in the bedroom hamper and then took a breath as she went to the kitchen. Once more into the breach, she mused darkly.

He was there, all right, Joe Buck, and his mutt was there, too, both of them sitting, Joe on a kitchen chair and Dog scratching at a tattered ear with one hind foot.

"He better not have fleas," Laurel said, standing in the door with her hands on her hips.

Joe Buck looked up from his plate. "Neither of us do," he said, deadpan.

"Enjoying my food?" she asked.

"Very much so, thanks. I made you a plate. It's on the stove."

"How thoughtful."

"Um," he said and went back to his scrambled eggs.

Laurel did sit down across from him with her plate. She was famished, and if she was going to have to spar with this big Indian, she'd need all the strength she could get.

"How's the arm?" she asked.

"Stiff. It'll work out."

"Maybe I should take a look at it, in case it's infected or something."

"I checked it out. It's okay."

"So you won't die of gangrene on my kitchen floor?"

"Not today," he said dryly.

She watched him as she ate. He'd showered—in her bathroom—and his hair was still damp, pulled back in the ponytail. The stubble of a sparse beard showed on his face, and she wondered about that—she'd always heard Indians had no body hair. But Joe Buck did. A little. A few very fine dark hairs on his face and chest, but the rest of him was all smooth, coppery brown skin over long, corded muscles.

He looked better, rested, a different person from the bloody apparition who'd burst into her car last night. A handsome guy with high cheekbones and a hooked nose and a wide, thin-lipped mouth. A Ute Indian, she thought, knowing absolutely nothing about the Utes, although she'd recently realized the state of Utah had been named after them.

"You didn't think to bring in the paper from the drive, I suppose," she said, chewing on the crispy bacon, and without warning she recalled with utter clarity the texture of his skin under her fingers, the way he'd smelled. She felt her cheeks grow hot and bent her head to eat.

"You want it?" he was asking.

"What?"

"Your paper."

"Oh, yes, I would like it. I always read when I eat."

"Never been married, huh?"

"How observant."

He ignored her remark, rose and went out to the drive, fetching the newspaper for her.

The fact was, she really didn't care if she read the daily paper or not. Having it delivered was a habit. But this particular paper she most definitely wanted to scan. While he did the dishes and actually got the bacon grease off the stove top, Laurel glanced through the paper for news of anything peculiar that might pertain to her Indian: an escaped convict, a thief on the loose, a mass murderer roaming the Four Corners area and picking up unsuspecting females with a wild tale...

"Disappointed?" she heard him ask, and she looked up sharply to find those black eyes fixed on her.

"I don't know what you..."

"Lying doesn't suit you," he said, folding his arms across his chest.

"I...okay, so I'd like to check you out."

"I told you, I'm a cop."

"Then let me call your headquarters and ask. I won't say anything else, I'll just ask if you're there. Maybe I'll get a description. That's all." That wasn't all, though. Holly would be coming soon, and Laurel could never involve her in a dangerous situation.

He studied her for a moment longer and then picked up the phone on the counter and walked it over to her, plunking it down on the Formica table. "Number's 555-3706. Go for it. Woman named Nancy Bearcross will answer. She's the dispatcher. She'll tell you anything you want to know."

"Good," Laurel said, dialing. She got right through. The woman, presumably Nancy Bearcross, was quite open on the phone once Laurel gave her a cock-and-bull story about having lost her purse near the casino the other day and Joe Buck returning it to her, and, gee, Laurel just wanted to say thanks.

"He's not here," Nancy said, "but I'll give him the message."

"Joe Buck, have I got the right name?" Laurel said.

"Sergeant Buck, that's him."

"A big guy, six-one or so? Long ponytail?"

"That's him. Always has that mutt with him, too. Dog."

"Right," Laurel said, meeting Joe's eyes.

"Anything else?"

"Ah, no, and thanks," Laurel said and hung up.

"Satisfied?" Joe asked, still watching her.

"Yes. And you can't blame me. This whole thing's weird. I just don't understand why you don't report what happened last night to the authorities. I mean, I can understand you not wanting to go to the police off of the reservation, that at least makes sense. But why not your own people? Surely you should file a report or..."

"Look," he said, spinning a chair around and sitting, knees splayed, arms resting on the back of it, "I don't know what's going on out there in the desert, but whatever it is, it's big. If I had to guess I'd say there was a million dollars' worth of heavy equipment and it wasn't out there for a picnic."

"So take it on as your own investigation at work."

He regarded her silently for a moment and then seemed to come to a decision. In a low voice he said, "I can't. I'm on suspension."

"What? I didn't hear you."

"Damn it, I said I'm on suspension. As of yesterday I got my butt kicked out of the office for two weeks."

"I see," she said slowly.

"No, you don't. Both Charlie Redmoon, my boss, and the superintendent think I'm a screwup and a maverick as it is. If I tell him I got shot, he'll have a stroke. And if I tell him I don't even know *why*..."

She cocked her head. "Okay, I believe you. Tell me one thing, though. Just why did he suspend you?"

He made a grunting noise that caused Dog to prick up his ears. "I didn't follow police procedure."

"Tell me."

"I went into a house alone to break up a domestic spat and almost got a round of buckshot pumped into my belly because I didn't call for backup. Are you satisfied now?''

"Yes," she said. "You *are* a maverick. Your boss is right. And you're pulling the same stunt all over again, aren't you?"

Laurel stood and picked up her plate then and walked to the sink, showing him her back, thinking. She supposed the events of last night made a perverse kind of sense now—at least Joe Buck's actions could be explained. Obviously he was feeling humiliated—he'd gotten suspended for almost getting shot and then he'd gone out and gotten shot! And he didn't even know why yet. The trouble was that she'd been inadvertently dragged into this mess. On the one hand it was certainly...intriguing. But she'd come to Cortez for a reason, a very important reason, and Joe Buck with all his troubles did not fit into the scheme. What if she offered to help him, at least let him lie low in her house for a while. What would happen to Holly Schultz?

Laurel finished washing her plate and sat it in the rack. She turned then and faced him, crossing her arms beneath her breasts, eyeing him as he was eyeing her. "I take it you have a plan," she said, crossing her ankles, her head cocked.

"The glimmering of one, yes."

"And does this 'glimmering' include me?"

He seemed to weigh that. He said, "Only to the extent of protecting you."

"Ha!" Laurel scoffed. "I don't need protection. I do just fine on my own, thank you very much."

"And if that dude who shot me got your license plate number? You can handle him?" There was a curl to his lip, a mocking, arrogant curl that made her hackles rise.

"Yes."

"You're a brave lady, but you're full of it," he said.

Laurel set her jaw. "I can handle myself, Mr. Joe Buck, *Sergeant* Joe Buck. Don't ever doubt that."

He was silent for a very long time then, quietly pinioning her with a hard glare. She couldn't help remembering how he'd handled her last night, panicking her, making her feel so helpless. And she wondered: Can I really handle myself? Maybe all her cockiness was put on. Maybe at heart, deep down where it really counted, she was just as scared and helpless as the next person. Oh, God, she thought.

"All right," she heard him say.

"What?"

"I said all right. I won't smother you."

"Smother me?"

"You know, hang out here till you're ready to kill me or something. But I can't let you go gallivanting around the country, either, not till I figure out just what's going on out on the reservation. Can you lie low?"

"Yes," she said emphatically.

"Good." Then he seemed to hesitate. "Uh, listen...about last night..."

"So, will you try whips and chains tonight?"

"I'm sorry. I didn't know what else to do. I had to get some sleep."

"You ever pull that kind of stunt again..." she said in a hard voice.

He held up a hand. "I won't."

"Okay." She continued to hold his gaze bravely. "So what is your plan?"

"Maybe it would be better if I kept that to myself."

"Going it all alone again? Isn't that what just got you in trouble?"

He gave a low laugh, admitting nothing.

"So tell me."

"Why?"

"Maybe I can help." She shrugged.

He laughed again and then sobered, his eyes rising to hers. "Well," he said, his face deadpan, "I figure I'm going to let the white-eyes circle their wagons and then I'll attack."

"You. All by your lonesome. That's real clever."

"I don't have a helluva lot of choice right now," he said. "If I had something concrete to take to Redmoon, well, maybe he wouldn't bite my head off for this bullet wound...." Joe raised his injured arm. "But as it is..."

"You want to prove yourself," she said. "Vindicate yourself."

"It's not that at all."

"Oh, really?" was all Laurel would allow.

Later that day, his torn and bloody shirt washed and the sleeves cut off to match, Joe told her he was going out. "I'll leave Dog with you," he said, putting on his wire-rimmed sunglasses.

She looked up from where she was typing at her messy living room table, which she called a desk. "So now you suddenly trust me?"

"Um," he said, "you've got a point. Let's just call it intuition." And with that he left, striding toward downtown Cortez and wondering just why he *did* trust her. There was something...

He rounded the corner onto the main street of the small, southwestern Colorado town and kept thinking about that and feeling uncomfortable. All his life Joe had lived and studied and worked among the whites, but he still had ambivalent feelings toward them. It was a tough situation for all native Americans. There was too much bigotry out there, that and the reality that it had only been a little over a century since his people had been soundly defeated by those pallid Europeans. Heck, Joe often thought, a hundred years was nothing. In time, though, the western tribes would be assimilated. History dictated it.

The streets of Cortez were crowded. Though the core was only a few short blocks long, a hodgepodge of brick buildings and false-front Old West structures, the town was filled to capacity in the summer. Recreational vehicles crammed the parking spaces and outlying campgrounds, motorcycles and rental cars filled the remaining spaces, and the ranchers and business folk complained constantly, though without the tourists the downtown would die.

They came to the Four Corners region for a number of reasons: camping, fishing, hiking, touring the ancient cliff dwellings. They came to gamble now, but only out on the reservation, a nation unto itself not governed by any laws but its own.

They poured down out of the snow-crowned San Juan Mountains into the heat of the high desert where the vast land was broken by towering red mesas and bizarre spirals of barren rock jutting from the desert floor.

They came to see the mountain to the west of Cortez known as the Sleeping Ute, because its silhouette resembled a man in repose, arms folded across his chest, toes sticking up. The saying among the Utes was that the mountain really was a "she," the folded arms actually a large bosom—some called her Dolly Parton. The tourists loved the joke.

They came to the saloons and leather shops and bought colorful ceramic bowls from the Ute Indian roadside stands. And they asked where the turquoise-and-silver shops were and had to be told that the Utes did not make jewelry. "Go to Santa Fe if you want jewelry" was the blunt suggestion.

They came in droves for three months out of the year, but the truth was that Cortez would never have survived if it weren't for the scattering of dryland ranchers and bean growers and the myriad of services the town provided to the adjacent reservation.

The Ute Indians roamed the streets of Cortez comfortably. Unlike their relatives to the south, the Pueblo Indians, the Hopi, the Navahos and Apaches, the Utes lived quite a modern existence. They had no true native dress, nor did they live in hogans or adobe structures. Their English was unaccented and full of hip jargon. They shopped with ease in the grocery stores and dined on Mexican and Chinese. A nomadic tribe from the Colorado mountains, the Utes had never settled for long in one spot—weather and hunting conditions dictating their movement—and thus their customs were far more flexible than those of their brethren. And so most of them fit tidily into Cortez society.

Joe stood on the street corner waiting for the light to change, and he thought about that, wondering why it was that some of his people fit in so easily while others would always straddle a fence. Couldn't the Utes maintain their culture and still exist in the modern world? Other societies did.

Joe was certainly trying to maintain a balance. The truth, the reality, was that, like it or not, the American

Indian, eventually, was going to have to come to terms with both the modern society that surrounded him and his native culture. It *was* going to happen, this assimilation, and depending upon each individual's reaction to this change it was going to be either difficult or smooth. He hoped he would play a part in it—he hoped he was worthy.

When the light changed he shook himself mentally and headed across the street to a saloon where he knew a lot of construction-type workers hung out. It could just be, Joe thought, that there was a legitimate operation going on out in the desert that he hadn't heard about. It was doubtful, but as a cop he wasn't going to eliminate any possibility.

He strode into the bar, took off his sunglasses and nodded to a few of the men he knew, then caught the bartender's attention.

"Well, hi there, Joe," Big Jim said. "Ginger ale as usual?"

"Not today," Joe said, and then he asked Big Jim casually about any new projects going on out on the reservation.

"On the res?" the bartender said, shaking his head. "Only thing I know of is a new oil find in the Southern Ute neck of the woods. Why? You looking for work, Buck?"

It took Joe a second to get it, and then he said, "Very funny."

Big Jim grinned. "Hey, it's a small town, buddy. Word gets around."

"Uh-huh," Joe said and he left, smarting, embarrassed.

He visited two other saloons, but no one was aware of any new project, and that was enough to tell Joe the operation he'd stumbled across last night was illegal. And then, of course, there was the wound on his arm.

Satisfied, he headed back down the street toward Laurel Velarde's house, devising a course of action. A safe course, because, he remembered, he'd involved an innocent person in this when he'd hopped into her car. He sure as heck had done that, all right.

Laurel, he mused. She *was* pretty, had a wholesome look about her, a healthy, girl-next-door type. She was a white woman, though, so he wasn't about to let himself dwell on the pale freckles across the bridge of her nose or her dark lashes, or the gleaming golden-brown hair that she wore in one thick braid down her back. He wasn't interested. Nonetheless, he was stuck with her for a time because, damn it, he'd gotten himself into a fix.

He came into the house quietly, and Dog, who'd probably smelled him coming two blocks away, only grunted and then went back to his nap. But Laurel nearly jumped out of her skin. "God, don't sneak up on me like that!" she yelped, her hand flying to her heart.

"Didn't want to disturb you," Joe said and he settled himself on her couch.

She took off big pink-tinted glasses and glared at him. "I've got work to do, all right? Don't you think it's time you and your mutt took off? I mean, it's been swell and all that, but..."

"I'm staying," Joe announced.

"Now just a darn..."

"I'm not going until I'm sure no one got your license number."

"My car's in the garage."

"I know that."

"So what's the problem?" She cocked her head and dangled her glasses from a finger.

"There isn't a problem," he said, "not yet."

She sighed. "And if I said I really wanted you to go?"

Joe smiled and shook his head slowly. "Sorry, Laurel, I'd feel like a real ass if I came back tomorrow to check on you and found you splattered from one end of here to the other."

"That's really...disgusting," she fired at him.

"I agree. But it's the reality of what a rifle shot can do to a person."

"You're trying to scare me."

"No, I'm trying to reason with you. I'll spend the night on the couch, and we'll both sleep in peace."

She considered him for a time, her green eyes fixed on his dark ones until she seemed to finally see the sense of it. "Just tonight," she said.

He nodded.

"And another thing..."

"Yes?"

"When, *if,* you get to the bottom of this thing going on, this construction or whatever, I want an exclusive, on-the-record interview."

A slow grin tugged at the corner of his mouth.

"I'm serious," she said.

"All right."

"What?" she said. "What are you grinning at?"

"I was just wondering," he said. "Is that all you want, an exclusive?"

It was Laurel's turn to smile. "Just what are you suggesting?"

"I'm not suggesting anything," he was quick to say.

"There's no ulterior motive here, Joe. You say you want to stay close, just in case some creep's out to get me. Okay, I buy that, I guess. So all I'm saying is I should at least get a story out of this."

"Uh-huh," he said, and watched her as she went back to work on her article. He sat there on her couch for a very long time after that, ignored, and stared at her, his dark-skinned face a study in inscrutability.

CHAPTER FOUR

HOLLY SCHULTZ RAN with a fast crowd. At fifteen years old she was learning how to work the system—whether at school, which was out for the summer, or at home on her folks' ranch. With the help of a rowdy peer group, Holly had it all figured out.

Her hormones were raging that summer in Cortez. Habitually an A student, Holly had let her grades slip that spring to Cs and Ds, and her parents, Earl and Fran, were at a loss. But the teenager couldn't have cared less, or so it seemed.

She was learning to work her dad like a good cow pony. Of course, she knew the second generation German-American Earl was a pushover for hard work. All Holly had to do to get off the ranch at night was put in a few long hours helping him.

There was always plenty to do on the three-hundred-acre cattle ranch, too. Irrigating, cutting hay, cleaning the barns, doctoring sick cattle, driving the tractor, riding out on horseback or in a pickup truck to inspect the herds, mile after dusty, boring mile. It was drudgery, plain and simple, but Holly pretended not to mind, just to put one over on her father.

It was a hot summer day when Holly and Earl rode in from the range where they'd been checking the spring's wealth of new calves. They found only one dead, its flesh already stripped, the small bones bleached white in the arid heat.

Holly put up her tack and began brushing Cinnamon's back, giving her mare a good portion of oats from a bucket. "I hate it when a calf dies," she said to Earl.

He, too, was putting up his saddle. "It's the way of nature, Holly, you know that."

"I guess," Holly said, sulking.

"It's a fact. Scientists have all this new mumbo jumbo gene-manipulation business going for ranchers, but common sense will serve you better. You let the weak die. Nature always knows better than these Ph.D.'s in their labs. Trust me on this, honey, and you'll be as good a rancher as any."

"I don't want to ranch. I want to live in a city, Dad. I want to do something. None of my friends are going to ranch."

He smiled indulgently. "You'll see. It's just youth talking. Give it a few years—you're still a child, Holly."

Holly was smart enough to bite back her reply. She was not a child. And she was sick of being treated like one. If only her parents didn't put so much pressure on her; she often thought that if only she had a brother or sister then they wouldn't spend so much time bugging her.

They ate an early meal that evening as they always did. Holly hardly touched hers, though, because she was on a diet, just like her high school girlfriends in Cortez. No way was she going to get fat hips and legs like her mom.

"Will you please at least eat your salad?" Fran urged at the kitchen table.

"I'm not hungry."

"You're a bean pole. I don't know why you want to look like that Jenna Reynolds. She's anorexic, Holly, and it's unhealthy."

"Jenna's not anorexic. You're always putting my friends down."

"Now, that's not true," Fran began. "It's just that I don't like that crowd you run with. They have absolutely no manners, and not a single one of them gives a hoot about school. I don't know what their parents are thinking."

"Now, Fran," Earl said, "Holly has some nice friends, too."

"Just name me one," Fran said, rising to clear the table. "They're a bunch of juvenile delinquents."

Holly felt tears well in her eyes. She sat mutely listening to her mother tear apart the only people in the world who mattered to her, and felt a familiar misery rise in her stomach.

At the sink Fran said over her shoulder, "Holly, tonight I want you to help me get caught up on the ironing. We can..."

"But... Dad!" Holly turned pleading eyes onto her father.

"Oh," he said, looking uncomfortable, "I did promise Holly I'd give her a ride to town, Fran. She wants to go to the movies."

"The movies?"

"That's right, dear. I promised that if she helped out today, I'd drive her to Cortez."

Fran leaned against the sink, drying her hands, and eyed her only child. "A movie. And that's all you're going to do, go to a movie?"

"Yes," Holly said, sulking again.

"And just who are you going to this movie with?"

"Mom, I'm fifteen! Why do I have to tell you who I'm going out with? You treat me like a two-year-old!"

"Now, honey," Earl said, but it was no use, Holly was already storming up the stairs to her room.

He did drive her to town. He'd promised, and really, Fran was hard on the girl, accusing her of things that seemed unfair, of drinking and speeding around in cars with older boys—things like that. And Holly was a sensible girl. She'd had a hard year. All teens had some rough times, he thought as he drove—Holly would pull out of it.

"Thanks, Dad," she said sincerely, shutting the pickup's door in front of Josh Holloway's house. "Josh'll give me a ride home after the movie."

"His parents don't mind?"

"Oh, no, they're real cool. They let him have the car whenever he wants," she added pointedly.

"Okay, honey, you kids have a nice time."

"Thanks, Dad, we will. And I won't be late."

The truth was, Josh's folks were in Canyonlands in Utah for the week, camping with their younger children, and Josh was supposed to be watching the dog and cat and working at the local garage. Josh fed the animals, all right, and managed to make it to work relatively on time, but nights were for partying, and the empty house that sat near downtown Cortez on a dead-end street was the perfect place.

Holly let herself in the back door and heard the stereo blaring. Her school friend Jenna and her cousin Kara from Durango were opening cans of beer in the kitchen. In the den were Josh and Luke and Steve, all sixteen now, with driver's licenses and even cars.

"Yo, Holly," Josh said from where he was stretched out on the couch drinking a Coors. "Thought you weren't gonna make it."

"My folks are such a pain," she said, popping open her own can of beer and plumping herself down on the floor, petting the dog. She tossed her long brown hair, trying to be casual, cool, one of the gang.

"Parents are jerks," Luke chimed in, and everyone agreed.

By nine that evening the party was going strong. Six other kids from high school got off work at local grocery stores and fast-food joints and stopped by, digging into the cases of beer provided by Josh's twenty-one-year-old cousin, who was such a creep, according to the kids, that he'd do anything to be "in" with the crowd.

By eleven the throng of skinny, tireless teens was pretty much drunk. And they were getting bored. If Earl and Fran Schultz were convinced Holly was being led astray by this group, they were quite correct.

"Hey, guys," Josh said, rising from an hour of lethargy, turning down the music, "let's go out to the reservation. We all have fake IDs. Let's see if we can get into the casino. Come on, it'll be a blast."

Not everyone went. But two carloads of very drunk teens, including a reluctant Holly, did make the eleven-mile drive to Towaoc where they flashed their phony IDs to the Indian security guard, who immediately ushered them straight back outside and called Law Enforcement.

"Shit," Holly said, sobering, leaning against the building. "My folks are gonna kill me!"

Jenna said, "Maybe that old man will come, you know, Charlie Redmoon, the captain. Then we're in for it."

"We better hope not," Josh said, his pimpled face very pale in the neon light from the casino.

Indeed, it was Charlie Redmoon who arrived shortly and took custody of the two carloads of now half-drunk kids. It was also Redmoon who took only their names and phone numbers, because, luckily for them, Charlie had been on duty since nine that morning and he was so tired his old bones were screaming for rest.

"Maybe I'll call your folks in the morning and maybe I won't. I'm sending you kids home, and I don't want to see your faces out here again." And he radioed for a couple of deputies and another patrol car to drive the scared teenagers home, then had to wait until his men arrived before he could fold himself back into the patrol car and drive himself home, his mind turning to the comforts of his old bed and his wife, Clara, resting beside him.

It was Fran who awakened her daughter the next morning. She stood over Holly's bed, hands on her ample hips, and tried to control the quiver in her voice. "Wake up, Holly. Holly."

It all came out then. Charlie Redmoon had called that morning and spilled the beans. "Why?" Fran cried. "Why, Holly? We try to trust you. We've given you everything you ever asked for. Why?"

But Holly wasn't talking. Instead, she was lying there feeling all sick and twisted up inside, a part of her scared to death and wanting to hug her mother for security. But there was another, emerging part of the girl, an independent woman crying to escape the child's body. The two disparate sides battled, day in and day out, and Holly was lost between them.

Fran was still hovering over the bed, her pale cheeks splotched with red. "And how are we to trust you to go to work tomorrow for that tourist lady in town? What is the woman going to think? That we've raised a criminal? Maybe I'll just call this...this Laurel Velarde and tell her you can't do the work! Maybe you'll just spend the whole summer out here where your father and I can keep an eye on you!"

Holly spoke then. With her face buried in the pillow she wept and pleaded and said she'd die if she didn't get to work in town like everyone else. "I won't do it again, I swear, Mom. I won't even go near Josh's house! Please!"

In the end Fran gave in. The truth was, she was at a total loss. For the life of her she couldn't fathom what had gotten into this child—her child, adopted at birth and the most precious thing on earth to her.

JOE BUCK WOKE UP restless and irritated and ready to take on the world. But at least his anger was focused. His arm felt a hundred percent better, and there was nothing to stop him from going after that dude who'd tried to cut his life short, nothing to stop him from getting to the bottom of whatever he'd stumbled across last night and proving he wasn't a screwup.

He swung his legs to the living room floor and grabbed his jeans, tugging them on, and heard Laurel in the kitchen, closing a cupboard door. Dog lifted his head and stared toward the kitchen and Joe thought, Yeah, I hear her, old boy. I heard every move she made last night, too, every rustle of the sheet....

Without asking, Joe showered, and then he put back on his jeans and the white T-shirt he'd worn under his ruined shirt. He'd have to do something about getting clean clothes, stop by his house today. He only hoped it was safe. And speaking of safe, he thought, what was he going to do with the woman?

"You weren't kidding about that couch," he said.

Laurel looked up from her bowl of cereal. "I warned you. Now maybe tonight you'll go home like a good boy and try your own bed for a change."

"Never mind that for now. I've got better things to do than sleep," he said, helping himself to her box of cereal.

"Oh? What?"

He liked that about this Laurel Velarde, the quick curiosity, the way she cocked her head and openly met his gaze with her green eyes. Yeah, there were things about her he liked, but there were other aspects he didn't admire quite so much. For one thing, she had a real sassy tongue. But worse, she was just too full of nerve for her own good. It hadn't escaped him, either, that beneath the quick retorts there was something hidden, some insecurity he'd bet she thought she'd hidden. He'd like to know more about that, though for the life of him he didn't know why he should care.

"Well," she was asking, "what better things are you planning?"

"I don't know how much you should be told," he said. "Maybe the less you know, the better."

"Don't be so mysterious. You dragged me into this. I can handle myself. And you said I could have the story."

"Always the reporter."

"Hey, I'm just trying to earn a living."

Joe regarded her for a long minute. "I need to go to the cabin," he said. "It isn't just to get my Scout. I've got a bad feeling about that guy who chased me. If he hunted around the area he may have found my car, gotten the license number. If the roles were reversed, I'd have covered the whole territory."

"You're a cop. He isn't, or he probably isn't, I should say."

"Yeah, but he was desperate enough to chase me with a rifle." Joe lifted his stiff arm.

"I'll give you a ride," she said.

He shook his head. "No, I don't want anyone to see your car."

"Right." She bit her lip. "How about tomorrow? We'll rent a car...." She stopped herself. "No, I can't. I have someone coming over tomorrow."

He waited for her to tell him who, but she didn't, and he wondered about that. "Never mind," he said then. "I can get a ride."

"You're sure."

"Positive. And I want you to stay inside while I'm gone. Okay?"

"I'll stay in and work on my climbing article. That suit you?"

"It's for your own good."

"Why, Joe Buck," she said lightly, "you sound as if you care."

"Hey," he said hastily, "I'd say the same thing to anyone."

After breakfast Joe walked over to his sister's café, which was only a few blocks away. But then, the whole of Cortez wasn't very big. He left Laurel alone, although he still had reservations, despite her promise to keep her car out of sight and to stay in herself.

He didn't like it. She could well be in danger. The night Laurel had picked him up, getting away from the dude in the truck had been his only thought, but if that guy really had seen her license plate number, it was only a matter of time before he could track her down. Joe had gotten her into this, and he sure as hell wasn't going to abandon her until he found out exactly why someone had tried to kill him simply for stumbling onto some kind of operation out in the middle of nowhere.

With Dog at his side, Joe strode toward Rose's café and couldn't get the image of Laurel out of his head. She was sarcastic and way too liberated, that was for sure, but grudgingly he admitted she was also the kind of woman who could make a man's blood burn. He saw her sitting at her table, those golden, tanned legs crossed, her arms lifting to knot the heavy honey-brown hair at her neck. She wore practically no makeup, and she didn't need it. Her green eyes were darkly fringed as it was, and to cover up those lovely golden freckles on her nose would be unforgivable.

He crossed the main street and passed the bookstore and tried to shake her image out of his mind. Dog looked up at him at the next corner and seemed to curl his lip. "Shut up, mutt," he said. "I can at least look at the lady, can't I?"

His sister Rose was indeed at work, but then, she put in seven days a week during the summer tourist months. Her husband, Frank Miller, a white man, worked hard, too, as a local food salesman for a Denver outfit. They did well, Rose and Frank. And their three kids, all in their teens now, were model citizens, a rarity for Indian kids nowadays, because too often the native American children were tugged in different directions and got torn apart in the process. Rose and Frank, though, had raised the kids carefully, trying to maintain a balance. Their children were doing fine in modern society while still being intimately aware of their culture. Someday, Joe believed, all Indian kids would be able to achieve that balance.

"Well, well," Rose said, looking up from the prep table where she was slicing ham. "What brings you in, little brother?"

"I need a favor—a ride, actually," Joe said, taking off his sunglasses, picking up a piece of the ham and popping it into his mouth. "Couldn't get my Scout started the other day. Flooded it. It'll be okay now, though."

"What's the matter?" she asked, pinning him with her eyes, "they take away your patrol car, too?"

"So you heard," he said.

"There are no secrets in this little town, brother. Sure, I heard, and so did everyone else. You got suspended." She shrugged heavy shoulders.

"So I made a mistake," Joe said defensively, embarrassed all over again.

"Hardly the first one. Charlie was right to discipline you. You're too damn arrogant, think you can handle everything all by yourself. I'm telling you, little brother, I worry."

He frowned and shook his head. "How about that ride?"

"I'm busy."

"You've got help. You'll be back by twelve, one at the latest."

"No."

In the end, of course, Joe got his ride. Rose, the eldest of the five Buck children, had pretty much raised her younger brothers when their parents had died young, their father in a car accident and their mother a year later, of heartbreak, it was said on the reservation. Rose had done fine, though, and all four brothers had had a shot at college, though Joe was the only one who'd graduated. And now the boys were scattered. Two worked in the Alaskan oil fields, a third lived on the reservation with his wife and two kids, and Joe, after his stint in the army as an MP, was now with local law enforcement. Or had been, as Rose pointed out more than once on the long drive through the reservation that morning.

"You should settle down," she said, steering the pickup truck, fiddling with the air conditioner. "If you had family, Joe, you wouldn't be so quick to jump into things feetfirst."

"I need a ride," he said, staring out across the huge, dry expanse of land, "not a lecture."

"Someone's got to lecture you. And by the way, where have you been the past few days? I called your house a dozen times."

"Here and there," he said.

"You got yourself someone?"

"Hey," he said, "the turnoff to the cabin's just around this bend, better slow down."

It was a bumpy ride along the seldom-used dirt track that led up to the base of a mesa where Joe had been on retreat. The cabin itself was known to the Utes as Morgan's Hut, named after Harlow Morgan, a white-eye ex-cavalry officer who'd gone mad back before the turn of the century and died at the cabin he'd built after thirty years of living there alone. Most of the Indians steered clear of the place, believing it to be bad medicine and haunted by evil spirits. Joe, however,

laughed at the old tales and had been camping out at
the remote site for years. Only once in a while did Dog
stare at the center of the single room and growl.

"Who do you see?" Joe would ask. "Crazy old
Harlow?"

Rose complained the whole way. First, she really
hadn't the time to be driving Joe all the way out there,
but secondly—and far more important—her pickup
was brand new and had never been out of Cortez.

"I could kill you for this, Joe," she said.

When they finally arrived at Morgan's Hut, she
dropped off her younger brother without even waiting
to see if the Scout was going to start.

"Hey," Joe said, standing there with Dog at his side,
"can't you even wait a . . ."

"I don't like it here, and that dog of yours got hair
all over my car, and you can just walk back if you have
to, Joe Buck," Rose said.

"What if my car won't . . ." Joe began.

She only glared at him. Then, before rolling up her
window, she shook her finger at him. "Don't you go
and forget the Sun Dance. It starts tomorrow, and you
better be there one of the nights."

"Have I ever missed it?" he muttered.

"I wouldn't remember," she said, then switched the
air conditioner on high and headed back down the
bumpy dirt track, her three-week-old red pickup covered in dust.

Joe watched her for a time to make sure she didn't
drive off the road or something and then turned and
looked at the old cabin. "What do you think?" he
asked Dog. "Has someone been here?"

He scouted the area, carefully studying the ground
and the tracks made by his own car and then Rose's. In

the baked-dry earth it was hard to make out one tire tread from another, but it did seem . . .

Joe dropped to his haunches and traced a ridge of dust with his hand. Beside him Dog was sniffing the air and then the hard dirt, the hair on his back raised. If pressed, Joe would have said that there had been another vehicle here with unmatched tires on the front and back. Of course, he couldn't be one hundred percent sure, but he was betting that the dude who'd shot him had found the cabin and his abandoned Scout.

He checked the car next, but Joe couldn't say if anything was disturbed.

The interior of the cabin told him nothing, either. He walked back outside, took off his sunglasses, lifted his eyes to the distance and wondered, and he could feel the tiny hairs on his arms rise—was that guy out there somewhere? Or maybe searching Towaoc or Cortez? Surely by now he'd have gotten Joe's name and address from the state motor vehicle division. But as Joe stood there and scanned the broken land, it was not his own safety he was thinking about.

He drove too damn fast back toward Cortez and even got stopped for speeding by one of Redmoon's rookies. "Oh, Sergeant Buck," the young Indian patrolman said, "sorry. I didn't know it was you."

Joe took his sunglasses off and glared at the kid. "You gonna ticket me or not? I'm in a hurry," he said.

"Ah, no, sir, you can go."

And Joe did, pushing the old beat-up car to its limit, worried about the pretty, long-limbed woman whom he'd put in danger.

Joe parked the Scout in an unused shed not far from his sister's café where he was sure no one would find it in a million years, and then headed on foot to Laurel's, Dog by his side.

He was on edge. Seeing those tracks up at the cabin had only brought home to him the very real danger he was in. And Laurel, yes, maybe she was in the same tight spot. Damn it! Joe fumed, he was a *cop,* he should have known better than to have involved a civilian. If he hadn't turned his gun in to Redmoon he probably would have been carrying it that night and been able to protect himself.

He took the blocks in long, agitated strides, and felt his jaw lock. What a mess, he thought, and he didn't even know yet what was going on out in the desert. But he would, come hell or high water he was going to get to the bottom of this.

Thank God, Laurel was at home, typing away. He'd been picturing her driving around Cortez, running errands, her white Honda with those California tags sticking out like a sore thumb despite his warnings to her.

"How's your article going?" Joe called from the kitchen as he gave Dog a bowl of water.

She came to the kitchen door and stretched, her breasts full and round beneath the T-shirt. Quickly Joe looked away. "It's coming along, I guess," she said. "My mind's not really on it."

"I hope you aren't worried. I mean, I'm sure you're safe as long as you keep your car..."

"It's not that."

"Oh," he said. And then he recalled something she'd mentioned earlier, about someone coming tomorrow. He felt a sudden pricking beneath his skin, an unwarranted irritation.

"Well," she said, "did you find what you were looking for?"

"What?"

"At the cabin, Joe, did you find anything?"

"Maybe," he allowed.

"Tell me," she said, and walked past him, opening the fridge, taking out a soda. "It's not fair to keep me in the dark when I can't even poke my nose outside."

"Of course you can go out."

"Not with my car."

"I'll rent you one. In fact," he said, "I was going to, anyway. I've got my Scout hidden and I need wheels."

"So," Laurel said, "tell me. Stop avoiding the subject. What did you find?"

He regarded her for a moment. "Tire tracks. A pickup truck."

"In case you haven't noticed, every other car in the Four Corners is a pickup. Why do you think this set of tracks belongs to the guy who shot you?"

"Because no one but me goes up to that cabin and the tracks were fresh."

"Oh, come on," she said, "no one but you goes there? That's absurd."

"The place is haunted."

"Uh-huh."

"I'm serious. There're dozens of spots on the reservation that we avoid."

"Because they're haunted."

"That's right. Take it or leave it."

She met his eyes for a moment longer and then sighed. "Okay. It's haunted. Fine. But you go there."

"I'm not afraid. It's a great spot to get away from it all, and I've never been bothered."

"So if a pickup truck has been there recently, you're saying it has to have been the same one that chased you."

"The odds are it is."

"Um," she said. "So you think this guy has a lead on you now?"

He nodded.

"That's bad."

"It's not real good."

"Then you can't go home."

"No, I'd say that would be a real stupid move."

"Um," Laurel said again, and she leaned against the counter and lifted her gaze to his. "You need a place to stay, then."

"Uh-huh."

"And it would be convenient to stay right here."

"It would. And," he added hastily, "I'd feel better if I could keep an eye on you. I got you into this."

"Yes, you sure did."

"Mad?"

"No. But I refuse to live like a scared rabbit."

Joe thought about that, then said, "You know, you're too cocky for your own good, lady. But I guess if I consider what you do for a living it makes sense."

"Being a writer?" she asked, her back up.

"It's the kind of thing you write about. Thrill-junky stuff. You really get off on that. But I'll tell you, I wish I had a dollar for every rock climber and hiker and white-water rafter I've had to go out and rescue in the past eight years. I'd be a very rich man."

She glared at him in silence.

"Sorry," he said, "but it's true. You white... Some folks," he said, quickly correcting himself, "haven't got a lick of good sense or any respect whatsoever for

Mother Earth. She can be gentle, but she can also strike with anger."

"What are you trying to say?"

"Oh, what the hell? You're basically selfish. You take and take from the earth and never give a thing back."

"You're a bigot," she said.

"Not true," he countered. "It's simply a fact that you folks are only just now learning how much you've screwed up the environment. You could take a lesson from us, that's all I'm saying. Try to understand that you've got to live with nature, not try to fight it. It's a very basic concept, Laurel."

And then she drew herself up. "You know," she said, "I really feel like I just got slapped in the face, Joe Buck. I try to write about enjoying nature and having a little fun without leaving a trail behind. That's possible, you know. It really is. And you don't know me at all. How dare you get off judging me, putting me in a tidy little box?"

He studied her for a time, an unreadable expression carefully in place. Okay, he thought, maybe he was judging her unfairly, taking his anger out on her because she was available.

But, damn it, there were a bunch of people out there on the reservation tearing up the land for whatever reason, and he was mad, good and mad.

"Joe," she was saying, and he had to focus, "don't put me in a category. I've been doing some thinking today and . . . well, I do want to help you. It's not just the story, either. Someone shot you, someone's out there on your land doing something obviously wrong. I *should* help."

"That seems to be a pretty flimsy reason," he said, "for putting yourself in harm's way."

She lowered those long-lashed eyes, and if Joe hadn't known better, he'd have said she was embarrassed. "Let's just say I want to help and leave it at that. Okay?" she said. "There are other things going on in my life right now, but I won't go into that. Just let me help however I can, even if it's just to give you a safe place to stay."

Joe weighed her words. He was used to being alone, working alone—he'd certainly never worked with a woman before, and yet...

He told himself he was giving in, though, because Laurel was better off with him than without him; he could keep an eye on her. It was easy for Joe to convince himself of that. Too easy.

"Okay," he said.

"Okay? I can help?"

"I said yes."

"And you have a plan, don't you?"

He nodded.

"So tell me what I can do."

He allowed a corner of his mouth to lift in a half smile and said, "Call a rental car agency."

"And then?" she asked with fire in her eyes.

"Then we go for a midnight ride. Okay?"

"Okay," she said, and pulled out the phone book while Joe stood by staring at her and wondering, What in hell have I gotten myself into?

CHAPTER FIVE

IT WAS NEARLY DARK and Charlie Redmoon was just getting ready to go home when Nancy Bearcross knocked on the door of his office and said that a man wanted to see him. Charlie sighed and gave a nod. "Sure, show him in."

The man was a complete stranger, a white man, a short but muscular fellow with a potbelly and a mustache. He had a broad smile on his face and he held out his hand. "Good evening, how are you? My name's Jack Tolliver. Glad to meet you."

Charlie merely nodded and extended his own hand, which Tolliver pumped enthusiastically.

"Sorry to bother you so late, but this won't take long. I'm looking for an old pal of mine, and I can't find him anywhere. I know he lives here, though, in Toe-way-oc."

"Toy-ak," Charlie corrected him.

"Right, that's it. Thought I'd try you here. You guys must know everyone on the res."

"Maybe. What's his name?"

"Joseph Buck."

Charlie grunted. "Joe Buck."

"Yeah, that's him."

"Oh, I know Sergeant Buck, all right."

"Sergeant Buck?"

"He's a law enforcement officer, works for me."

"Wow, I hit the jackpot, didn't I?"

"Where do you know Joe from?" Charlie asked, not exactly suspicious, but curious.

The man seemed to hesitate a split second. "The service," he said. "Old drinking buddies, you know."

"Joe doesn't drink."

"Well, he sure as hell did then," the man said, and gave a laugh. "Well, see, I was in this area so I thought I'd look him up. You know, remember some good times."

"Joe isn't here right now. He's, ah, on vacation for a couple of weeks."

"So, is he still in town?"

"Probably, unless he went off hunting for a few days. He lives about a mile from here, back on the highway toward Cortez, then a dirt road on the right. He has a small place a few hundred yards from the highway. If he's home his old Scout will be there. Be careful of his dog, though."

"Watchdog, huh?"

"Mean thing. Real protective."

"Does Joe have a family these days?" Tolliver asked.

"Joe? Not him, nobody but his dog."

"Good-looking young guy still?" Tolliver asked.

Charlie shrugged. "I guess so. Wish he'd cut his hair, though. Guess his hair was short when you knew him."

"Short? Oh, yeah." Tolliver lifted off his baseball cap and ran a gnarled hand over his own crew-cut gray hair. "Shaved right off, practically."

"You live around here?"

"No, ah, I'm from Denver. Doing some work in this area. Construction."

"You bidding on the new casino?" Charlie asked.

"Oh, no, not that. Some roadwork for the state, actually. The Durango area.''

"Needs it."

"Sure does. Well, I'll be going now. I really do appreciate your help, Chief, ah, Captain. It'll be good to see Joe again."

When he was gone Charlie sighed and hitched up the belt of his blue uniform. Now he could go home.

He drove his official police vehicle. It was a Ford sedan covered with such a heavy layer of fine beige dust that it matched the landscape. Sometimes he got calls at night, though, and he had to be ready to go anywhere. Like last night when those kids had tried to get into the casino. He'd have whupped his kids something fierce if they'd ever pulled a stunt like that; though, of course, when his kids had been young there'd been no casino, no tourists, nothing of any interest to Cortez teenagers in Towaoc. He wondered what these kids' folks were doing about it. Mrs. Schultz had been real upset, the Holloways hadn't even been home and the others had either laughed it off or yelled at Charlie for bothering them.

He drove the short distance to his bungalow-style house, and could smell meat barbecuing as he drove up. Clara was doing deer steaks tonight. His mouth watered at the thought.

He pulled into his dusty drive and up beneath an old metal roof, his makeshift carport, thinking about that fellow Jack Tolliver. Joe had lots of white friends, having been away to college in Durango, then in the army. He'd even traveled some, to California and Chicago once. A real sophisticated Indian, Joe Buck. And a pain in the neck. Smart, tenacious, an intuitive policeman, but he just couldn't follow procedure. Trouble was, Joe had always been too much of a loner for his own good.

Well, the bottom line was still the same. Charlie'd had to suspend him, and Superintendent Thomas had wholeheartedly agreed—Joe Buck needed to be brought down a peg or two. But now Charlie was shorthanded in the middle of the summer tourist season. That was not good.

He got out of the car and admired the last lingering red light on the horizon, shucking his workaday skin and stepping into his at-home one. Behind him the eroded buttes and chimney rocks jutted redly into the sky. He looked at the familiar Sleeping Ute Mountain, checked the trappings of his traditional role in the tribe—the tepee poles stacked neatly by his carport, the canvas, the sweat lodge, the shade house—took a deep breath of sage-scented air and went into his nicely kept, asbestos-sided bungalow to have that steak dinner with his wife.

Clara broke the news to him when they were almost through eating: "Delbert Ray came by. His father, Gary, is real sick, and he'd like you to go out there and do a cure."

Charlie sighed. He was tired. But as the medicine man of the tribe, the healer, he had to go. Clara knew it, and so did he.

"I told Delbert how busy you are at work," Clara was saying, stacking dishes in the sink, "but he said it was important. His father won't go to the clinic."

So many of the old ones refused to go. Sometimes Charlie didn't blame them, although he didn't discount modern medicine. He only wished the Cortez doctors felt the same way about his medicine. "What's the matter with Gary?"

Clara sighed. "The same thing. He's sick, vomiting, weak. Like he was poisoned. Like the others, Charlie."

Lately, for months, in fact, there had been this vomiting sickness. Some recovered, some got worse. Animals sickened, too, in unnatural ways. The earth was out of kilter. Yes, poison. "All right, I'll go," Charlie said heavily.

"I'll go, too," Clara said. "I'd like to see Gladys again, anyway."

They drove in Charlie's pickup, following the path of his headlights west on a dirt road to the Rays' place, a few miles outside of Towaoc. It was a thing Charlie did several times a month, visiting tribal members who needed his help, either for mental or physical dysfunctions. The Utes did not see the mind and body as separate. Religion and medicine were the same thing.

Evil, illness and imbalance were its antithesis. To be cured, one only had to restore the natural balance. Charlie had always felt the particular talent within himself, the strength to follow the spiritual path that others lacked. Charlie also felt himself to be the vital link between the old and the new, and when one of his people needed him, he went.

Delbert awaited him, looking tense. "My father is very sick," he said in the old tongue.

Clara went into the kitchen with Delbert's wife—this was men's business—and Charlie got his paraphernalia ready.

The old man had white hair and thin arms ropy with sinew. His color was bad, but he gave Charlie a weak smile. "Welcome to my house," he said. "I am sorry you had to come so far, my brother."

"It is my duty and my pleasure," Charlie replied respectfully.

Charlie and Delbert helped the sick man outside, where he reclined on a mattress on the porch. Charlie would have liked to do a sweat bath, but he judged Gary to be too weak. This ceremony would have to do.

He directed Delbert to build a fire of cedar. Smoke was one element of the cure. He got out his bone whistle and his eagle's wing, the links to the spirit world; he closed his eyes and cleared his mind.

The smoke wafted over them in the warm darkness. Overhead the stars hung in vast clusters, wheeling in age-old patterns across the night sky, and from inside the women's voices could be heard, sparkling and flowing like a mountain stream.

"I am ready," Gary said.

Charlie picked up some dirt, a handful of Mother Earth, and sprinkled it on Gary. He blew the bone whistle and fanned the eagle's wing over the man's supine body. He muttered prayers in a low, deep voice in the old language, calling on Grandfather the Creator for good blessings from the four directions. The old man, eyes closed, moved restlessly. Delbert sat very still, watching, lending his spiritual support.

When Charlie was through he was offered strong black coffee and fry bread by Gladys, Delbert's wife, and they all sat on the porch near the old man and spoke companionably.

"This sickness, I've heard of others who had it south of here," Gary said faintly. "And there are dead animals in great numbers out on the land."

"There always are, Father," Delbert said.

Gary shook his head. "There is something out there, a poison. It got into me when I hunted. Animals are dying from it. It is very bad."

"What poison?" Charlie asked, but the old man only shook his head tiredly.

Clara and Charlie left then, accepting Delbert's thanks, a gift of dried beans from Gladys, and began the drive back to Towaoc.

"Will he recover?" Clara asked.

"I don't know. He's old and very sick."

"Do you believe there's a poison in the land?"

Charlie shook his head sadly. "There's something. The balance is disturbed. We have to find a way to get back to the right path. I don't know."

"Perhaps the Sun Dance will help," Clara said.

"Yes, we can all hope for that. The young men will have to dance very hard, be very strong this year."

"Maybe it's a virus going around," Clara suggested, trying to be open-minded.

"I don't think so, Clara. I just don't think so."

Charlie drove, very tired now, his eyes straining through the darkness to see the road. He was glad Clara was with him, although he'd never admit it to her. She probably knew it, anyway, though. There wasn't much he could keep from Clara.

Her voice came from where she sat in the passenger's seat. "How is Joe Buck doing?"

Of course she knew about Joe's suspension. She liked Joe and had told Charlie he was handling the young man badly. Charlie shrugged at her question. "How would I know? He's not at headquarters. He's at home, I guess."

"He must be very, very angry with you. You know, a young man like that, you can't take away the one outlet he has, and that's what you did."

"Listen, Clara, Joe's a menace. He puts himself and his brother officers in danger. I gave him a hundred chances, and this time he had to be disciplined."

"I know, but..."

"He'll live. He's only ashamed because he knew he was wrong. Basically Joe's a fine officer, a true asset to the tribe and the force. Trouble with him is that he's a loner. He needs to find himself someone and realize it's okay to need somebody once in a while."

"He's a good boy," Clara said.

"He's not a boy."

"We knew his parents, Charlie. To me he's a boy."

Charlie grumbled under his breath. "He'll learn. Someday he'll learn that we are all one and must work together."

The night fled before the headlights, then closed in around them. They were almost home. Charlie let himself yawn.

"You're tired," Clara remarked.

"Yes."

"You've been working too much," she said. "And now with Joe Buck off..."

"I know, I know."

"I hope no one calls you from headquarters tonight."

"Danny Willets is in charge. He knows better than to call unless it's an emergency."

"There are so many emergencies these days."

"The casino," Charlie said.

Clara, the staunch defender of anything that provided employment on the reservation, said nothing.

"I could retire," Charlie said.

Clara stared at her hands. "You could."

"I've come all the way up in the force. I've done my best. Caught a lot of lawbreakers, Clara."

"You've done a good job, Charlie."

"It's getting harder now. All these white men coming to gamble. Strange people."

"You deserve time off."

He frowned. "Time to do what, Clara?"

His wife sighed. "Whatever you want. Write down all those old stories."

"I'm not a writer. I don't know how to do that. I'm a policeman, that's what I am."

"You could go into business with my brother Felix any day. He's asked many times."

"Smelly sheep."

"So, you picked the one job that was as close to being a warrior as you could, and nothing else will do?"

Charlie grunted.

"Stubborn old coot," Clara said lovingly as they pulled into their driveway.

In bed that night, on their accustomed sides that neither would dare change, they talked a little in the dark room.

"Be nice to Joe when he gets back to work," Clara said. "He needs understanding. I wish he'd find a wife, Charlie."

"Not likely," Charlie said, yawning.

"Such a handsome boy." Clara dropped her bombshell gently. "He would be a wonderful captain if you retired, don't you think, Charlie?"

"Joe Buck?"

"Yes, that's who we're talking about."

He sighed.

"Now, Charlie, all he needs is some responsibility to bring out the best in him. Isn't it always that way? In the old days, didn't the war chief take the wildest of the young men to battle?"

"Oh, Clara."

"When you retire..."

"I'm not decrepit yet."

"No, no, of course not."

"I refuse to be a damn farmer," Charlie said.

"Yes, dear, I know."

"Maybe raise horses. Send some to the races. Gilbert's got a fine stud...."

"You certainly could."

Charlie lay in the sagging old bed that fit his own lumps so well and felt sleep coming over him. "Man stopped in tonight," he said, staving off the sweet oblivion. "Friend of Joe's from the army. Looking for him."

"That's nice," Clara said sleepily.

"White man from Denver."

"That's nice, dear," she said in the old tongue.

CHAPTER SIX

IT SEEMED VERY FAR TO JOE, driving the rutted dirt road, a track really, out to where that equipment had been two nights ago. He could hardly believe he'd walked and run as far as he had before he'd gotten to the highway. And the rental car, a highway-sprung Taurus, made it even slower going.

"You're sure you know where we are?" Laurel asked again.

"Yes, I'm sure."

"How can you tell? It's all the same. It's all dark. Maybe we're lost."

He gave a short laugh. "Where're you from?"

"Berkeley, I told you."

"Would you get lost driving around Berkeley?"

"Of course not."

"There you are."

"But this isn't a city," she said.

"It's where I live. I know it," he explained.

"But what're you looking for?"

He turned the wheel hard to avoid a particularly big rock. "I'll know it when I see it. Like I said, I'm parking this car before we get there. We're walking."

"Yes, you told me. How far?"

"Two, three miles. I don't want us driving up onto anything like I saw the other night."

"What if they're there again?" she asked, and for the first time Joe noted a touch of caution in her voice.

"Then we retreat, very, very quietly."

"And what are you going to do if they're not there?"

"Boy, you're full of questions."

"Well, listen, my life is at stake here, too. I have a right to know."

"I knew I was crazy to let you come along," Joe said.

"Why, because my questions bug you or because my life's at stake?" she asked matter-of-factly.

"Both," he muttered.

Laurel was quiet for about thirty seconds and then started in again. "Will your dog bark and get us in trouble?" she asked. "Maybe you should have left him home—or we'll leave him in the car."

He risked a sideways glance at her that he figured answered her question and switched his eyes back to the rutted track he was following.

"These late hours are tough," she said.

"You didn't have to come."

"Oh, sure, and miss all the excitement?"

"Have you always been like this, sort of, well . . ."

"Venturesome," she finished for him. "Isn't that a nice word? I think I read it in *Alice in Wonderland,* or maybe it was *Pride and Prejudice.*"

"Yeah, Alice in Wonderland, that's you."

"I'm not an airhead. I'm not dumb," she said defensively. "And who're you to talk? The maverick cop on suspension."

He saw a big bush off to the left, sagebrush. He took a look around and figured he was about the right distance from the spot. Better too far than too close.

"What're you doing?" she asked in alarm when he pulled off the track to bump across the ground.

"Parking."

"Here?"

"Check the numbers painted on the wall and the color of this level," he said dryly.

"I'd never find this place," she said, holding on to the dashboard as he drove around the bush and nosed into it, bouncing over rocks and hillocks of bunch grass. He stopped the car and turned off the head-lights, and abruptly they were encased in darkness.

"Where's the flashlight?" Laurel whispered.

"You don't have to whisper."

"Yes, I do. I always whisper in the dark."

"It's right here." He reached over in the darkness only to find her hand. It was a smooth, small hand that jumped a little when he inadvertently touched it. "Here, this is it." And he moved the flashlight so that she could feel it.

"Okay," she whispered, and for the first time Joe wondered if her bravado wasn't all facade.

The moon was up, a half-moon that cast a great deal of silvery light. Even their shadows showed faintly on the rough ground. It was warm and dry, and the scent of the high desert was as familiar to Joe as an old friend. He knew exactly what direction the site was, he knew the ground he'd have to cover, how long the trek would take. The only thing he didn't know was how Laurel would do.

"Okay," he said. "It'll take an hour or so from here. We're staying off the road. You have to follow directions, you understand? No arguments, no questions."

"Yes, sir," she said smartly.

"I'm not kidding."

"Let's go. Let's get this over with."

He switched the flashlight on. "Okay. Follow me and watch your footing. All I need is for you to twist an ankle or something."

"I'll keep up, don't worry," she said.

He started out, Dog at his side, the flashlight beam spearing the blackness. He could hear Laurel behind him, her footsteps a little uncertain at first. He could smell her scent, a fresh, female aroma, and if he listened closely, he'd be able to hear her breath, quick and light.

For a moment he turned his thoughts inward, shutting out the physical sensations she aroused. He didn't like having her here, it felt all wrong. He never hiked or camped with anyone, least of all a woman, and he never should have agreed to this—damn, nosy magazine writer.

"Tell me again," she was saying behind him, "what exactly did you see out there?"

"I've told you three times already."

"The more you tell it, the more you'll recall."

"Is that a reporter thing?"

"Just humor me," she said, and he heard her step on a twig that snapped loudly.

"Okay," he said, "I saw trucks, a couple of big machines like bulldozers, one with a long arm. My guess is that someone was burying something. I couldn't tell what."

"Hmm."

He walked on, careful to keep the light down. If someone was driving along the dirt track they were paralleling, he didn't want him to see the light; it'd stand out like a beacon in the unrelieved darkness.

"Why do you figure out here, and why in the middle of the night?" Laurel asked.

"I don't know."

"And you say the police didn't know anything about a project on the reservation?"

"Nope. Neither did any local contractors, and they'd have heard."

"So it's got to be something illegal," she declared.

"Good deduction, Watson," he said.

"Okay, Sherlock, what could be going on out here? What could they be burying? And who are they?"

"How many times are you going to ask me that?"

"I'm just thinking out loud," she said.

"Well, keep it to yourself. We sound like a herd of elephants out here." He turned to glance at her then, and all he could see was the pale oval of her face and her shorts-clad legs gleaming like white marble in the moonlight. She was moving along easily now, striding, her arms swinging, relaxed. He had to admire her, however grudgingly, because she was keeping up just fine, not complaining, and seemingly unafraid. Yeah, he had to give her credit for determination and guts. But that was all he'd give her.

He wondered how he'd arrived at this place with a strange woman he'd known for just about forty-eight hours now. Very curious. And he wondered why he kept thinking about her when his mind should have been on the deadly serious problem that lay ahead.

Sure, she was pretty and she had spirit. She had a mouth on her, too, and a sense of humor. But she was a white woman, and he'd sworn never to get involved with a white woman again, not since college. Oh, he'd learned his lesson, that was for sure. Stacy Eubanks, that had been her name, and they'd been in love,

young, innocent love. But her parents had had a fit
when they'd learned he was an Indian and yanked her
out of college, and that had been that.

Yeah, it had been a real learning experience, all
right.

"How far?" Laurel was asking.

"Another mile or so. Tired?"

"No, no, I just wondered."

"Let's rest for a minute. We'll have to walk back to
the car, too, you know."

"Hey, I'm okay. If you need to rest, fine."

He smiled to himself at the nettled tone of her reply.

"There's a nice flat rock over there." He swept the
flashlight beam toward it.

So they stopped and sat on the boulder that had been
washed down out of the San Juan Mountains a million years ago. She pulled her knees up to her chest and
hugged them, her face turned up to the stars, her white
throat exposed. "There's the Big Dipper," she said.
"And the North Star and Orion."

"We have other names for them," he said.

"Tell me," she said.

"You say that a lot. 'Tell me.'"

"There are a lot of things I want to know."

"Like what?"

"Well, I want to know what's ahead of us, what you
saw the other night. I want to know what your tribe
calls the stars. I want to know more about you."

"Curiosity killed the cat," he said.

"Is that a Ute saying?"

"No, it sure isn't."

"You learned it at school," she said.

"I learned a lot of things at school."

"Uh-oh, sounds ominous."

"Education can be enlightening. It can also teach you things you didn't ever want to know."

"Isn't that experience you're talking about, not education?" she asked.

"Maybe."

Dog was sitting beside Laurel, and her hand was on his head, resting there. His tongue was lolling out and he looked dazed with pleasure. Joe looked away.

"This isn't a bad dog," she admitted. "Why didn't you give him a better name?"

He shrugged. "Couldn't think of one."

"How'd you get him?"

"Found him."

"Oh, come on, tell me a better story than that."

"Well, he'd been thrown out of the house with the rest of his litter because it was raining."

"Raining?"

"There's a belief among the Utes that a dog attracts lightning, so they threw the puppies out into the rain. Combs and mirrors attract lightning, too, in case you didn't know."

"Where was his mother? What happened to the rest of the litter?"

"The mother was hit by a car on the highway, and the rest of the litter died."

"Oh, God, how awful."

"So I took him home."

"You have a soft heart," she said.

"Don't read anything into this," he said. "He's just a lousy dog."

"Um," she replied, looking up at the firmament, the moonlight settling on her face and neck like a spangled scarf of the finest silver thread. He felt a twinge in his belly and turned his face away quickly. Yet he knew her hand still rested idly on Dog's blunt head with its tattered ears, and it was as if he could feel the ghostly touch of her hand on his own head.

"Where's your man?" he heard himself asking.

"My man?" She gave a tinkling, mocking sort of laugh, stroking Dog's ears, and the spurt of emotion he felt at her reply irritated him. She was a women's libber, he decided, that's what she was, or just too tough and independent for most men to handle. It didn't surprise him a bit that she wasn't married—who could stand that mouth of hers and the endless questions? Still, once more he sensed something deeper in this woman, something she hadn't revealed to him—yet.

"Let's go," he said, rising.

She stood, brushing off the seat of her shorts in an unconscious gesture, and they started off again.

"Tell me something," she said after a while. "Is this where your tribe originally lived? I mean, I know how often they moved tribes in the past."

"This barren land? No, we were always mountain Indians. We lived in Colorado and Utah. We called ourselves the People of the Shining Mountains, *Nuche*. The old men say we left our ancestors in the rocks and they're waiting there. Someday they'll tell us to go back."

"Oh, that could cause some problems."

"Yeah, the Ute had the very last Indian uprising and maybe we'll start again."

"What uprising was that?"

"The Meeker Massacre, 1879. We killed the Indian agent up there in Meeker. He was a real nerd, and that was the last straw. They moved us all to this reservation and the Southern Ute reservation just next door, and there's one in Utah, too."

"It's terrible what we did to the Indians," she said softly.

"A bad case of do-gooder's guilt?" he sneered.

"Don't be nasty."

Women, they always wanted to change you. White, Indian, it didn't matter. Women were too hard to get along with, asked for too much from a man. He'd learned that years ago. And they sure never stopped talking. Then, as if to punctuate his musings, she was asking him yet another question. God, did she ever quit?

"Is your tribe related to the Anasazi? I mean, you live in the same area."

"No," he replied patiently. "The Anasazi were here thousands of years before we were. They were farmers who lived in pueblos or cliff dwellings, and they disappeared more than six hundred years ago. The Ute came later, probably from the north, although no one knows for sure, and we were always hunters. Different folk."

"Uh-huh, so the cliff dwellings over in Mesa Verde and the Ute Tribal Park have nothing to do with the Ute?"

"Nope, not a thing. We knew of them, of course, but never went near them. They're haunted by spirits. Unhealthy."

"Of course."

The shrouded land stretched away from them like an ocean. Joe headed straight as an arrow for the site. They were close now, right about where he'd first heard the sounds of the trucks. And like a good sailor, Joe could read this endless ocean of his that appeared featureless to the uninitiated. That rock, that gully, that clump of rabbit brush—they were all familiar, emblazoned on his brain like signposts. He listened as he walked, but tonight there were no outlandish machine noises, only the normal night sounds.

"Are we close?" he heard Laurel ask in a whisper.

"Yeah, we're getting there. Over those ridges."

And they headed on into the silver-etched blackness, following the tunnel of his flashlight beam.

SHE WAS GLAD she wasn't alone out there in this land of forever, although she never would have admitted it to him, not in a million years. She trusted his dog's senses and she trusted his, although she wasn't sure why. Certainly, she had little enough reason to trust him or any man.

She'd never known an Indian before. Native American, she should remember, that was the preferred term. Until moving to Cortez she'd only seen them stereotyped in movies, either all bad as the old cowboy movies depicted them or all good in the newer, more politically correct films. She was sure they were really somewhere in between, like people everywhere, and she was trying to figure this man out so she could come to grips with the bigger picture. He was a hard one to pin down, though. Sarcastic, arrogant—a maverick, even—seemingly attuned to the white world, educated. Yet some of his attributes were a little different from those of other men she'd known. A way of talking about natural things as if they had a...well, a soul. The way he moved, the look in his eyes at times, his uncanny knowledge of where they were right now, the way he fit into his surroundings, walking lightly on the land, as if it were a garden full of the rarest of flowers.

So okay, she admitted to herself, she wanted the story of what was going on in the desert, if there was one. She was curious, and she did have a stake in solving this mystery after the other night's happenings, but she'd become fascinated by this man Joe Buck.

Handsome. Oh yes, he was handsome, the kind of Indian every Hollywood casting director would die for. Tall, well built, a great face, chiseled and bronzed, straight black eyebrows, a strong, aquiline nose and a wide mouth shaped just right for the rest of his face. And those eyes, even when he kept them carefully neutral, still hinted at an unfathomable knowledge, something ancient and eternal.

There was another thing about Joe Buck that piqued her interest. For all his pride and macho attitude, he was incredibly vulnerable. He was so humiliated at being suspended that he'd set off on this quest so that he could vindicate himself in his boss's eyes. She knew that intuitively, and yet she liked that, finding a chink in his armor. It made him, well, human.

She wondered what he thought of *her.* He'd asked her: Where's your man? He should only know! Oh, there'd been men since high school, since Gray, but never had she really made a commitment to any of them. Couldn't, really, after Gray's betrayal. It had scarred her badly, at a very early age. Funny that most men seemed to turn out to be Grays. Oh, their hair was different, the way they walked and dressed, but the men were the same—they all wanted to control her. She'd always made a point of being the one to say goodbye before the hurt began.

And who needed a man, anyway? She was living life on her terms, and if sometimes—just sometimes—she got a little lonely, she had her friends ... and the hope of meeting Holly Schultz.

Soon, maybe, Holly—her daughter—would come into her life, and she'd have an ally with whom to take on life's challenges. But of course she couldn't count on that. Holly might not know she was adopted, might not want to know her. What would it do to her relationship with her adoptive parents—in a sense, her real parents? Better to deal with that tomorrow.

She followed Joe Buck's admittedly attractive broad back across the arid land, not knowing where she was or where she was going, but knowing she wanted to be there. Sure, he was handsome, but she was terribly afraid he'd be like all the rest. Yes, she was definitely better off without a man, no matter how attractive.

Suddenly he stopped and held up a hand. Her heart gave a lurch.

"What?" she asked, whispering.

"Tire tracks."

She looked down but couldn't see anything. He knelt and felt the earth with his hand, and then she could see where the flashlight shone that there were indeed deep tracks in the dust-dry ground, broad tracks made by heavy vehicles that seemed utterly out of place here.

"Are those from the trucks you saw?" she asked.

"Yeah," he said thoughtfully.

They went on, carefully now, because they weren't sure what lay ahead. She marveled at how quietly Joe could move, a big man like him, and his dog was a phantom, a mere shadow cast by the half-moon. She couldn't help feeling as if she'd traveled back in time: he was an Indian brave and she was his captive—or maybe his mate. She imagined him in buckskin breeches, his torso bare, painted in war stripes, perhaps. Did Utes wear war paint? She'd ask, but not now, later. He'd be wearing a headband, too, the way he'd worn the bandanna the other night before he'd wrapped his arm in it. And feathers or bear claws around his neck, resting on his smooth brown chest. She followed him and couldn't keep the image from her mind, eclipsing the time, the place, the mystery ahead. And finally she had to force her attention back to where they were because she stumbled, not watching, and he stopped and regarded her questioningly.

"Let's go," she said impatiently.

"You tired?"

"No, are you?"

He turned and went on. Once he had to help her down an escarpment as they took a shortcut the trucks hadn't been able to navigate. As his big hands spanned her waist, her knees betrayed her and went all watery. Abruptly they were face-to-face, chest-to-chest. Her breath caught, and she imagined that he held her too long like that, although it was surely only a second or two. She pushed away, unable to meet his eyes, glad for the darkness. Well, even if she didn't *need* a man, apparently she was not immune to Joe Buck's potent masculine appeal.

They finally came to the end of the tracks. All Laurel could see was a flat, semicircular area torn up by tire tracks, a sort of natural amphitheater surrounded by low ridges.

"This is it," Joe said, shining his flashlight around. "I came from that direction—" he pointed "—and that's where I was when they saw me."

"Nobody's here. I don't see a thing," she whispered, disappointed.

"Well, they were here."

"What did you expect to find?"

He shrugged.

She kicked a loose stone. "I thought there'd be something here."

"There is, in the ground," he said grimly, and then he started walking back and forth across the area, shining his flashlight down, occasionally kneeling to feel the earth. Laurel stayed where she was and watched him. It seemed so silly now, looking for something intangible. But someone had chased Joe and shot him, so there must be *something*.

He stopped then and dug in the ground with one hand, holding the flashlight on the spot with the other. She hurried over.

"Did you find something?" she asked, her heart giving a little jump of excitement.

He just handed her the flashlight so he could dig with both hands. His knuckles rapped on metal then, and he sat back on his haunches. She shone the light down into the hole he'd dug, and saw a round metal rim.

"What is it?"

"A drum, a metal barrel, I think," he said, then he leaned forward and brushed more dirt away. "Good thing they just dug this up or I'd never have been able to get down to it. Should've brought a shovel."

"They buried metal drums?" she said, staring down at it.

"Yeah, that's what they did, all right. Lots of them."

"What for?"

"Damned if I know."

"What's in them?" she asked.

"Good question, Watson," he said, reaching down to dig more dirt away. "Let's see if there's anything here that gives a hint."

He got his pocketknife out to scrape at the barrel. The top of the drum was slightly rusty, and Joe was digging deeper on one side.

"Ridiculous, I need a shovel," he said again.

Laurel watched, impatient. So far there was only this rusty old metal container. But as Joe cleared more soil away, something stenciled in black paint on the side of the drum came into view.

"What on earth?" she whispered, going down on her knees beside it.

"I'm not sure," he said, scooping more dirt aside. "It looks like..."

They both stared hard at the uncovered symbol, an internationally recognized symbol enclosed within a diamond—a circle surrounded by three curved wedges and below it a word.

Laurel suddenly felt faint. "It can't be," she breathed, the blood draining from her face.

Joe simply squatted there unmoving, staring in disbelief.

"It's...it's radioactive," she whispered, her fingers beginning to tremble so that the light from the flashlight wavered.

"It's nuclear waste" came Joe's hoarse, outraged reply.

"Oh, no," she began, "oh, my Lord. Joe..."

But he'd suddenly gone rigid, his whole body so tense that Laurel felt her heart burst with fear. Dog was growling now, too, and Laurel's limbs turned to water.

"What?" she whispered.

"Shh," he said, and rose in one quick movement as she watched him, her heart doing a tap dance in her chest as he listened intently. Dog growled again, his hackles rising. Then Laurel could hear it, too—an engine.

Joe swore, kicked dirt into the hole, grabbed her hand and pulled her along, extinguishing the flashlight. She couldn't see a thing then, but she ran, following him, her hand in his. Up, the ground uneven under her feet. She tripped on something, and Joe's arm was around her waist, practically lifting her off her feet, snatching her over a rise and down behind a rock and a clump of brush. She lay there where he'd pressed her, her breath coming quick and hot, her pulse pounding in her ears.

He put a finger on her lips. She lay there, cheek pressed to the dust, and she could hear a truck grinding over the rough ground in low gear and see the jerky swing of its headlights along the top of the ridge that hid them.

Joe was crawling now, moving to the top of the rise. She wanted to cry out to him, to pull him back. Her mind screamed danger! She couldn't, though. He needed to see who it was, didn't he? He couldn't cower there behind the hill. Well, neither could she. She began crawling, crablike, up toward the ridgeline, following him.

She reached the top, her knees and palms skinned, her heart leaping. Joe saw her and shot her a ferocious look, but it was too late to send her back. They both lay there, behind some sagebrush, and peeked over into the amphitheater.

There was a dusty white pickup parked there now, its engine idling, its headlights illuminating a great part of the area. A man was standing silhouetted in the glare, hands on his hips, a baseball cap on his head. Laurel couldn't see any more than that. It scared her, though, that angry stance. She breathed shallowly, trying to be absolutely quiet. Then the man turned on his own flashlight and started examining the ground. She could follow his progress by the beam of his flashlight, darting here and there, stabbing into the shadows.

Adrenaline coursed through her veins. What if he saw the hole Joe had dug?

As if her thought caused it to happen, the man stopped, his light shining down at the spot. He seemed to be studying the hole, standing there for too long while Laurel held her breath, paralyzed. She felt Joe's hand on her arm, warning her, and the hairs on the back of her neck stood up.

The man moved then, looking around, the light swinging from side to side, reaching out into the darkness, brushing the ridge right in front of them so that they both ducked. Laurel's mouth was dry, her chest constricted, her belly churning. What if he saw them? What if he had a gun? He'd had a gun the other night. He'd shot Joe!

Laurel couldn't breathe. She wanted to scream, but her throat was frozen. She could feel Joe's tautness on one side of her, Dog's crouched form on the other. Quiet, she had to be quiet. This was what it was like to be hunted, this stark, helpless terror.

Minutes—it seemed hours—must have passed, an interminable time. Laurel's chest ached and her eyes

were gritty with staring. Finally, the dark figure with
the flashlight returned to his pickup and climbed in.
The truck swung around, churning up dust, and went
back into the night.

CHAPTER SEVEN

LAUREL LET OUT A PENT-UP breath and just lay there for a minute, then she rolled over on her back and took in a deep gulp of night air. The stars swam in front of her eyes. "Holy cow," she whispered.

Joe was getting up, brushing dust off, mumbling something. He was only a dark mass standing above her.

"What?" she asked faintly.

"EMC-451," he replied.

"Come again?"

"EMC-451. The license number of that truck."

"Oh."

"I'm damned sure it's the same one that chased me," he said, then he looked down at her. "Hey, you okay?" He switched on the flashlight.

"Sure, just a little winded from holding my breath for an hour or so."

"Close call," he offered.

"Too close for me." She reached a hand up to him. "Please, help me up. I'm weak as a kitten."

He enclosed her hand in his big warm one and pulled her up without effort. She stood, facing him, shoulders slumped. Dog whined and pressed against her leg. "It's okay," she said, petting his back, but she was really reassuring herself.

"Well, we found out something," Joe said.

"That I'm a sniveling coward."

He ignored her. "Radioactive," he said, "God."

"I can't believe . . ."

"Well, believe it," Joe snapped. "But we got the license number."

"EMC-451," she repeated dutifully.

"Good memory." He brushed at her shoulder. "You're dusty."

"I'm not surprised." She slapped at her shorts, rubbed her T-shirt. "I was trying to bury myself in the dirt."

"You should have stayed down behind the rock," he said.

"You're right. I should have. Next time I will."

"There isn't going to be a next time."

"You're absolutely right. This was insane," Laurel said.

"But effective."

"No wonder your boss put you on suspension."

"Now, listen, I'm a damn good cop. I get results. I solve problems. This is how I work." He hesitated. "And you wanted to come along. You pushed it."

"I did." She sighed. "It's not your fault."

"Okay. You ready to walk back to the car?"

She stood there still shaken. "We've got to tell someone, maybe the FBI. This is . . . horrible."

"No," he said.

"No, what?"

"Look, this is my land, damn it, Indian land. If you think for one minute I'm going to let the feds take this over . . . no way. You know what they'll do? Slap a few hands."

"But Joe . . ."

"No buts. We're onto something here. Something big. We get to the bottom of it and then I go to my boss."

"But couldn't he help now? Joe, I really think..."

"You think too much. Just let me do things my way. All I'm going to do is find out who's behind this before I file a report."

"Sounds like you want to prove yourself so bad you'll risk anything."

"Not true," he said quickly, and then he seemed to relent. "Maybe, I don't know. I need to give this some thought. But right now I want your word this is between us."

"Okay," she said, hesitant. "For a while, but if we don't..."

"We will nail them. I will," Joe said vehemently. "Now let's get the hell out of here before our pal comes back."

"You don't have to twist my arm," she said. "Besides, it's past my bedtime."

"Right," he said.

When they got started, following the tire tracks out of the amphitheater, Laurel remembered just how far it was back to where they'd left the Taurus. She was drained. All she could think of now was crawling into bed and sleeping forever. But first they had to walk three long miles in the dark, then they had to drive all the way back to Cortez. She quailed at the thought, then straightened her shoulders. She'd got herself into this, just as she'd gotten herself into a lot of bizarre situations, and she'd darn well get herself out. And she'd never admit to Joe Buck how tired she was, because he'd only remind her, once more, that she'd wanted to come along. Oh, yes, he'd remind her in that dry way he had, in his low, rich voice that was like melted chocolate.

They walked, Joe in front, then Laurel, then Dog, trotting along tirelessly. The landscape looked to her like an old black-and-white movie, a profusion of shades of gray, with lousy film quality and soft focus. Nothing looked familiar, not a rock or a hump of dirt or an outcropping of crumbling shale. She just put one foot in front of the other. They'd get there sooner or later. Joe knew the way.

Halfway there they stopped for a few minutes to drink some water out of a canteen Joe kept hooked on his belt. Laurel hadn't realized how thirsty she was; she must have sweat a lot from pure terror. She gulped half of the canteen down, then handed it to Joe and couldn't help watching how his strong throat worked as he drank.

"Are you warm enough?" he asked, finishing. "It's cooling down."

"I'm okay as long as we keep moving."

"Not too tired?"

"I'm okay," she repeated, damned if she was going to admit any weakness to this renegade.

"I could go on ahead and get the car, drive it back and pick you up," he offered.

"Oh, sure, and I could stay here alone in the middle of the desert at night."

"I'll leave Dog with you."

"No, let's go."

They went on, the half-moon tilting to the other side of the night sky now, casting long, oblique shadows of dusty black. Off in the distance Laurel heard a coyote yip and howl, then another answered, then another.

Dog pricked his ears and stopped for a moment, sniffing the air.

"Come on, Dog," Joe said.

"Do coyotes attack people?" Laurel asked.

"Nope. Too smart."

"Oh."

"They can make trouble, though. The coyote caused wars between people, according to Ute legends."

"How's that?"

"It's just an old story," Joe said, striding alongside her now, occasionally guiding her with a hand against her back.

"So, tell me," she urged him. What she didn't let on to Joe was that his voice somehow gave her comfort in the eerie shadows of the night. "Just how did the coyote cause these wars?"

Joe gave a short laugh. "Well, it was like this. Before there were people in the world, Sinawaf the Creator began to cut sticks and put them in a big bag. This went on for a long time until the curious Coyote couldn't stand the suspense any longer. One day when Sinawaf was gone Coyote opened the bag. People came spilling out, speaking different languages and scattering in all directions. When Sinawaf returned there were only a few people left, and he was very angry, because he'd planned to distribute them evenly. With Coyote's unequal distribution there would be war, each group trying to gain land from its neighbor. The only people remaining in the bag were the Ute, and they stayed right there in the mountains where all this happened."

"That's a nice story," Laurel said.

"Strangely enough, the Ute don't have a migration legend, which most Indian tribes have. No one knows exactly where we came from."

"You probably know more than I do about where you came from—and where you belong. You must have a sense of who and what you are that's very clear."

"Oh, yeah, an Indian has a great sense of where he belongs in the tribe, but not the sense of self you're thinking of. An Indian is first and foremost a member of a tribe. Your system of society and government is rooted in individualism, not in the tribe, and so it causes a lot of conflict for us."

"Do you feel that conflict? You seem so..."

"Civilized? White? There's a term for that—apple, meaning red on the outside, white in the center. I understand that blacks have a similar concept."

"You seem pretty well adjusted, better than half my friends."

"I do my best."

"Don't we all," Laurel mused.

They were walking along together, the flashlight beam dancing over the rough terrain. "What a night," she said. "Actually, that first night was crazy, too." Her legs were tired but pleasantly so now that they were almost back at the car. "And I thought Cortez was a dull little town."

"Why did you move here?" Joe asked.

"Well, it's not a permanent move," she said.

"But why Cortez?"

"Oh, to do the article on the Ute Tribal Park," she said quickly, hating to trivialize the burning importance of her real reason.

"I'd think you'd just get a motel room," he said. "You don't move to an area every time you do an article about it, do you?"

"Well, no. But this one is . . . in-depth. I have to get a feel for the area, you know."

"Not really."

"Well, I do. And I like my things around me. I hate to live out of a suitcase. Of course, it's not like I have a big house of my own in California or anything. It's pretty easy for me to pack up and go."

"Footloose and fancy-free," Joe remarked.

"Very," Laurel said emphatically.

He shone the flashlight on something ahead of them, and a metallic reflection struck Laurel's eye. "The car," she said gratefully. "You found it!"

"You ever hear of an Indian getting lost?" he asked drolly.

She sighed as she slumped against the back of the car seat. It felt good to sit on something soft, to relax. She glanced at her watch in the car's dome light as Joe got in the driver's side. Almost two-thirty in the morning!

Then there was the long, slow drive out along the rutted track, the Taurus bouncing and bottoming out. Laurel thought it would never end, but it did finally, and then they were on the highway that eventually went through Towaoc and back to Cortez.

"What are you going to do now?" Laurel asked, her eyes scratchy as she stared at the highway ahead.

"Find out who that truck belongs to."

"And then?"

"It depends on who it is."

"Hmm." Laurel looked down at her hands in the dim light. She couldn't see very well, but they looked dirty. She scrubbed them on her shorts as if she'd touched the deadly substance in those drums. "Joe?" she said.

"What?"

"I don't know about you going this alone."

"It's already decided."

"But the FBI..."

He laughed without humor. "You ever read about the mess they made on the res in North Dakota? The Leonard Peltier thing?"

"They can't all be incompetent," she said.

But all he said was, "No. No FBI yet."

"Joe Buck on the warpath," she muttered.

"You bet," he growled.

The casino lights were the only ones on among the scattered buildings of Towaoc. There were still cars parked in the huge lots as they drove by.

"One of my brothers works there," Joe said. "He's a dealer. Makes darn good money."

"How many brothers do you have?"

"Three and Rose, my sister."

"A big family."

"Yeah, pretty big. How about you?"

"I'm a spoiled only child. My parents got divorced when I was just a kid. My mother's remarried."

"Does she live in California?"

"Yes. Sausalito, just north of San Francisco. My stepfather's a stockbroker in the city."

"You were a rich kid?"

"Rich is a nebulous word. We had enough."

"How about love?"

"Oh, my mother loved me to death."

"Controlling?"

"Everyone wanted to control me then, Joe," she said.

"But not anymore, I take it."

Laurel was feeling ill at ease. "Stop interrogating me," she said. While she wanted to learn more about

Joe, she wasn't prepared to reciprocate yet. The memories were still too painful.

Joe was silent for a time, then he said, "Look, I know it's late, but I'd like to stop at my place and check it out. You aren't too tired, are you?"

"Who, me?"

He turned off the highway just past the town and drove up a long driveway, the car lights finally reflecting off his small house.

"This is yours?"

"Yup. Home sweet home. You want to wait here?"

"No, I'll come."

"Curious, huh?"

"Always."

The front door was obviously unlocked, and she could see Joe stiffen as he turned the knob. He swore under his breath when he pushed the door open and switched on a light.

"Oh!" Laurel said.

A television set was upside down on the floor, shards of glass everywhere. Joe looked at it, legs spread apart, hands on his hips. His mouth was a hard line.

"Somebody's been here?" Laurel ventured.

"I knew they'd trace me through my car," he said angrily.

"They know where you live," she said softly.

"Yeah, that guy in the pickup. Damn. I really can't stay here now."

Laurel looked around at the austerity of the living room. So this was where Joe lived.

Dog was sniffing the floor, following a scent. He growled and went down a hallway. Joe followed, Laurel right behind him.

His bedroom. A bright red-and-black blanket tucked in army-style on a narrow bed, a dresser, a feathered wall hanging. The bedroom window was broken, glass on the floor under it.

"Damn."

"He got in here," Laurel mused aloud.

"This is personal now," Joe said grimly. "I'm going to find that son of a buck if it's the last thing I do."

She stood there watching him. His anger was justifiable but scary; Joe looked fierce when he scowled like that. Suddenly she felt sorry for the man—or men—who'd broken in. She didn't doubt for a moment that Joe would find them. She shivered a little.

"Okay, only a couple more things," he said, "then we can go. Nothing I can do here."

He went to his closet and reached in. When Laurel saw what he'd retrieved, she paled.

"Do you really think you need that?" she asked.

Joe was holding a shotgun and putting a box of shells in a duffel bag. "Best to be prepared," he said, opening drawers and piling clothes in the duffel.

She looked away, shaken. "Sure, uh, well, I'll wait in the car, okay?"

When he came out a minute later, he put the bag and gun in the back seat, Dog hopped in and Joe silently slid behind the wheel. Knowing the gun was there made Laurel uncomfortable; it hammered home as nothing else had done the implications of what was going on. Were there really men looking for her? Did they know her license number, too? Joe had warned her to keep her car in the garage, but could they have seen her license when she picked Joe up that night? What if they'd found out her address from her license number and broken into *her* house? She shivered again.

"Cold?" he asked, driving the dark, silent highway toward Cortez.

"No. Yes. Do you think they know where I live?"

"We'll find out."

"Oh, God . . ."

"Don't worry."

"Okay, whatever you say."

She held her breath as they drove into Cortez. She held it all the way to Cottonwood Street. She held it till her temples pounded and her chest hurt. She was still holding it when Joe turned into her driveway and shut the Taurus off. Then she let it out, sitting there in the dark with him, the only sound the warm engine ticking over.

"Well?" she whispered.

"I'll go in first. Give me your keys."

"You don't really think . . . ?"

"No, I don't, but it's better to be sure."

"Okay."

"You wait here," he said, "and no funny business. No following me."

"I swear I won't," she said in a small voice, getting her keys from her pocket.

He got out of the car and leaned over, taking the keys from her. And then he lifted the shotgun from the back seat, unzipped the duffel bag and opened the box of shells. He broke open the gun, loaded it and closed it with a loud click. His dark eyes met hers—she could feel his gaze rather than see it. "Don't come in until I signal that it's okay."

He walked to the front door, a tall, dark figure, his dog beside him. She could see him there, unlocking the door, opening it, very slowly, then he and Dog slipped inside, two shadowed apparitions. Her eyes were glued to the front door. She rubbed them, afraid to blink. Her heart pounded a slow, turgid beat. Then one of those awful, unbidden fantasies that seemed to last forever seized her mind: the man was inside, got the drop on Joe, shot him, and Laurel was there, watching the police zip his long body into a black plastic bag, so sad, so alone.... She shut the fantasy down firmly.

And then the light went on in her living room, and Joe appeared silhouetted in her doorway, gesturing for her to come in.

She ran to him, almost sobbing with weariness and gratitude, her knees weak with relief.

"Hey, it's okay," he said, putting a hand on her arm. "No one's been here."

She rubbed a hand over her face. "Thank heavens." Then she slumped down on the couch, stretching her scratched and dirty legs straight out in front of her.

"Yeah, I know how you feel," Joe said, putting the gun in the coat closet.

"I doubt that." She looked up at him. "You're staying here for sure tonight. I mean after what we just saw at your place."

"It's for the best," he said.

She waved a hand. "It's all right. There isn't much left of the night, anyway. But tomorrow...tomorrow there's someone very important coming to see me, so you've got to be out of the way."

"Okay, I'll be out of your hair, don't worry."

"So, good night, Joe. Thanks for the adventure. And—I get the bathroom first."

Her bed had never felt so good. She slid between the sheets, sighing with pleasure, feeling the tiredness in her body all the way down into her bones. Then her heart gave a little lurch. Tomorrow—oh, God... She lay there, suddenly wide awake, only too aware of Joe Buck rustling around on the couch in her living room, and thought about the coming day.

Tomorrow was the day Holly was to start work. Tomorrow an utter stranger, a fifteen-year-old girl Laurel had never seen, but had dreamed about for all those years, would walk through her door.

Tomorrow.

CHAPTER EIGHT

JOE DROVE THE RENTED Taurus toward Towaoc the next morning and thought about Laurel. He searched his mind for a word to describe her mood and finally decided she'd been preoccupied all morning, distant, quite unlike her usual cocky self. It was as if she'd gone to bed one person and woken up another. Well, he thought, he hardly knew Laurel Velarde. He'd already sensed she had secrets, odd dark corners of her life, and maybe it was none of his business, but she'd brushed off all his questions, telling him only that she had an important meeting that afternoon and he needed to be out from underfoot.

An important meeting.

"You aren't taking your car out?" he'd asked before leaving for Towaoc.

"No, Joe," she'd replied, "I'm staying right here."

"Good, good," he'd muttered, envisioning a man coming by her house, someone visiting, maybe from California—someone tall and blond, a real suave dude.

When Joe pulled up across the street from the BIA police headquarters, Charlie Redmoon's official car was still there. He checked his watch. Why hadn't the old man gone on home for lunch? But it wasn't ten minutes later that Redmoon did appear and climb into his car and drive off, and Joe got out and crossed the dusty street, Dog dutifully at his heel.

"Well, well," Nancy Bearcross said when he poked his head in the door, "the big stud's back."

"Yeah," Joe said, taking his sunglasses off and determining how empty the building was, "but this little visit is going to be our secret, sweetheart."

Nancy's black eyes narrowed.

She was a big woman, the police dispatcher, probably close to more than two hundred pounds of female. The casual observer would have assumed she was married, had children, the whole nine yards. But Joe knew Nancy was single, single and very much sought after. Hell, there wasn't a day that three or four of her male friends didn't stop by to invite her to a movie in Cortez or a moonlit drive out onto the reservation. Nancy Bearcross might have been overweight, but each solid pound was all woman. She possessed a singular animal magnetism, all right, and Joe himself wasn't immune to it.

"You look good," Nancy said. "I've been thinking about you, Joe Buck. I was going to call you and suggest a sweat bath with the old ones to get your head straight, but you look fine. Oh, and some chick called to thank you for finding her purse. Never off duty, eh, Joe Buck?"

Joe sat on the edge of her desk and casually leafed through some papers. "You know it, and I'm fine," he said.

"You're not angry with old Charlie?"

Joe shook his head slowly. "Not really. I suppose from his point of view I screwed up."

"Humph," she intoned, shifting her bulky weight, "and what about your point of view, Joe?"

"I'm still thinking about it."

"I bet. So why the visit?" she asked. "Charlie told you he didn't want to see your face for two weeks. And you've got that look."

"What look?"

"That shifty look, like you're ready to go on the warpath."

"That's what I love about you," he said. "You're so trusting." He leaned over then and gave her a lingering kiss on her satin-smooth brown cheek. "God, you taste good. How do you do it?" he asked.

"My secret," she said, and pushed him away. "Now, why don't you just tell me what you want?"

Bantering words back and forth, still engaged in their flirtation—a familiar game—Joe finally got it out.

"Now let me get this straight," Nancy said, tossing a heavy black braid over her round shoulder. "You want me to risk my job for you and call Denver and check out a license plate number?"

"It's no big deal," Joe said, looking wounded, and Dog gave a big sigh as he settled in a corner.

"It's a big deal if Charlie or the superintendent get wind of it. This office is off-limits to you. You *and* that stinky mutt."

"No one's going to find out unless you tell them."

"I don't know, Joe...."

"Dinner," he said. "I'll buy you the best dinner in town."

"Peking duck at the Chinese restaurant," she said.

"Peking duck it is. Now will you make that call?" Shifting, Joe reached into the back pocket of his jeans and handed her a slip of paper with the pickup's license number on it.

"You know," Nancy said, her eyes following his movements, "that's some pair of buns you got on you, Sergeant Joe Buck."

"You've got some pretty fine curves yourself, sweetheart."

Nancy held the slip of paper between two fingers. "Dinner and what else?" she said.

"It'll be your night," Joe replied smoothly. "I'm all yours."

"Promises, promises," she said, and reached for the phone.

Five minutes later Joe had the name, Mountain Construction Company, with an address in the Denver suburb of Lakewood. It wasn't much, but it was a start.

"So who or what is this Mountain Construction?" Nancy asked.

"Huh?" Joe muttered, thinking.

"I asked what was going on."

"Ah, nothing," he said.

"Sure," she replied.

He stood and walked to the window in the small cinder block structure. The unpleasant scenario was coalescing in his head, some nuclear plant out there unable to get rid of its waste. What better solution than to dump the stuff on an Indian reservation, especially one way the hell out in the boonies?

And then, too, there had been those rumblings on the reservation for months now, rumors flitting around among the old-timers about Mother Earth being poisoned and the life flow of the land drying up, withering, scattering like dust before the wind. Well, maybe the rumors were true.

"Joe?" Nancy was saying, coming up behind him. "What is it?" But he didn't hear. Instead, he was battling a strong rage that was rising within him. The land of his people might not be worth much, not in terms of white man's money, but this was the land of the Utes, despite the fact that no one could ever own the earth, and it should be respected, kept pure and clean so that it could continue unharmed.

My God, Joe was thinking, they had to be stopped.

"You big dummy," Nancy said. "You aren't going to tell me, are you?"

Joe finally turned and pasted a smile on his lips. "It's nothing," he said, "really. Someday I'll fill you in." And he bent and gave her another gentle kiss.

Nancy sighed. "Get out of here, you good-looking hunk of man, before Charlie comes back."

"I'm going," Joe said, and pulled open the door, letting in a blast of hot, dry air, while Dog took off for the car. "And thanks."

"Don't you go getting yourself burned," Nancy said to his broad back, "playing with fire the way you do, Joe Buck."

After leaving police headquarters, Joe stopped at the gas station in Towaoc to give Dog a drink of water while he formulated a course of action. He knew he could always park himself at that remote dumping site and just wait until those trucks showed up again, but there were two things wrong with that scenario. First, he couldn't arrest a group of men, some of whom were most likely armed, all by himself. And second, he might have to wait for months before they showed up out there again, especially now that they'd been alerted.

He *could* go to Redmoon. But he knew he wouldn't, not yet. Or, as Laurel had suggested, he could still go to the federal authorities.... No, not in a thousand years, he thought, not until he got to the bottom of this and could present them with solid evidence about what was happening on the land.

But he did need help. He held the hose behind the gas station for Dog to lap up the water and admitted to himself that he really did need help—Laurel's would be just the ticket, too, what with her press credentials and that wholesome, innocent look of hers.

He took a long drink of water himself and then got a candy bar from the vending machine and shared it with Dog while he strode to the phone booth and dropped a quarter into the slot, dialing Laurel's number. If she refused to help him, Joe decided while the phone rang, then so be it, he'd go it alone. Nothing new there.

"Hello?" she said after the third ring, and Joe was positive there was tension in her voice.

"It's me. You okay?"

"Of course I'm okay," she was quick to reply.

"You alone?" he asked, a tingle edging up his spine.

"Yes, I'm alone. Look, Joe, I'm real busy, though. I'll, ah, talk to you later," she said, and then she simply hung up.

He stood there for a long moment, staring at the phone in his hand, and a picture flashed through his mind—Laurel was not alone at all. There'd been this man standing next to her, holding a gun on her....

"Shit!" Joe whispered, his blood freezing.

IN REALITY LAUREL WAS NOT fine. She was a bundle of raw nerves, and if she'd pulled back the kitchen curtain once to look for the teenager to come up the drive, she'd pulled it back a dozen times.

She was besieged by questions: What would Holly think of her? Who did she look like? Laurel? Gray? Both of them? Would Holly notice a resemblance—or care? And what if she did care? How would the Schultzes feel to learn that Laurel had contacted their daughter?

She paced the kitchen and pulled the curtain back again and strained to see down the street. It was three o'clock; Holly was supposed to be here. Maybe she'd forgotten, decided not to take the job after all.

At five minutes past three Laurel went outside and turned on the sprinkler, trying to look casual—just starting the afternoon's gardening, folks. But nonetheless she kept swiveling her head, checking the street.

At ten past the hour, sweat trickling down between her breasts and dampening her underwear, Laurel was squatting by a flower bed, pulling some weeds, her mouth dry, her heart thudding. Where was Holly?

She didn't know what to do, whether to keep working or go inside and try to write. Oh, God, she couldn't write; she couldn't even concentrate.

Her daughter. The only time she'd seen her had been when she'd just been born, a squalling infant, all wrinkled and red and yet so beautiful. A beautiful little girl. Her *child*. And just outside the delivery room had been the Schultzes, Earl and Fran, though Laurel hadn't known who they were then. God, how she'd hated those faceless people! How she'd hated the world!

She rested on her haunches, a weed in her hand, waiting. The suspense, the trepidation, the anticipation, built in her like foam on a boiling pot. Any second it would boil over. Where was Holly?

When she finally came it was almost an anticlimax. A tall, coltish girl with a honey-brown ponytail walking carelessly, casually, down the sidewalk, then hesitating at Laurel's driveway.

Laurel rose too quickly, the weed forgotten in her hand, and devoured the girl with her eyes, absorbed the freckles, the nose and mouth, until Holly noticed her. Brown eyes—Gray's eyes—turned toward her, and Laurel abruptly felt faint. She swayed and put a hand to her head. The girl stared at her, puzzled.

"A head rush," Laurel said faintly. "Got up too fast."

"Oh," the girl said. "Uh, excuse me, but are you Mrs. Velarde?" She stopped and looked awkwardly around, one skinny knee bent, her hands clasped.

Laurel swallowed, still feeling dizzy. "It's, ah, Miss Velarde," she got out.

"Oh, sorry."

"That's okay, it's a natural assumption," Laurel said inanely, and then it was as if the world ground to a halt and time hung suspended above the hot, weedy little yard. Laurel stared at her child, the flesh of her flesh, and recalled with astounding clarity her pregnancy, the shame and fear and that sense of complete abandonment. The pain of the birth came back to her, the wrenching seconds that she could see the doctor and nurses handling the red-streaked infant, the impression of arms and legs and little toes and fingers. The tremendous *love*. And then the newborn was gone, covered in a hospital blanket and taken away while the doctor uttered kindly platitudes, and all Laurel had been able to think was, my life is over.

The months of healing her wounded heart had passed eventually, and she'd finally, a year behind her friends, gone off to college and journalism school at Berkeley. She'd tried desperately not to think about the baby, though over the years a part of Laurel could instantly calculate the child's age, right down to the hour. But most of the time she was able to keep that inner knowledge buried, and with maturity life had taken on meaning. Still, on the girl's birthdays—though she knew neither the child's name nor whereabouts, Laurel was miserably depressed.

The years fell away, fulfilling years that saw Laurel building a career that suited her temperament, because there'd always been a wild streak in her, a need to challenge the parameters of life.

Of course she denied the other, deeper reason that drove her to try everything, every new taste and smell and experience. She sold articles to a travel magazine, which had landed her at her present job, and the amazing thing was that *Travel Adventure* had called *her*.

She'd traveled, all right, and made a passable living to boot. But always there'd been that emptiness, that sense of loss. Where was her child? Was she happy, healthy? And then one day she simply couldn't stand the pain any longer and she'd mustered up the nerve to call the private investigator.

Oh, he'd milked her dry, that was true, padding his expenses, contacting her dutifully every week to tell her he was making "real progress." The months had gone by, the years. All in all he'd taken Laurel for over thirty thousand dollars—the total of her inheritance from her estranged natural father. But in the end the investigator had come up with her child's name and the address

of the ranch in Cortez, and Laurel figured he'd possessed that knowledge for some time—but she didn't
care. Holly Schultz. Her child had a name and a life in
a safe but isolated corner of the world. And Laurel
wanted to see her.

"...Sorry I'm late, Miss Velarde, but my dad had to
drop me in town and I walked..."

Laurel felt the earth begin to rotate again and she
shook herself mentally. "Ah, that's all right, Holly,"
she said, clearing her throat, "the day's still young."
And then they both just stood there. "Say, maybe we
should have a soda or something before we get to work
on this awful yard. You want one?" she offered, realizing that she was staring too hard and her heartbeat
was frantic.

"Sure, that would be nice," Holly said, and she followed Laurel into the kitchen.

Later, much later, Laurel would laugh about the incident, but at the time she could have throttled Joe
Buck. One second she was searching the fridge for two
sodas and the next the back screen door was banging
open and there was Joe, crouching, Dog growling at his
side, Joe's eyes searching the room.

"What in God's name do you think you're doing?"
Laurel demanded, straightening.

And poor Holly. He'd scared the wits out of her and
she'd let out a shriek.

"Joe," Laurel said as he came upright, a bemused
look on his face. "What are you doing?"

"I, ah," he began, and he stared at Holly Schultz as
if she was a leper. "I thought you were, ah, you know,
maybe in some kind of, ah, trouble here."

"Oh, hell," Laurel said as she placed her hands on
her hips and glared at him.

"I mean, when I called from Towaoc you sounded..."

"I know what you're trying to say," she ground out. "But as you can see, Sergeant, we're both fine."

"Uh-huh," he muttered.

"Now, if you don't mind," she said, "Holly and I have some work to do."

"Ah," he said, "yes, I can see that," and he kept right on staring at the teenager.

After a long moment Laurel said, "Joe Buck, this is Holly Schultz. She's here to help me with some yard work. Holly, this is Joe. He's with the BIA police. He's, ah, a friend I met here."

"We've met," Joe said, "haven't we, Holly?"

The girl, who was still cowering near the living room door, looked at her tennis shoes. "Yes, sir, we've met," she said in a whisper, and Laurel wondered about that.

"Well," Joe said, "I'll be going, then."

"Yes, do that," Laurel said pointedly. "We'll talk later, okay?"

"Yes," Joe said, backing out the door with Dog. "Later, then." And he was gone.

"That was weird, Miss Velarde," Holly said when Laurel finally handed her the Coke.

"It's Laurel," she replied, popping open her own can. "You can call me Laurel."

"Well, anyway, Laurel," the girl said, uneasy with the familiarity, "he's a really scary dude, Sergeant Buck."

"I don't know about that," Laurel said, and wondered again just why her child happened to know the Indian policeman, but she let the notion go—she had far more important things to discover about Holly Schultz.

For a time they rattled around the toolshed at the end of the drive, looking for gloves, and a shovel and spade. The lawn mower worked, though, and there was even some gas left in the old, dented red gas can. Of course, Laurel couldn't have cared less about the lawn and weedy flower beds. But it was a way to work companionably with Holly. They cleared out the shed and made two piles, one for usable stuff, the other for trash.

"Yuck," Holly said, holding up a greasy rag with spiderwebs on it, and they both made a face and laughed, and Laurel felt the first of the ice begin to melt.

On her knees, pulling weeds out of a flower bed that ran alongside the short drive, Laurel said, "How do you like school here?"

The girl waved a fly away. "It's okay."

"Just okay?"

"Well, I guess my friends are all there. It's okay."

"Grades not so good?"

"They're okay. I got a D in English, though, and my mom's pretty piss . . . mad about it."

"Um," Laurel said. "Maybe English is hard for you. Grammar and all that."

"It's not so hard," Holly said. "History and math are worse."

"But you got better grades on them?"

"A little," she admitted reluctantly.

"Well," Laurel said, "sometimes high school is tough. I was no rocket scientist, myself."

"You got bad grades?" Holly asked, perking up—a comrade in arms.

"Sometimes," Laurel said, thinking about the end of her senior year, the pregnancy. I was pregnant with you, she thought, but she'd never say it aloud. Yet maybe the opportunity would come, maybe someday she'd get a chance to tell her baby everything.

Surreptitiously, Laurel studied her daughter as the heat of the summer's day drifted around them and side by side they worked and sweated. She was a pretty girl, Laurel decided or would be pretty, but Holly was still at an awkward age where her teeth were too big and her limbs too long and thin. Gawky. But then Laurel had been, too. She'd hated her nose and her hands, and when everyone said she had lovely eyes she hadn't believed a word. And those freckles . . . As much as Laurel enjoyed summer, the sun only made them stand out all the more. She could see the same pattern in her child. If there was a big difference between them, it was in the eyes. Laurel's were green and Holly's were dark velvety brown, like Gray's.

Laurel thought about him, too, that afternoon. She hadn't seen Gray Baxter since high school, but today for some reason his face was as plain in her memory as her own. Odd, she mused, but then she supposed her memories were very keen just now.

She'd told Gray she was pregnant on graduation night. He'd taken it well, not getting upset, kissing her. He was such a calm person, that was one of the things she'd loved about him, so even-tempered and logical.

He'd said to her in his cool, measured way, "Laurel, you know I love you, and this is my responsibility, too."

Oh, she'd loved him so much, then. "I don't know what to do, Gray," she said, and the feeling of being able to share her secret was such a relief that tears came to her eyes. She could never tell her mother, who would find a way to control even this situation.

"We'll take care of it together," he said. "We're both too young to start a family, Laurel. You know that. I've got to finish college, and you do, too."

It had dawned on her then what he meant, and a chill had settled over her. She knew he was right, but her mind balked.

"But Gray, I..."

He smiled at her. "It was a mistake. No use paying for it all our lives." And he held her tenderly, patiently convincing her of what needed to be done.

Handsome, smart, ambitious Gray. She'd heard years later that he'd become a lawyer. It figured.

He drove her to the clinic the following week. He'd taken care of everything, even made the appointment. He said he would come in with her, wait, drive her home, and she cried in the car on the way there, unable to stop, ashamed of her weakness, and Gray began to get impatient.

"For God's sake, Laurel," he said. "It's not like you're doing something terrible."

At the front door of the clinic, her feet simply stopped carrying her forward. "I can't," she said.

"Laurel," Gray began, exasperated.

"No, I can't. Take me home."

"Don't be ridiculous, you're making a big deal out of this."

"It *is* a big deal," she sobbed. "Take me home."

"I won't take you home. Either you go in there and get this done or I won't take any more responsibility, Laurel," he said in a tone she'd never heard before. "I won't ruin *my* life over this!"

She stopped crying and stared at him, and she knew then what was happening. He was just like all the others, trying to make her do what he wanted. "Gray, please," she said, her chest so tight she could barely talk.

"No, Laurel, I know what's right."

The tears spilled over again, but she was past caring. "You said you loved me!"

"I won't go down with you, Laurel."

Then she ran from him, across the baking-hot asphalt parking lot of the clinic, and she stopped in a park nearby, sweating, nauseated, and threw up on the grass, utterly spent, utterly humiliated.

And that had been the last time she'd seen Gray Baxter.

AT FIVE, AFTER THE LAWN was mowed, they took a sandwich break and sat at the kitchen table together.

"What time is your dad coming?" Laurel asked, her mouth half full of what Laurel called a gourmet peanut butter and jelly sandwich.

"Around five-thirty in town, I guess. He had to go to Durango and get a part for our tractor."

"Um," Laurel said. "I imagine ranching is hard. I've really never been on one, myself, much less worked one."

"It's okay."

"You don't sound very convinced," Laurel observed as she studied her child's face. *My child,* she kept thinking.

"It's kinda boring, I guess."

"Um. No friends out there?"

Holly shook her head and her ponytail swung over a shoulder. Automatically, Laurel reached up and touched her own hair, braided as usual. "My friends all live in Cortez," Holly was saying, "and I'm the only one stuck out in the boondocks." She made a face.

"You won't be out there forever," Laurel said carefully.

"If my dad has his way, I will."

"I see," Laurel said. "Don't your parents want you to go to college? I mean, agricultural college or something like that?"

Holly frowned. "My dad's so against me leaving I can't even tell you. It's like... weird."

"Um." Laurel considered that. Perhaps, because Holly was an only child, her father was afraid to let her go. Maybe he was too possessive, or maybe Holly was exaggerating. It was hard to tell. Half of her almost wanted to believe that the Schultzes were bad parents, but the dominant half just wanted to know that they were good to Holly, that they loved her as if she were their own.

Laurel took a drink of ice tea and mused. In a couple of years Holly would be old enough to make her own decisions, maybe even the decision to come and live with her. And Laurel would never stifle her child— she'd show her the world, buy her the most beautiful clothes, send her to the best college. Whatever Holly wanted. It *could* happen.

She thought about the Schultzes a lot. The investigator had been certain the parents had not told Holly about the adoption. Did Holly Schultz ever look at her mother and father, notice the lack of resemblance and wonder? And what about the Schultzes? They probably loved their little girl, perhaps even doted on her, spoiled her. If she were taken away from them... Laurel winced inwardly at the thought of what they'd go through, then stopped herself. She'd have to wait and see. She'd just taken the first step, and that was all she could do for now. Evidently Earl and Fran were second-generation Germans. Strong, sturdy, hard-working stock. And big on discipline. In the investigator's report he'd written that they were apparently quite strict. Well, Laurel thought, that wasn't all bad. And yet Joe knew the child. Cortez was a small town, but not that small. She picked up their plates, put them in the sink and wondered if she had the nerve to ask Joe about Holly, just how and why he knew her. Or maybe it was better not to know.

She'd promised herself not to do anything rash when she'd come to Cortez. First off, she'd planned to just *see* Holly. That was the most important thing. Then she'd have to feel out what the girl's family was like. She'd told herself a million times she'd never do a thing to hurt Holly. If her folks were good people, if she was happy, well... Laurel would have to decide what to do then.

If, however, she found out that the Schultzes were abusive or neglectful—or anything short of wonderful—she'd have them in court so fast their heads would spin! It had happened lately that courts were awarding custody of an adopted child to its natural parents when the adoptive ones were found lacking, sometimes even when the adoptive parents were good people.

She had to be careful. The most important thing here was her daughter's happiness, and she'd never do anything to jeopardize that.

Well, she'd completed the first step. She'd seen Holly. She'd seen her daughter. That would have to be enough for now.

They went back to the yard and put away the gardening tools and the mower and locked up the shed. Then Holly said she had to meet her dad soon in town, and Laurel paid her in cash, giving her a handsome tip. She really had been quite a help.

"Gosh, thanks, Laurel," Holly said, stuffing the money into the pocket of her shorts.

"You know," Laurel said while they stood at the end of the drive, "there's so much to be done in this yard. If you're free I could really use some more help tomorrow. What do you think?"

"That would be great."

"Now you're sure you aren't supposed to be helping at the ranch tomorrow?"

The teenager shook her head and her beautiful ponytail swung, catching the golden afternoon light. "No, I can come tomorrow."

"You need a ride or anything?"

"No, my mom or dad come to town just about every day, anyway."

"Let's say two o'clock, then. Or whenever you can make it. I'll just be here working on my article."

"That's so cool," Holly said. "Wait till I tell my friends you're a writer."

"I'll tell you all about it tomorrow," Laurel said. "It's been pretty exciting."

"Wow," Holly said. "Okay." And then she left, waving and smiling and heading up the street. For a long time Laurel stood at the end of the drive and stared after her, watching the way her hair swung and how her long legs ate up the distance. She felt an enormous melting inside, a warm flow of love that she had never experienced before. There was a kind of sadness, too, that so many years had been wasted. But maybe she could make up for all that lost time. Maybe today was the start of a relationship between them, whatever form that might take.

CHAPTER NINE

HOLLY SCHULTZ unconsciously hummed one of her favorite songs from Wilson-Phillips as she walked up Cottonwood Street away from Miss Velarde's house. Laurel. She wanted to be called Laurel, Holly reminded herself. What a neat lady. A writer. Wow. She'd been all over, traveled. That's what Holly wanted to do—get away from dull old Cortez, stuck out in the middle of nowhere—and see the world. It was out there, all the excitement and big cities and things Holly couldn't even imagine, yet here she was, held down, kicking and screaming, and made to go to school and boring stuff like that.

She put her hand in her pocket to feel the crisp bills Laurel had paid her and she smiled to herself. It was easy work; Laurel would never know how easy after ranch chores, and Holly never got paid a penny for those. It was easy and she made money and it got her off the ranch. Besides, she liked Laurel. Tomorrow she'd ask a million questions about her job and where she'd been.

Holly was supposed to meet her father at five-thirty in front of the City Market. She was headed that way, ambling along. He'd ask her about her day and what the lady was like and what work she'd had to do, then he'd tell her about the new part he'd picked up in Durango—oh wow, real exciting—a tractor blade or something. And then when she got home she'd have to repeat everything for her mother. Then there they'd be, the three of them, sitting around the dinner table like every night, saying the same boring things, and the whole world beyond that same old place would be buzzing and humming, people doing things, having a blast, all without Holly Schultz.

She couldn't stand it. Her feet took her in a different direction, not toward City Market, but toward the Holloways' house, where Josh was having the guys over, she was sure, because his parents were still in Utah camping.

She set her jaw and began to walk faster. She was going to party with her friends, that was that. She had to. Inside her the hunger for her friends, for fun, for experiences, was so undeniable that she didn't care if her father waited for her in front of City Market for hours. She had things to do. Her parents were old and boring and they didn't understand her; they only wanted to keep her shut in and controlled. And besides, Holly reasoned, her dad wouldn't wait too long at the market. He'd figure she'd gotten off early and made her way home. It was no big deal, it had happened before.

She walked faster now, practically running. She was almost there, and her heart quickened with gladness. They'd all be there at Josh's, and there'd be beer and maybe something stronger, and music. Things would be happening.

She burst in through the front door as if she'd reached a sanctuary, and they were there, twenty kids at least, hanging out, draped over chairs or on the floor, the stereo blasting, beer cans sitting around.

"Hey, Holly!" Josh called out, grinning.

"Thought you couldn't make it," Suzy said.

"Well, I'm here," Holly said, tossing her ponytail.

"Come on in, get yourself a brew," invited Chris.

"Don't mind if I do," she replied, and went straight to the kitchen, opened the refrigerator and pulled out a cold can of beer.

Janie was necking with Rob Jarvak; Holly wondered if they'd gone all the way yet. She'd like to ask Janie what it was like. Did it hurt? Did you like it? She wondered when she herself would do it, with whom and where it would be. She'd wondered about that endlessly.

Holly drank the first beer quickly. She sat on the couch next to Josh, her legs folded up Indian-style. Josh had a kind of glazed look and he smiled a lot. A bottle was being passed around—some clear stuff. Holly took a swig and nearly choked.

"Good stuff," Josh said.

"Who's got the Eagles CD?" Ricky McCoy was asking. "Come on, where is it? I wanna hear that one they do... you know, the fast one."

"Shut up, Ricky," someone said.

Laughter came from the kitchen. The television was on, some dumb program that nobody was watching, and it added to the din.

Holly wandered around, a little unsteady, and she was happy. Someone handed her a piece of bread covered with peanut butter and jelly, and she took it. Dinner. She thought that was pretty funny. She and Laurel had just had the same thing. A neat lady... "Gourmet peanut butter and jelly," she explained to anyone who would listen.

She was in the den, watching Josh sleep. She cocked her head. He looked about ten years old. That was funny, too.

Ricky came into the den and assessed Holly. He was older, a junior, Holly thought. She held her half-eaten piece of bread out. "Would you care for some gourmet peanut butter?" she asked drolly.

"Who're you? Oh, I know, Holly. That's right, isn't it?"

"That's me, Holly Schultz."

"You're cute."

"Gee, thanks, Ricky," she said, trying to be the sophisticate, but her heart sped up and she felt a thrill run through her.

He came close to her. She could see the pimples on his face, but he had whiskers, real whiskers like a man, and he shaved! She tilted her chin up to him and put a come-hither expression on her face.

"You're okay, Holly."

"You're not too bad yourself," she said daringly, enjoying the power she felt. He was male and she was female, and she sensed the vibes between them. Her body thrummed with expectation.

Ricky pulled Josh off the couch. "He won't care. He's out." They sat down. Ricky tugged her into his arms and kissed her. He smelled like beer, and his whiskers scratched. His hands were all over her, and Holly felt thrills of fear and excitement and pleasure crackle through her like forks of lightning.

They kissed, forever, it seemed. He put his tongue in her mouth, and she didn't half mind it. She felt daring and all-powerful. This was great! She was having a new experience!

Ricky pulled her down and lay next to her. He kissed her again, and she closed her eyes, and that was when the room started going around, spinning horribly, sickeningly.

"Uh," Holly said, trying to sit up.

"What's the matter?"

She shook her head mutely.

Ricky pulled her down again, and for a moment the world still spun in that sickening vortex, but then it settled down, and she could feel Ricky kissing her and hear the music and the voices, but it was all very far away.

She let herself go. It was too hard to fight, and she was so comfortable there, all warm and cozy with Ricky beside her. The last thing she heard before she faded completely was Ricky's voice. "Oh, shit, she's passed out."

JOE CAME BACK just after six that evening, knocking politely at the door, Dog slinking silently beside him. Laurel let him in, caught off guard by the intrusion. She'd just been coming down from the incredible sensation of seeing her daughter, and she'd hoped to savor it alone for a little while longer.

"Sorry about this afternoon," Joe said. "You sounded funny on the phone. I thought..."

"You thought the bad guy had a gun to my head and made me hang up, I know."

She thought about that then, for the first time, really. Joe Buck, the protector, *her* protector. She'd only known this tall, handsome man for a very short time, and yet he was strangely closer to her than any man she'd know since Gray.

Joe cared. It wasn't forced or even his so-called policeman's instinct. He cared about her welfare, even though he'd deny it vehemently. And that was both funny and a little scary.

She lowered her gaze as he said again, "I really am sorry I frightened you two."

"Well, never mind. It's over. No harm done."

"I'd like to make it up to you," he said.

"It's not necessary." Laurel turned away from him and went to sit at the kitchen table.

He wasn't about to give up so easily, though. "The tribe is having a dance tonight. Actually, it's been going on all day, and it'll go on tomorrow, too. The Sun Dance."

She cocked her head and looked up at him. "Are you asking me out?"

"No, Laurel, I'm trying to keep an eye on you, and my family expects me to show up at the dance," he said bluntly.

"Oh."

"Well, what do you say?"

"You don't want me along. I'd be in the way," she said.

"What's this? You're shy?"

"Well, no, but..."

"Aren't you writing an article about the reservation?"

"You know I am, on the outdoor sports angle."

"This is most definitely outdoors, but as far as sport..." He shrugged. "And there's food, a big feast, in fact."

She drew a breath. "I *would* like to go," she said. "But I think we should keep this all in perspective."

"All what?"

"You know, this being together so much. It's just business as far as I'm concerned." She looked up to catch those black eyes fixed on her. "What I mean is, I've got other things going on in my life right now and... Well, I guess I'm not explaining myself very well."

"Oh, I think I get the drift," he said, and she could have sworn there was a touch of anger in his voice, but she must have been mistaken.

Laurel changed into white slacks and a lavender T-shirt, but she was still preoccupied, trying to hold on to the moments she'd spent with her child, praying there would be many more moments to treasure. Maybe even a lifetime's worth.

While she combed out her hair, letting it fall to her shoulders, Joe changed clothes in the bathroom. He appeared wearing clean blue jeans and a turquoise-and-black western-style Roper shirt in an Aztec design. Around his waist was a beautiful silver-buckled, hand-tooled belt. His hair was in its usual ponytail, and he'd tied a red bandanna around his forehead. He looked great, and she felt that familiar, irritating quickening of her pulse.

"Well, I'm ready," she said, sticking the pad and tape recorder into her purse.

"Got a rain jacket?" he asked.

She looked at him askance. "Joe, it hasn't rained here in a month."

"Bring a jacket," he said. "It'll rain tonight."

When they got into the Taurus, it felt crowded to Laurel, as if Joe were too big, leaving her with no space, no air to breathe. For a long time they said nothing to each other, and it made her nervous. She searched her brain for an opening gambit, but everything she came up with seemed somehow suggestive.

They drove out of Cortez back toward the reservation and took a road that led up the side of the Sleeping Ute. Dog sat with his head out the window.

"Okay," Laurel finally said, "now give me some background on this Sun Dance."

He shot her a sideways glance at her from behind his sunglasses. "Are you really taking notes?"

"Isn't that why I'm here?" she said, and she switched on the tape recorder.

Joe finally told her the history of the annual ritual, and she began to realize how personal it was to him. "Do you want me to switch this thing off?" she asked carefully.

But he said he didn't mind, so she taped his explanation of the rite. He explained there were four days of fasting, dancing and meditating, and that the Sun Dance was a search for power, both for yourself and for your people. The dance had been enacted annually for a hundred years.

He didn't say anything more for a while, and she had to prompt him.

"So why, exactly, is this called the Sun Dance?"

He gave her a shrug and said, "The Utes believe they came from the sun. It's a kind of quest, I guess, to get back in touch with our Creator." Joe thought. "I know a guy who believes Indians dance to show the Creator they're here, still going, still making tracks on Mother Earth."

"Interesting."

"You sound like an anthropologist."

Laurel turned the recorder off. "Sorry, I don't mean to. I'd probably sound the same listening to a priest or a rabbi explaining his faith. I *am* interested." She looked at him. "Is this your faith? Or am I getting too personal?"

"You sure are."

He was pensive for a time, then, almost reluctantly, he said, "I'm not sure if it's my faith. All I can say is, it makes as much sense as any other set of beliefs I've come across."

"You're going tonight because your family expects you, not because you're joining the ceremonies?" Laurel said.

"Is that a question?"

"Yes."

"Well, yeah, I'm going because my big sister, Rose, would never forgive me if I didn't, but I like the dance. It…well, I have to say it touches something inside me."

"Tell me about your family."

"Tell me, tell me," he said. "Don't you ever let up?"

"Look, you invited me to this shindig, and I assume I'm going to meet some of your family. I'm only asking about them, for heaven's sake." She sighed. "You mentioned Rose. She's the one who gave you the ride to get your car, the one who has the café in Cortez, right?"

"That's her," he said, and he did go on to tell Laurel about his family, a little, anyway. There was Rose's family, then there was Lawrence and his two sons. That left Joe's married brothers Hank and Gerry, who both worked in the oil fields of Alaska.

"They're getting stinking rich up there," Joe said. "The pay's super." And then he went back to talking about Rose, obviously the matriarch of the Buck clan now that both parents were dead.

"So you, Joe Buck, are the only one still single?" she asked.

"Looks like."

"How come?"

"You want to get back to discussing religion?" he said, staring straight ahead.

Joe drove on, winding up the big hump of rock, the Sleeping Ute, the last bastion of the Rocky Mountains in Colorado's southwestern corner. Silence hung between them for a time, and Laurel felt the need to fill the void. "So tell me what you did today," she asked, "other than scaring the two of us half to death, that is."

He ignored her barb and said, "I was going to get around to that. I found out about the truck's license number."

Laurel sat up straighter. "Well?"

"It belongs to an outfit called the Mountain Construction Company, with an address in Lakewood, a suburb of Denver."

"Mountain Construction," she mused.

"It doesn't mean a whole helluva lot. I called the phone number Nancy Bearcross gave me."

"And?"

"I got an answering machine. That's it."

"Shoot." Laurel thought for a minute. "Someone has to go to Denver and check out that address."

"Yeah."

"You," she said.

"I was thinking along the same lines."

"I had a productive day, now that you ask," she said after a while.

Joe just shook his head. The woman was absolutely indomitable. "Uh-huh," he said.

"That kid's going to be just fine. She's a good worker."

"Holly Schultz?" He looked at her skeptically.

"What's the matter?" she demanded.

"You're asking for trouble."

"What on earth do you mean?" Laurel said, her back up. "She's a sweet girl, as nice as anyone. We got along just fine!"

"Hey, I'm sure she's a nice girl, but she's been having problems. Getting into trouble. Drinking, smoking dope, stuff like that. The other night I heard Charlie had to go pick up Holly and her pals out at the casino. They were trying to get in."

"Holly?"

"Holly and a few others. Drunker than skunks. I think it's strictly peer pressure, but if she keeps going in this direction things'll only get worse."

"Look," she began, "this is really none of my..."

"And her folks, the Schultzes, that's Earl and Fran, are probably going nuts. They're good people, ranchers, solid, churchgoing folk, though I don't know that that's much consolation to them now."

These last words hurt even more; the Schultzes were good people. Oh, she half wished Joe had said they were awful parents, and then she'd have more reason to hope...

"Yeah," Joe was saying. "That kid's driving them crazy. She's trouble."

And suddenly Laurel broke. "She is not! She's just a teenager, that's all. She's rebelling. It's natural."

"Natural, okay. Hey, take it easy."

"Well, I did that kind of thing when I was her age. I was awful. Got into all kinds of trouble."

"Oh, is that so?"

"My mother didn't handle it very well, either, even though people would have said she was a good parent. But she was really a total control freak."

"I'm glad you can keep it all in perspective," he said dryly.

"It was a long time ago," Laurel said. "It's all over now."

"And you never get into trouble anymore."

"Only when big Indians kidnap me in the middle of the night," she said under her breath.

They were getting close to the site of the dance. The dirt road was lined with pickups and RVs, dozens of them. "Are we almost there?" she asked coolly, her arms folded tightly across her chest.

"Yeah," he said. "I guess we'll have to park and walk."

Walk they did, but it really wasn't very far, and soon Laurel could hear the thumping and booming of the drums, rhythmic yet still muted, and oddly she felt her pulse fall into line with the steady beat. She looked over at Joe; yes, he felt it, too. Behind them, slinking, was Dog.

"We should have left him in the car," she said.

Joe looked over his shoulder. "Nah," he said. "Dog's never missed a Sun Dance."

There were a lot of people, handsome brown-faced people, the men dressed mostly in cowboy-style clothes, bright shirts and high-heeled boots, jeans. The women wore skirts and moccasins and fringed shawls in rich colors; they were clustered together in groups, laughing and gossiping. Children ran around getting underfoot, but no one spoke a harsh word to them. And it soon became clear to Laurel that this was strictly a tribal function, and she felt honored to be included.

JACK TOLLIVER WASN'T included, however. He'd heard about the Indian ceremony, this Sun Dance, by accident when he stopped to fill his truck with gas that evening.

It was a big deal, everyone went—every Indian, that was. And when he heard that he perked right up. If the whole tribe was there, then *his* Indian would be, too. So he asked directions from the young local kid who was filling the gas tank.

"It's up in that meadow up the side of the Sleeping Ute," the kid said. "But you can't go, mister, it's only for Indians."

Uh-huh, Jack thought. "Well, thanks, anyway," he said, "too bad, I guess."

Of course, he drove straight to the foot of the mountain, and soon his truck was rattling up the road, climbing higher and higher. It was getting dark, and his headlights pierced the dusk as he took the switchbacks. He was on to something now, and his ulcers had even stopped jabbing him. If he found Joe Buck up here, if he recognized him—and he was damn sure he could—he'd hang around all night if he had to, follow him to wherever he was nesting these days and take care of the problem.

He skidded around another switchback and smiled to himself. Jack had a quick ear, all right. He heard things—a talent he had, he supposed, like picking up on this Sun Dance thing back at the gas station.

He parked as soon as he saw the other vehicles lining the road, pulling off pretty far so that his truck wouldn't be noticed if that Indian was parked close by. Wouldn't want to get spotted, not when he was this near.

Okay, he thought, he'd just walk right on in as if he owned the place, say he was a tourist or something if anyone bothered to ask. He'd have a good look-see. Maybe, real casual-like, ask a few questions.

He strode up the road and he could hear noise, drums and such, a lot of people talking. It was close now. And then he came to the place where the road met the meadow, where he'd start looking for that damn Indian.

It was there that the three men came up to him. They were pretty big dudes. "I'm sorry, this is a private gathering," one said.

"Yeah, well, I was invited," Jack replied.

"Okay," another one said. "Who invited you?"

Jack thought hard. The men stood in his path, their faces very serious, respectful but serious. One had feathers in his hair, another had stripes painted on his cheeks. And they *were* big. Jack cursed silently.

"Hey, look," he finally said, "it was this guy I worked with. Tom something. He said I could come on up."

"Tom something," one of them repeated.

"Yeah," Jack said. "I know I know his last name."

"Well, as soon as you remember, let us know," the third one said. "We'll be glad to find him for you."

"Right," Jack said, defeated. "Maybe next time." And he gritted his teeth as he turned away, his stomach in spasms.

He left the meadow behind, and the noise receded as he walked back down to his truck. He swore to himself, even mumbled some choice words out loud. His gut was really hurting, and he'd made this long trip for nothing. He couldn't find that damn Indian, Grant was going to come down hard on him and, to add insult to injury, when he reached his pickup it was blocked in, and there wasn't another soul in sight.

"Great," he muttered. But there was always tomorrow.

CHAPTER TEN

LOOK, JOE, it *is* going to rain," Laurel said, pointing at the looming clouds.

"Of course. It's a sign from the Creator, a blessing."

"Oh." She gave Joe a look and then followed him through the crowd, feeling a little self-conscious in the mass of Indians, trying to absorb the atmosphere, the way she always did when she was scouting an area to write about. And she had to admit grudgingly she was glad to have Joe with her.

The drumbeats were closer now, and ahead of them in a clearing Laurel saw a corral, a large round structure made of logs and cottonwood branches, with an opening to the east. In the center of the corral stood a pole, a cut tree shaped like a big Y with willows laid across the fork.

"What's that?" she asked, pulling at Joe's shirt.

"It's where they'll dance later. The pole is a kind of channel to the Creator."

She simply *couldn't* pull out her notebook here and start writing. It would be too rude. She'd have to remember it all. The drumbeats, the people, the sky darkening with thunderheads.

She heard Joe mutter something. "What?" she asked.

"Charlie Redmoon's here. I was hoping to avoid him," he said grimly.

"Your boss?"

"He's a medicine man. It would've been too much to hope he'd stay home tonight."

And then a short, rotund older lady was approaching them, a broad smile on her face. "Joe," she said, beaming. "It's so good to see you, Joe Buck." And she pulled his face down to kiss him on the cheek.

"Aunt Clara," Joe said, disengaging himself, "this is Laurel Velarde. She's a magazine writer."

"So nice to meet you, Laurel. Are you doing a story on us?" Clara asked.

"Well, maybe. It's all fascinating."

"Come say hello to Charlie," Clara said. "This isn't police business, Joe."

"I don't know, Clara. We had some words."

"Come, come. Never mind. This is more important," and then Clara said something in Ute, Joe managed a half smile, and he steered Laurel after Clara's round figure.

"She's Charlie Redmoon's wife," he explained as they walked. "She knew my parents."

"She's not really your aunt?"

"No, but she could be. We're all one big family, really. That's how the older ones think, anyway."

"So, we're meeting with the dread Captain Redmoon," Laurel said, trying to diffuse the sudden tension.

"Not here. Here he's a medicine man, an elder. He's one of the leaders of the dance."

And Laurel spotted him at once—a short man with a round face and a big belly. He had a calmness about him, though, a kind of power, she guessed. An eagle-

bone whistle hung around his neck, and he held an ea-
gle-wing fan.

"Charlie, say hello to Joe and his friend . . . Laurel,
was it? She's a writer. Behave, old man, and she may
put you in her story."

Charlie said something in Ute; Joe replied. A greet-
ing, obviously. Then Charlie turned to Laurel. "I hope
you enjoy the ceremony," he said politely, but she
could tell his mind was elsewhere, perhaps with the
bank of black clouds that was moving in relentlessly
from the west, ever closer to the Sleeping Ute. Faint
growls of thunder could be heard, and far-off forks of
lightning flared, drawing the distant mountains from
the darkness.

"It will rain," Charlie said.

"It looks like," Joe replied, and then Charlie was
moving away, called by a young man with ocher paint
on his bare torso.

Joe took her past the corral, winding through the
crowd. Laurel followed, feeling the drums beat inside
her, hearing snatches of the unfamiliar language. This
was a different world than hers, an exotic, colorful
world where the things that mattered were very basic.
And Joe walked among his people, tall and proud, at
ease, like a prince. Laurel looked sideways at him and
marveled that this man was still part of his tribe but
part of her world, too, a policeman, and just as comfortable there.

He turned and glanced down at her, and she looked
away quickly. But all he said was, "I'm looking for
Rose. If I don't check in I'm in deep trouble."

"You're making me nervous," she whispered. "Rose
sounds pretty tough."

And then Joe stopped short and looked down to where Laurel had unconsciously put her hand on his arm. "Well, well," he said, "so Laurel Velarde is human, after all."

Rose Miller did make Laurel nervous, though she never would have admitted that to Joe.

Rose was a formidable woman, obviously in control of her husband and three teenage sons, Jesse, Ken and Lyle, who were all camped out at the perimeter of the gathering with folding chairs and their own cottonwood-branch shelter. With them were Lawrence Buck and his family: wife Janet and sons Adrian and Bryan.

Laurel was instantly beset by too many people and names and stood there in vague confusion while Joe introduced her.

Rose was a tall, stout woman, older than Joe but with the same great cheekbones. She gave Laurel a swift once-over, then turned to Joe and gave him a big hug. "So you made it, little brother."

"I promised, didn't I?"

"You got here just in time. The dancing is going to start soon." She turned to Laurel. "I hope you enjoy the ceremony," she said tonelessly.

Laurel felt the woman's resentment, or perhaps only a mild distrust, a protectiveness toward her younger brother. "I'm glad Joe asked me to come. I'm a writer and I'm doing articles on this part of the country. This should make a wonderful story."

Frank Miller spoke up. "Laurel, don't mind Rose. She thinks she's Joe's mother. We're all glad you're here."

"Thanks," Laurel said, and gave Frank a smile.

Laurel looked at Joe's family. Obviously the Bucks ran to males; there were a bunch of handsome bronzed youngsters there, five cousins. How nice, Laurel thought, thinking of her own family—herself and her mother and that was all, until her stepfather had come along, but that sure hadn't made for a happy family. The boys were now engaged in a touch football game with another clan, and soon Joe was dragged into it.

"You'll ruin your good shirt," Rose called after him and Laurel thought, uh-huh.

She watched the men and boys then and shook her head at their antics. Joe was tackled a couple of times in the touch football game, but he gave the teenagers as good as he got.

"Sorry," he said, returning, brushing himself off, "it's a family thing, beating each other up."

"Oh, I don't mind," Laurel said, "it was kind of fun seeing you get knocked around," and she felt Rose's eyes on her, appraising. The whole while Dog sat just at the edge of the trees, tongue lolling, watching the ongoing game closely, as if he'd like to join in but felt it beneath his dignity.

Above the gathered throng the sky was turning darker, the sun going down behind the ominous line of black clouds. A breeze stirred the trees, and lightning flashed far off to the west. Still the drums kept up their rhythm, faster now, and the children began to quiet down.

"The dancing is starting," Lawrence said. "Boys, listen up, time to go watch." Five handsome boys dusted off and lined up respectfully.

Joe took Laurel's elbow, bending close to her. "Sorry, it's family stuff. Hope you don't mind."

"I think it's . . . special, the things you do with family. Don't worry about me, I'm taking it all in," Laurel said, acutely aware of his hand on her arm.

The mood in the meadow was changing; she could sense it. A seriousness settled over the place, an aura of significance. This wasn't a square dance, an evening's fun. This was a tie to the tribe's past, a symbol of the identity of each person watching, a living faith that had not lost its meaning.

The drums picked up their tempo even more as the Bucks made their way toward the corral, where all the people were gathering. Charlie Redmoon was there, in the circle by the inner pole, surrounded by fifteen young men, the dancers. They wore long colorful skirts and had bare torsos painted with red and ocher. In their hands they held eagle feathers and around their necks hung whistles of eagle bone.

Primitive, Laurel thought, but in the sense of raw power, closeness to the things that matter, the Creator and Mother Earth. Yes, she'd have to remember this.

It was dusk now, the clouds covering the sun in a premature sunset. Thunder shook the ground and wind caught the dancers' skirts. They began, slowly, a cadenced movement toward the center pole and away from it, back and forth, a tide of brightly hued figures. They blew their whistles, and the drums thudded on and on.

Laurel watched, mesmerized. Back and forth, bare feet stamping, shuffling, hopping, prancing, each dancer had his own style, his own way of approaching the Creator. It was beautiful and intricate.

People in the audience sang and chanted. The dancers had been doing this on and off for two days; they ate and drank nothing.

After a time a fire was started in the corral, a big, smoky bonfire, to light the dancers. The drums went on, the chanting narcotic. Laurel just stood, mesmerized, but all this was familiar to Joe. He'd said it touched him, and now Laurel knew why. And she was beginning, also, to comprehend the strength of tribal ties. A ceremony like this was so compelling, so potent, that it had to create a center that held its people, a center from which, if they wished, they could travel, but it would forever be there for them. And they could always renew the bonds at a dance, like this one. Such security, Laurel thought enviously. How lucky Joe is.

Overhead the clouds blotted out the stars, the moon, the last rays of the sun. It was black, close and black, and a jagged flash of lightning knifed down, very near, because the thunderclap followed it swiftly, shaking the ground.

"The Creator sends his blessings," someone said.

The first drops fell, hitting the massed crowd. Lightning sizzled across the sky again, catching the dancers, freezing them in stop motion. They paid no attention to the rain or the lightning, locked into their dancing, back and forth, back and forth, and Laurel felt the rhythm inside her, as if her blood pulsed to it, and her heart beat to its tune. Next to her Joe was very still, and even through their rain gear she could have sworn she felt the heat from his closeness, the beating of his own heart, strong and steady.

The drums, the singing... Someone heaped more wood on the fire and it flared up, and the rain kept coming, sweeping in sheets across the meadow. No one cared, though; they merely pulled on coats or shawls and turned their faces up to gather the blessings.

There was a break shortly after. The dancers were exhausted. Their women brought them fresh willow sprigs so that they could touch the cool greens to their skin, a small refreshment. The crowd eddied, broke, quiet for now.

The Bucks went back to their shelter, all squeezing under it to get out of the rain.

"Well, what did you think?" Rose asked. "Is it worth a story?"

"Incredible," Laurel said, awed.

"Yes, it is, isn't it?" Rose replied.

The family spoke of the dance then, comparing it to other years, discussing the styles of the dancers. Jesse, Rose and Frank's oldest, was studying to become a dancer. "Maybe next year I'll be ready," he said.

Laurel realized it was a source of family pride to have raised a dancer.

"Did you ever dance?" she asked Joe.

He shook his head. "I was too busy with other things, never could find the time. I've been sorry ever since. My brother Hank did it, though, and he was pretty darn good."

An unbidden picture flashed in Laurel's head—Joe dancing, his broad brown torso glistening with rain and paint, moved by his closeness to the Creator, stamping, shuffling, lit by lightning. The tiny hairs on her arms rose.

Rose and Janet began setting out a feast then, food they'd brought from home and from Rose's café. Casseroles of beans and corn and a big elk roast, food enough for an army. Thermoses of coffee, containers of ice tea, cakes and doughnuts and pies.

They ate, sitting on folding chairs, the young ones on the ground, in the darkness, lit only by the bonfire. The rain pattered on the roof of the shelter, dripping a little, but it was a fast-moving storm, blowing off to the east now, and the ground was damp and fresh-smelling. Laurel was hungry, holding her plate out for seconds.

"This is wonderful," she said. "Thanks for bringing me, Joe."

"It was my pleasure," he said.

Frank Miller asked Laurel where she was from, and she told him Berkeley. "Isn't that where they have riots and things? And earthquakes?"

Laurel laughed. "More earthquakes than riots these days."

"Are you going back when you're through with your research?" Frank asked.

She felt a little uncertain about her answer. "Probably."

"You like that busy place?" he asked.

"Sure, I was raised there. I'm used to it."

She helped the women stack plates and plastic cups. "It was awfully nice of you to feed me, unexpected as I was," she said.

"No problem," Rose replied. "Any friend of my little brother is a friend of mine."

Laurel didn't believe a word of it. Rose was just an overprotective big sister. Well, she'd like to tell Rose that she and Joe weren't romantically inclined, not one bit. But this wasn't the time or place.

"It's getting late," Joe said, coming over to where Laurel was scraping dishes. "You ready to go?"

"Sure, just a minute." She looked at him. "Is it okay if we eat and run?"

"Yes, I have permission," he said. "And I'm getting up early tomorrow. Got things to do."

"Going to Denver?"

"We'll talk about it later," he said pointedly.

They said goodbye to everyone, making their way back across the crowded meadow. The drums were starting up again, and off to the east the storm flickered and pulsed, raining blessings on someone else now.

"That was really something," Laurel said as they walked back to the car. "And I enjoyed meeting your family."

"Yeah, Rose certainly took you to her bosom, didn't she?"

"You're her little brother. She doesn't want you getting mixed up with the wrong kind of woman."

"Which is you, right?"

"I would have assured her that there wasn't a thing between us, but I didn't think it was the right time."

"She wouldn't have believed you, anyway."

Laurel stopped short and looked up at his face. "Oh," she said, "and why not?"

"I just mean Rose suspects that every female has ulterior motives."

"Well," Laurel said indignantly, "maybe some of them do, but not me."

"I know that."

"Maybe I really should set her straight, then. Or maybe you should."

"I will, don't worry."

"You do that, Sergeant Buck," Laurel said, and she started toward the car again.

They reached the Taurus, which was very out of place among the four-wheel-drive trucks and campers. Dog jumped in and Laurel threw her purse, recorder and pad on the back seat. "Well, I didn't take any notes," she said. "And I should have recorded the drums and the chanting, but, I don't know, it was so...so full of reverence, I just couldn't."

"The Bear Dance is in the fall. If you're around," he said, shrugging.

"This fall? I doubt that I'll still be here." A pang struck her as she said that. By then—God knew—anything could happen. She *could* still be in Cortez, near Holly. But she wouldn't worry about that now. There was just tomorrow, tomorrow with her daughter. Then she'd see.

Joe drove back down the Sleeping Ute Mountain. It was fully dark now, the storm past, the stars out in their unbelievable multitudes.

"There're more stars here than in California," Laurel mused.

"Same sky. It's just the thin air up here lets you see them more clearly," Joe said.

Laurel lay her head back on the seat. "Oh, it's so beautiful here at night. You're closer to the stars and the moon. And don't give me some scientific explanation, Einstein—I say it's closer."

"Okay, it's closer."

He drove on, down and around the curves of the Sleeping Ute. A rabbit froze in his headlights, and he had to brake for it. "So," Joe finally said, "about tomorrow..."

"Um." Laurel's eyes were closed, the cool night air from the open window washing over her.

"I do plan to drive to Denver and check a few things out, Mountain Construction for one, Rocky Plains Munitions for another."

"Um. What's that?"

"Rocky Plains? It's a plant where they used to put together nuclear warheads, up until a few years ago when they were closed for pollution violations. Been in the news a lot. I know there's nuclear waste sitting around at that plant, because the people who live around there complain constantly. The groundwater and land have been contaminated."

"But it could be some other nuclear facility that buried those drums. How do you know they're from Rocky Plains?"

"I don't for sure, but I figure it this way. Any out-of-state company would need all sorts of interstate shipping permits, and if they lied about what they were carrying, they'd get caught at one of the state line inspection stations. Besides, that pickup had Colorado license plates."

"If it's all true, and I'm in on it...what a story," Laurel breathed.

"Story be damned! They're poisoning our land."

"You promise you'll go to the authorities pretty soon, though? You said you would."

"Not yet, Laurel, not yet. I told you, they'll screw it up. And besides, I don't have enough to go on yet. For now, this is my baby."

"Our baby," Laurel pointed out.

"Our baby, then. I want to get to the bottom of it and present a tidy little package of proof to old Charlie."

"I bow to your authority, Sergeant Buck. I wouldn't dream of messing up your investigation," she said. "Not for a few days, anyway."

"That's the way it's going to be, Laurel. When I get done with these creeps no one's going to pull a stunt like this again on a reservation. They won't even think about it."

"Yes, sir," Laurel said, "Joe Buck is definitely on the warpath."

"Okay, so that's settled. There's one more thing, though."

"What?" she asked.

"I want you to go to Denver with me tomorrow."

She gave him an amused look.

"I'm not kidding. I want to do some serious snooping, and I'd stand out like a sore thumb in the city. Also, I think your press credentials might come in handy."

"Well, I can't tomorrow," she said. "Holly's coming."

"Call Holly and tell her you have to go out of town for a few days. I don't want you to be alone in Cortez, anyway. Too risky."

"It's too late to call now."

Joe made an impatient noise. "Call in the morning."

"I wanted to..."

"Laurel," he said, "what's important, you pulling some weeds with that kid or us getting to the bottom of this crime?"

"Well, I..."

He turned onto the highway and headed toward Cortez. "Come on, Laurel. What about your story? You really disappoint me. All that talk about being venturesome."

"You think I'm scared to go with you."

He said nothing.

"I have work to do, the article I'm writing, my house..."

"Bull. I'm calling you on that. It's that kid, isn't it? What's so damn important about her?"

"Nothing," Laurel said quickly, her heart thudding. "She's a cute kid is all."

"So you'll go with me?"

Laurel looked out of the window at the dark land rushing by. She'd wanted to see Holly so much. Her flesh cried out to see the girl, to touch her, and she'd promised to tell Holly all about her job. Even more, she'd decided to draw Holly out about her getting into trouble. Laurel knew the feelings so well, remembered the rebellion and confusion and craving for excitement. She could talk to Holly, maybe help her, give her the benefit of her own hard-earned wisdom. She'd wanted to see her tomorrow so very much....

"Well?" Joe pressed.

Laurel sighed then turned to look at his profile. "Okay, I'll go."

"Good" was all he said.

When they got back to her house there was a message on her answering machine. She pushed the playback button, listened to the usual clicks and whirs, then a strange woman's voice came on. "Miss Velarde, this is Fran Schultz. I know Holly worked for you today. We're terribly worried because she never met her father, and she still isn't home. It's 11:00 p.m. and we're very upset. We thought you might know where she is. Please call if you do. Thank you very much."

Laurel's heart constricted, and she was glad Joe was in the other room. Holly had mentioned that she had to meet her father. Laurel had seen her set off walking. What had happened to her? Horrible images ran through her brain—rape, murder, kidnapping.

Was this what it was like to be a mother? The worry, the dread? It was probably nothing—Holly'd met friends, gone out, sure she had. Laurel would have done that when she was Holly's age, and her mother...oh, God, how her mother must have suffered.

It was almost 1:00 a.m., but Laurel called the Schultzes, anyway. The phone rang once, then was snatched up. A man's voice barked, "Holly?"

"No, Mr. Schultz, it's Laurel Velarde. I'm really sorry, but I'm worried about Holly, too. She left here at five-thirty, and I haven't seen her since. She still isn't home?"

"No."

"Have you called the police?"

"Yes."

Laurel could feel the man's anger and fear as if he were present. "Please, Mr. Schultz, promise you'll call me the minute she gets home, no matter when it is. I won't be able to sleep a wink until you do."

"That girl," he said, his voice choked. "That girl."

"You'll call me?"

"Yes, ma'am, we'll call."

She put the phone down gingerly and sat there at her messy desk for a moment, head hanging.

"What's the matter?" she heard from behind her.

She turned slowly. Joe stood in the doorway, arms folded across his chest, his expression unreadable. "Holly's not home yet," she said.

"Not surprising. I told you about her. Probably out raising hell."

"Her parents are worried. So am I."

"Why are you worried, Laurel? She isn't your kid."

She looked away and said nothing.

"Well, I'm going to hit the sack. Early morning. We're leaving by eight."

Distractedly, she said, "I can't go, not if they haven't found Holly yet."

"What the hell is this, Laurel?"

Her temper flared. "It's only natural. The girl's not home. It's late. She left here this afternoon, and no one's seen her since."

"You can bet her friends have seen her."

"I won't go if I don't know she's safe," she said stubbornly.

"Have it your way," he said, dismissing the whole thing.

Laurel went into the bathroom, closed the door and felt her heart thudding in a slow, heavy rhythm. Strange, it felt strange to worry about another human being so much, but she couldn't stop herself. She brushed her teeth and met her eyes in the mirror over the sink, and they looked scared.

In her bedroom she put on her nightgown and brushed her hair. She'd never sleep, not a wink. She'd worry all night. She could hear Joe moving around in the living room, and she wanted desperately to go to him, tell him the truth. Then he'd understand. But somehow she couldn't. Not Joe. He'd twist everything, he'd think she was crazy, coming here like she had. He'd think she was plotting to get her child back, to mess up everyone's life.

There was something else, though, another reason she didn't want to tell Joe about her child. It was so silly—it had happened over fifteen years ago—but she just didn't want to admit to him she'd made such a stupid mistake. To appear so vulnerable in Joe's eyes was unthinkable.

She got into bed, slid between the sheets. Her body was tired, but her mind still raced. She was reaching to turn the light off when she heard the phone ring in the other room. Her heart leapt into her throat, and she flew out of bed and raced barefoot to the phone, totally ignoring Joe on the couch.

"Yes?" she said into the receiver.

"Laurel?" a small slurred voice said. "Miss Velarde? My parents made me call. It's Holly. I'm sorry..."

"Holly," she breathed, her whole body sagging with sheer relief. "Oh, thank God, Holly."

And that was when she realized that Joe was watching her again, his dark Indian face utterly expressionless.

THE SUN DANCE WENT ON into the wee hours, and already there was the faintest pearl glow in the east. Out on the desert, many miles from the Sleeping Ute Mountain, a red-tailed hawk lay writhing on the ground near a clump of purple sage.

It'd been dying for two days, ever since it'd caught and eaten a rodent near a spring that lay close to the amphitheater where the drums were buried.

It flapped a wing, tried to rise, but the agony was too great. By the time the first rays of golden sun inched over a distant mesa and touched his mottled feathers, the bird lay still.

CHAPTER ELEVEN

THEY LEFT FOR DENVER later than Joe had wanted, but then it had taken Laurel an hour to shower and pack.

"What on earth are you ironing for?" Joe had complained.

"You want me to look professional or not?" she'd called back from the bedroom. "I can't pull out my press credentials in a city and be wearing cutoff jeans."

So he'd driven Dog out to his brother's in Towaoc, fuming the whole way—women. And when he'd got back she still wasn't ready. She was packed, okay, but she was on the phone with an editor or someone from that magazine she worked for, and so Joe had yet another cup of coffee at the kitchen table while he leafed through a copy of *Travel Adventure* that Laurel had lying around.

He had to admit there were a couple of interesting articles in it. In fact, Laurel Velarde's name was on one of them, a piece about heli-skiing in the Canadian Rockies. The photographs were nothing short of spectacular, and the writing was pretty good, at least Joe thought so. He loved the description of her arrival by helicopter at a lodge in the middle of the Bugaboo Mountains with a blizzard on her heels. And the way she wrote about the hairy helicopter ascents, the ski runs down precipitous avalanche tracts . . .

Joe had closed the magazine and finished his coffee by the time she finally entered the kitchen and announced she was ready.

The drive from Cortez into Denver was a long eight hours in the best of conditions. First there was the entire breadth of the Rocky Mountain chain to be crossed, and then there was foothill country to negotiate, and finally the drive north on the plains paralleling the mountains. It was going to be a very long day.

Their clashing of wills began over the air-conditioning—and that was before they'd even reached Durango, a scant thirty miles to the east of Cortez.

"It's freezing in here," Joe said, adjusting the dashboard control.

"Freezing?" Laurel immediately turned it straight back on. "I'm frying. The sun's right on me."

"If you weren't so gussied up," he muttered, eyeing her beige linen skirt.

"I'll be glad to put on shorts, and then let's just see how far my credibility gets us."

"Yeah, well," he said, "that's if we even get there."

They drove along in silence for a time, Laurel staring mutely out the window, Joe with his jaw locked, and she tried to touch base with her feelings. She was on edge. This trip was costing her at least two days that she could have spent with Holly.

On the other hand, she thought as the silence stretched on interminably, there was an excellent chance she might be on the cutting edge of one terrific story. She'd never considered being an investigative reporter—in reality she was trained in an entirely different genre, but to let this opportunity slip through her grasp was unthinkable.

The scenery drifted by the window, more green and lush now that they were ascending the western slope of the Rockies, lovely country, really, jutting mountains and thick evergreen forests rising to a hot blue summer sky, huge valley ranches stretching as far as the eye could see. She felt herself begin to relax a little and then admitted that this foray was about Joe, too, and as hard as Laurel tried to deny that his nearness was having an effect on her, she had to face the unsettling truth.

She sighed, recrossed her legs and gave him a sidelong glance. After a moment she said, "Pretty country." It was a peace offering, the best she could muster.

"Real pretty," he agreed, and she could detect a softening in his tone.

"Sorry we got a late start," she added.

"Um," he allowed. Joe Buck was not like any man Laurel had ever known. For one, he was thoroughly honest. And he had a sense of humor, was able to laugh at himself and at life despite a whopping ego.

He was arrogant, though. Too proud for his own good, she'd learned. This business with his boss, the medicine man, certainly wasn't getting Joe anywhere with his career. And going off like they were to Denver . . . Joe and Laurel out to save the land all by themselves. Lord only knew what they were up against! In that light she supposed she was as bad as he was. Mavericks. The both of them.

"I liked Charlie Redmoon and his wife," Laurel ventured. "A policeman and a medicine man. Weird."

"From your point of view it would be," Joe said. "No offense meant."

"But it works, for him, anyway."

Joe nodded slowly. "It did work. The trouble is the reservation's changing."

"The gambling."

"That and the rise in tourism. It was happening, anyway. Just too many damn people in the world."

"It's hard on the land," she said. "Everywhere I go it's the same. I did an article last year on rock climbing in Yosemite National Park, you know, on El Capitan, and you wouldn't believe it. You need a reservation a year in advance just to climb it."

"You're joking."

"I'm dead serious."

"I thought everyone was leaving California."

"Not everyone. And the land, the parks and rivers, well, they can't take much more."

He turned and glanced at her then and seemed to decide something. "There's been talk lately of bad spirits, people and animals getting sick, rumors," he said, switching his gaze back to the road.

"You mean . . . on the reservation?"

He nodded.

"You think it's because of the radioactivity? The drums are leaking? But how could it affect people so soon?"

"Let's assume I happened to stumble across just one unloading," he said. "Maybe it's been going on for years."

"Oh, wow," Laurel said, letting that sink in, and then she felt an anger kindle in her, a disbelief and horror that anyone, no matter the stakes, would do such a thing. Sickness. "That's awful," she whispered.

"Pretty bad," he said, and they both became very quiet.

The miles fell away behind them. The small rural towns. Pagosa Springs, Del Norte, the city of Alamosa on an immense dry plain where farmers grew potatoes. They stopped and grabbed a bite to eat in Fort Garland, where once a U.S. Army fort had existed. They'd killed Indians then—with bullets.

Back in the car and passing the site of the national monument to the old fort, Laurel said, "You must hate this place."

"Sure do," he said.

She studied him and cocked her head. "What was it really like?" she asked. "Growing up on a reservation, I mean."

He snorted. "It's another world. Tough."

"But there must have been good times, too."

"I wouldn't have traded it for anything."

"And your family. There was lots of family."

"The whole tribe is my family."

"How about school? You went to college...."

"In Durango, yes."

"So?"

"I learned a lot."

"Such as?"

He gave a short laugh. "Such as it's better to stick with your own kind."

Laurel pivoted and stared at him. "That's...terrible. What if everyone in the world felt that way? My God, Joe, we'd never have peace anywhere. The world's just getting too small, we have to change our thinking, our beliefs. And that includes you, too."

"Lecture over?"

"Yes. But I wish you'd give that some thought."

"Why?"

"Because you're a decent man."

"Um," he said.

She tucked one leg under the other and kept watching him. "So at school," she said, "you must have made a few friends."

"I made male friends. I played football." He shrugged.

"And lady friends?"

"Oh, there was a lady, all right," he said. Again he shrugged, but it was too nonchalant.

"So what happened?" she ventured.

"Why do you want to know all this stuff?"

"Because I do."

"She dumped me. Or, let me say, her parents yanked her out of school when they found out we were hot and heavy."

"Bigots," Laurel said carefully.

"The worst kind."

"And so that was the end of your relationships with...white women?"

He mulled that over. "Let's just say I'm too much of a loner for steady relationships of any kind."

"But you must date. Go to dinner, a movie, you know."

"Hey," he said, "I've got Dog for company, don't I?"

"Oh, I forgot," Laurel said, and was struck by a peculiar sense of protectiveness for this man.

As the miles ticked away and they passed through the Front Range city of Pueblo and turned north to Denver on the interstate highway, Laurel found out a lot about Joe Buck. Oh, it was no easy task getting information out of him, but then no man she'd ever met opened up as a habit. Still, she learned that he took frequent sweat baths with the older men, and he be-

lieved strongly in the affinity between man and beast—
he admitted that shape shifting, the ability of man to
take on the form of an owl or a coyote or a bear, was
in his opinion a possibility.

"You're kidding," Laurel said.

"Not really," Joe replied easily. "Oh, I'm not talking about me physically changing into a coyote, but it's
possible to see Mother Earth, to smell and feel and
sense the land as a coyote does."

"It's a . . . spiritual thing?"

"Absolutely. You take a night walk on the land, and
anything's possible if you're receptive."

"I'd like to feel that," Laurel mused aloud.

"Would you?" he asked, skeptical.

"Yes," she avowed.

They talked about her, too. And Laurel was embarrassed at times. She enjoyed discussing her job, her
present life. But it was her past that hurt. "My mom
got so hung up on her new life when she remarried,"
Laurel told him uneasily. "I guess I was left out. You
know, emotionally."

"And your blood father? Your natural father?"

She gave a bitter laugh. "I was lucky to get a birth-
day card."

"He's dead?"

"Yes. He left me some money, but only because
there was no one else to inherit. The State of California gave it to me."

"So you were rebellious?"

"Oh, yes."

"How about friends? You went to a girl's school,
didn't you?"

"In Berkeley, yes," she said. "I did have good
friends there. Thank God for that. A few of us got very

close when we worked on the student newspaper. We were quite a mix.''

"All troublemakers?''

"No. Well, some. I suppose I was the worst, though. But we hung together. We could have been sisters, in fact.''

"Still in touch?''

"Yes. This Christmas we even plan on a reunion. I can hardly wait.'' She thought about that and smiled— what if Holly could be there with her?

"So, you've never been married?'' Joe asked, breaking into her thoughts.

"Heavens, no,'' she said too quickly.

"And just what does that mean?''

"If you must know,'' Laurel said, "I had a bad experience once. When I was pretty young. It's hard to... trust.''

"I'm sorry to hear that,'' he said.

Sorry, she thought. Yes, it was a shame not to trust—not parents because they were too wrapped up in their own selfish lives except to issue her constant orders. And men, well, Gray had taken care of that.

"And what about Cortez,'' Joe was asking. "How long are you planning to stay?''

"I wish I knew,'' she said before thinking.

It was a strange day, Laurel began to sense as they neared Denver. Strange in that she and Joe had finally talked—they'd actually had revealing conversations without the need to hide behind light banter. She mulled that over. She must have looked at him surreptitiously a hundred times that hot afternoon and wondered.

Being cooped up with Joe was an unsettling experience at best. He was just too much man, too damn attractive with his strong brown forearm draped over the steering wheel and those muscular thighs. It was a good thing, she told herself, a real good thing neither of them was interested in *that* way. A girl could look, though, couldn't she?

They reached Denver by four in the afternoon, though Lakewood—the suburb where Mountain Construction was located—was still another twenty minutes through heavy, late-day traffic.

And it was hot. The nearer they got to the downtown core of Denver, which they had to traverse, the hotter and steamier it got.

"I thought Denver was mild and dry," Laurel said, switching the air conditioner to high.

"All cities have crappy climates," Joe said.

It was a problem finding the Lakewood address. Twice they made wrong turns and twice Joe pulled to the shoulder of the road and took the map from her.

"Can't you read a map?" he said.

After the second insult to her directional talents, Laurel swung open the door and got out. "I'm driving, you read," she said, and walked around to the driver's side, sweat breaking out under her arms.

It was nearly five by the time they located the address. Laurel pulled up in front of a long chain link fence. Trash clung to the wire in the hot wind. Laurel stared out the window. "You're sure this is it? You have the right address?" she asked.

"I got it right," Joe said under his breath, and they both just stared at the empty lot with an old, abandoned trailer sitting on it.

Joe took off his sunglasses and swore.

Laurel sat in silence stewing. They'd come all this way, all those long miles for this. "It's just a front," she said after a time. "Mountain Construction doesn't even exist. It's a front for someone who's covering up the real company."

Joe swore again.

They left the site a few minutes later, Laurel still at the wheel, Joe telling her to drive around the area, as if they might stumble onto a big lot with millions of dollars' worth of heavy, earth-moving equipment on it. They found nothing.

"This is just great," he said, pounding the dash with a fist.

"That's really going to help," Laurel said. "Why don't you just kick it in?"

"I will if I want," he fired back.

"What a child you are," she said loftily.

They went to a motel then, one that Joe knew. Laurel stared at it. "It's a dump," she said.

"You want nice? Okay, I'll take you to nice, lady, but I'll be damned if I'm paying for two rooms. You can share with me."

"Over my dead body."

"Then I guess we stay here," he said, getting out, reaching into his back pocket for his wallet and shooting her a cold smile. By the time they were checked into their adjoining rooms Laurel could have throttled him. She got into a cool shower and fumed. Okay, so they'd come hundreds of miles only to find an empty lot. Okay, it was infuriating. But to take it out on her... How dare he!

She stood beneath the cold running water for a long time and found every reason on earth to despise the man. And my God, she thought, earlier today in the car she hadn't been able to take her eyes off him!

Laurel dressed in summer white slacks and a dark green scoop-neck cotton shirt. She blew her hair dry and braided it and took up her purse, heading for the door, starving. She'd treat herself to the best darn meal.... Keys. Damn! Joe had the car keys.

Gritting her teeth, she knocked on his door and pasted an indifferent smile on her lips. She knocked again. He was there. The car was there, anyway. He answered a moment later, pulling open the door so fast she jumped.

"Give me the car keys," she said, recovering. "Please, I should add." She noticed then that he, too, had showered. His bronzed chest was bare, drops of water still gleaming on it, and the top two buttons on his jeans were undone. She tore her eyes back up to his and felt the afternoon heat bludgeon her.

"Look," he said, making no move to fetch the keys, "I was a real ... ass just now. I'm sorry."

She simply stood and stared at him, suddenly uncertain.

"I'm just disappointed," Joe went on. "I really expected to find something today."

"Well, yes, I did, too," Laurel said with caution.

"I want to make it up to you," he was saying, "the biggest, fanciest dinner in town. When this is over I'm going to charge all my expenses to the BIA, anyway. What do you say?"

She looked down at her feet for a moment. "Well, I..."

And then he seemed to take a step closer, and the scent of soap assailed her. "I'm apologizing," Joe said in a low voice. "I'm not very good at this."

"You're, ah, doing fine," she said, and then had to clear her throat.

"Where would you like to go?"

"I, ah..."

"How about Chinese? All women like Chinese, don't they?"

Laurel looked up and cocked her head. "All women?"

He gave a dry laugh. "Nancy Bearcross does, anyway," he said.

"The dispatcher at your headquarters?"

"She gets around," Joe said with a slow quirk of his lips.

"Uh-huh," she said. "Well, if we all love Chinese, then chop suey it is."

"There's a place just down the road. We could even walk, stretch our legs. Okay?"

"Okay."

"I'll just get my shirt...."

She stood in the open door and watched him and marveled at his abrupt change in mood. When was the last time a man had just up and apologized to her when he'd been a real jerk?

She pondered that as she watched him tug on his shirt. With his back to her he tucked it in, hoisting his jeans over his narrow hips. When he turned and said, "Ready?" she could only nod, and Laurel realized her chest was tight.

It was five long blocks to the restaurant. And it was still very hot out. They passed two more motels and a used car lot, a couple of fast-food restaurants, even a strip joint. "Nice area," Laurel remarked, and Joe grinned and put his hand on the small of her back as they crossed a side street.

The restaurant was crowded, and they had to wait in the bar for a table. Joe had a nonalcoholic beer while

Laurel sipped on a white wine with soda and ice. It was close and intimate in the bar area, and she couldn't help noticing the stares Joe got—some awfully bold stares by more than a few women.

Well, why not? Laurel mused, her shoulder against his arm in the close quarters. Especially here, among the pale city faces and big-bellied, middle-aged men. And she felt curiously proud, proud and protective of her companion. Get a grip, she told herself more than once. They were merely comrades-in-arms.

Their table was as intimate as the lounge had been, a table for two squeezed into a corner near the waiters' station. It was dim, too, with only a single stub of a candle to light the entire table.

"I'm gonna need glasses soon," Joe remarked, holding the menu eighteen inches from his eyes.

"How old are you?" Laurel asked.

"Thirty-four," he said, "going on forty lately." He raised an eyebrow at her.

"Thirty-three," she said. "Honest."

In the crowded little room with its dime-store Chinese decorations and the singsong chatter of foreign voices, they ordered two dinners, one hot and spicy and one mild, a pot of tea and steamed rice. It was enough for an army. "You never have a drink?" Laurel asked.

He shook his head. "We hold it worse than the Irish," he said. "When I was a teenager I tried it a couple times and found I was the cheapest drunk on the reservation."

"Good for you," she said, meeting his dark eyes. "I mean, at least you realized it." And then she ventured, "That's an admirable quality—honesty, that is."

The light from the candle seemed to dance in his black eyes when he asked, "Are you honest, Laurel?"

"Me? Usually." But then she thought about Holly. She looked up to catch those penetrating eyes still on her. "I guess I could work harder at it," she said.

"We all could," he offered.

They cracked open their fortune cookies with the last of the pot of fragrant jasmine tea and pulled out the fortunes.

"What does yours say?" Laurel asked.

"You are destined for great success," he replied. "Original."

Laurel read hers, holding the small slip of white paper between her fingers. She felt a flush rise up her neck.

"Well, what's yours?" he asked.

"The usual dumb remark."

"Come on, I told you mine," he said.

She wished she could refuse, but it would make matters worse. "Silly," she said.

"Out with it."

"You will meet someone tall, dark and handsome," she mumbled.

"Will you?" he asked, and his eyes met hers in mocking challenge.

They finally turned to the subject of Mountain Construction, which was why they were there, after all. It sobered them both.

"We're dead in the water," Joe stated. "It's got to be a holding company, something like that, for some big outfit. They've probably covered their tracks all the way to the Cayman Islands."

Laurel frowned. "We can go to the city records department tomorrow, at least look up the business license. Someone has to be paying the fee."

"Yeah, but I'm betting it's just another dead end."

"Maybe," she said, thinking, her chin propped on a fist. "But I think we should give it a try."

"Um," he said.

"Well, do you have a better idea?" she asked.

"We have to get inside the Rocky Plains plant, talk to someone there."

"They won't tell us anything we want to know."

"They might, inadvertently." He looked at her keenly. "You'll have to do it with your press credentials. Interview somebody."

"Me?"

"That's why you're here, remember."

"Okay, fine. Tomorrow we'll do just that."

"You should be happy. It's all for your big story, right?"

"No," Laurel said. "It's more. It's much more than a story now."

"Is that an honest reply?" Joe challenged.

"I won't dignify that with an answer."

It was cooler and nearly dark by the time they walked back to the motel. And there were some real hard-core types out now, too, lounging on corners, hanging out in front of the fast-food joints. Gang members. Joe tucked her arm under his and walked a little faster than usual, both of them keeping their eyes straight ahead.

"It's sick," Laurel said as they passed a group in leather jackets who whistled at her and threw racial slurs in Joe's direction.

Back at the motel, breathing a sigh of relief, Laurel said, "If I hadn't been with you, would you have reacted?"

"No," Joe said, standing at her door. "I'm not that stupid."

"Glad to hear it," she said, and twisted the key in the lock. "Well, good night. I enjoyed dinner. Thank you."

"My pleasure. It's the least I can do after dragging you all the way to Denver."

"Maybe tomorrow," she said hopefully.

"Yeah, maybe we'll luck out at the records department."

"Well," Laurel said, still just standing there, and it was Joe who finally moved. He bent his head and brushed her forehead with his lips. Her surprise soon turned into the warm liquid feeling of pleasure.

"Be sure to latch the chain on the door," he said.

"I will, and good night," she said again, smiling foolishly, ducking inside. She could still hear him, though, even after both their doors were closed and locked. The motel walls were paper thin, and she could hear him stirring around for a time before all was quiet. But even then he was still with her, too vivid in her mind's eye, his long brown body stretched out on that bed just a few short feet away. Tall, dark and handsome.

CHAPTER TWELVE

LAUREL DIDN'T SLEEP WELL. At midnight she convinced herself the restlessness was pure anxiety over the sleuthing she was about to do—leaping blindly into an area about which she knew very little. By the morning the truth was seeping in. It wasn't the interviewing; it wasn't all the thoughts about Holly. No, she realized as dawn crept over the urban sprawl, it wasn't any of those things, really. It was Joe Buck who had gotten under her skin.

She'd never meant to let that happen. Holly, a possible relationship with her child, that was the future, and there was no room for a third person, for even a thought about someone else.

And yet . . .

She took a shower and dressed in her city best and put him from her thoughts. Someday, maybe, in the distant future, there would be time for a man, but not now and certainly not Joe Buck with his misguided pride that might one day get him killed. She put on makeup and stood back to observe herself in the bathroom mirror. For once she looked professional. Good, she thought, the sooner she helped Joe collect his information the sooner she'd be back in Cortez.

They ate at a restaurant next door, and Joe seemed as preoccupied as she was.

"It'll go fine today," she assured him, buttering her muffin. "Like you said, there's only one outfit in the state that produces radioactive waste. It's got to be this Rocky Plains Munitions."

Joe pushed his half-eaten plate of food away. "Yeah, and we'll walk right in—you'll walk right in—and they'll say, 'Well, of course we're burying nuclear waste on the Ute reservation, anything else you want to know?'"

She shook her head at him. "Aren't we in a swell mood."

"I'm really ticked off," he said, sitting with an arm stretched along the back of the booth, staring grimly out the window at rush-hour traffic.

"Well, stop being a pessimist," she said. "Are you forgetting the Freedom of Information Act? They have to tell us about their disposal practices. It's the law, Joe."

"And they'd never consider lying," he said derisively.

Joe read the map as they drove to the Lakewood City Hall where they first planned on checking out Mountain Construction's business license. His mood was no better. "Turn here," he said, pointing at the next intersection.

"Right?"

"Yes." And then when she got in the wrong lane, he said, "Your other right, Laurel."

"Oh," she said, veering, getting honked at while he grabbed the dashboard.

At least the Lakewood city clerk was quite agreeable when Laurel flashed her press credentials, introducing Joe as her photographer. "I'm trying to locate the main office of Mountain Construction Company."

"Yes," the woman said, "that should be on the license. If you'll give me a few minutes?"

"Sure," Laurel said, smiling. "What do we do when, if, we get an address?" she asked Joe when the lady disappeared.

"It depends."

"You're not going to try some crazy kind of confrontation, are you?"

"No, I'm only collecting information."

"You're sure?"

"No shoot-outs, Laurel. I gave Charlie my handgun. Remember, I'm on suspension. And my shotgun's at your house."

"The suspension hasn't slowed you down much," she noted.

The clerk returned to the other side of the counter, and Laurel waited eagerly.

"Here it is," the woman said. "Mountain Construction."

Laurel and Joe bent their heads over the business license. They read the document carefully, both of them, then read it again. Mountain Construction Company was a wholly owned subsidiary of Mountain City Corporation, P.O. Box 1403, 12101 Alameda, Lakewood, Colorado, the same street address they'd already checked out.

"Shoot," Laurel said. "Useless."

"Let's ask for the license of this Mountain City Corporation," Joe suggested.

"It's a dummy corporation. You won't find a thing," Laurel said, bitterly disappointed.

"It's worth a try, seeing as we're here." He gave the clerk an apologetic smile.

She was not so patient this time; however, she got them the license for Mountain City. It displayed the same address in Lakewood.

"This isn't going to work," Laurel said as the heat smote her when they left the building.

"I thought I was the pessimist," Joe said.

"So what do we do now? Rocky Plains?"

"It's our best shot."

"Joe," she said, unlocking the car door, "what are we going to do if we strike out there, too? Aren't the head offices for the FBI right here in Denver? We could..."

He leaned across the hood of the car and stared at her. "We do this one step at a time, okay?"

"Yes, Sergeant Buck," she said curtly as the sweat began to dampen the back of her neck.

Joe gassed up the car at a nearby service station while Laurel telephoned the head office of Rocky Plains Munitions and made an appointment with a man named Patrick Drynan, in public relations.

"I'll leave your name at the front gate," the woman on the line said.

"And my photographer," Laurel said.

"I'm sorry, Miss Velarde, but we can't allow pictures. National security, you understand."

"Of course," Laurel said agreeably. "He can drive me in and wait in the car. All right?"

"That will be fine."

An hour later Joe and Laurel were driving north toward Boulder along the high plain that butted up against the foothills of the Rocky Mountains. Traffic was light, the land opening up into grassy prairies once they passed through Golden, the home of Coors Brewery.

It was actually pretty country, Laurel was thinking, until she saw the sign: Rocky Plains Munitions Plant, and it all came crashing back, the fifty-five gallon drums buried in the desert, the sickness Joe had mentioned.

"Hard to believe," Joe was saying quietly, echoing aloud her very thoughts.

They passed through the main gate with no trouble whatsoever. "Efficient," Laurel said.

"Yeah, for a plant that's been fined a dozen times in as many years for safety violations they're real sharp," Joe muttered.

"That bad?"

Joe nodded as he steered up the long road leading into the facilities—offices and plants and warehouses that could not be seen from the road. Even air traffic was prohibited in this corridor—again, national security.

"It seems to me," he said, "and don't quote me on this, but I remember a big flap not so long ago when a Colorado grand jury slapped a huge fine on them for spraying, that's spraying, nuclear waste on the ground to see if it would evaporate."

"You're joking," she breathed.

"No, I'm not. And you know how they got caught? Some neighboring housing project complained of a green fluorescent ooze seeping into their sewage treatment plant."

"Unbelievable."

"Well, believe this—it isn't real hard to figure these same upstanding civil servants might just dispose of tons of waste out in a remote desert. What's the worst that can happen? They get fined again by the EPA? And who's going to shut them down? Nobody. These dudes are hand in glove with the U.S. military establishment."

"They've got it made," Laurel said. "Pretty sad."

"I'll tell you what's even sadder," Joe said. "There's something like a half a century's worth of nuclear waste to be disposed of and no place to put it."

"You mean..."

"I'm no expert," he said, pulling into the visitor's lot and parking, "but the Denver papers cover the subject pretty closely, and I've read about only one or two states that allow waste disposal, and Colorado isn't one of them."

"Wow," Laurel said. "So we have to figure they've either set up a fake company, Mountain Construction, or hired that company to bury those drums illegally."

"That's about the gist of it," he said, and then he did a curious thing: he reached over and covered her hand with his. "Nervous?" he asked.

Surprised and suddenly uncertain, Laurel could only stare at the long brown fingers lying on top of hers. His hand was warm, she thought stupidly.

"Laurel?" he said.

"No," she said quickly, "no, I'm really fine. I'll plaster a big grin on my face and grill this Mr. Patrick whatever his name is...."

"Drynan."

"Right. Anyway, I'll question him till he squirms."

"Don't get him on the defensive."

"Joe."

"Okay, you're the reporter." And then he squeezed her hand before letting her go, but Laurel could feel the phantom touch of his fingers on hers. She took a big breath before entering the main offices, and she let it out slowly, squaring her shoulders and leaving Joe Buck behind.

Patrick Drynan was slight, a slim man with a bald spot on the top of his head and a wrinkled summerweight gray suit. He had nice teeth and he smiled a lot. She started in gently, mentioning what an attractive facility it was and questioning him on how many employees there were. He answered her in a friendly manner and seemed to know his stuff, but then he would—Patrick Drynan spent his entire day giving interviews, painting a nice picture of the nuclear weapons facility.

"But there's been some bad publicity over the years," she said after their initial niceties. "I'd like to hear your side."

"Oh, yes, I'm aware that there's been some trouble with the press over Rocky Plains. But that's all changed now. The EPA did fine us, but it's been appealed. Tests show the area is perfectly safe, perfectly safe." He liked to repeat things. "And we have a new manager. The DOE, that's the Department of Energy, checks on us regularly. There hasn't been a problem, Miss Velarde. We stick to the letter of the law."

Laurel busily took notes. "I will certainly include that in my article, Mr. Drynan."

"Now, what publication did you say you write for?"

"I'm a free-lance writer. I'll submit this piece to *Time* or *U.S. News* or *World Report*. They usually like my stuff." She met his gaze with utter sincerity and a smile akin to his. "Tell me more about converting to peacetime uses," Laurel said. "That's really the thrust of my piece."

"Well, of course, and it should be. Nuclear power is the only alternative energy source for the future. Safe, efficient, clean. Yes, very clean." And on he went while Laurel took copious notes she'd never look at again.

"So, you see, the taxpayer of this country benefits greatly from our work here," Drynan concluded. "You can quote me on that, Miss Velarde."

She looked up from her pad. "Oh, I will, I certainly will." And then she realized she'd started repeating things as he did.

"One more thing, Mr. Drynan. I'm aware that nuclear waste needs to be disposed of carefully. How do you take care of that problem? Do you bury it here?" she asked innocently.

The PR man steepled his fingers and smiled broadly. "Oh, my goodness, no. Not here. We contract out waste disposal. It's a very specialized process. And very expensive, too, very expensive."

Laurel grinned like the Cheshire cat, but her underarms felt damp. She held her pencil ready and asked casually, "Oh, who does the disposal, Mr. Drynan?"

"Now that's an interesting question, and your readership should be informed of the changing industry," he said, delighted to switch the subject. "You see, Miss Velarde, since the end of the Cold War the aerospace industry in this country has been scrambling to make up for the loss of military contracts. Obviously our nation doesn't need as many weapons and such."

"Uh-huh," Laurel said, taking notes.

"So, to make a long story short, because the aerospace industry has the technology, it has taken over the process of handling nuclear disposal. It's really quite lucrative, what with government contracts and all that."

"Um," she said, her eyes down, her pulse racing. "And so who does Rocky Plains use?"

"Why, that would be Blackwell International, right here in Denver. They do a terrific job for us, safe, efficient. And they're a pleasure to work with, a real pleasure."

Laurel kept writing. She wrote down Blackwell International and underlined it twice. Her hand shook. "What does Blackwell do with the waste, do you know?"

Another wide, white smile. "Well, really, once they pick the containers up here it's out of our hands. I really couldn't tell you. That's what we pay them to do."

"But it goes to a safe repository," Laurel said, her head bowed over her pad, her heartbeat racing now.

"Of course, of course. Everything is done to the letter of the law. We wouldn't stand for anything less."

"Of course." Laurel finally looked up. Mr. Drynan was enjoying himself; he liked to be interviewed. "Thank you so much for your time, Mr. Drynan. You've been so helpful." She stood and gathered her bag and her pad. Her knees were rubber. "Oh, one more thing, in case I need to pursue this for my editor," she said.

"Yes?"

"Could you tell me who at Blackwell is in charge of the disposal?"

"Hmm, let me see." He held up a finger. "Just a sec." He buzzed his secretary on the intercom. "Teresa? Please look up the name of Blackwell's man, the one who deals with us . . . yes, Teresa. Oh, good, that's the one. Thanks."

Laurel stood there, trying to look politely expectant, hoping Mr. Drynan didn't notice the sweat beading on her upper lip.

"It's a Mr. Jack Tolliver," he said. "Jack Tolliver of Blackwell."

Laurel scribbled it on her pad and beamed. "Thank you so much. I do appreciate it. If I need to call you for more information . . . ?"

He waved a hand. "Oh, any time at all, Miss Velarde, any time."

Laurel practically strutted out to the parking lot. She couldn't keep from grinning. She was bursting to tell Joe.

"I got it!" she said triumphantly, sliding in beside him. "Wow, I got it!"

"Care to share it with me?"

She leaned toward him and let her smile broaden even more. "Blackwell International disposes of their waste. Jack Tolliver is the man who's in charge of it."

"Good work," Joe said slowly. "Blackwell, they're the . . ."

"Aerospace giants, right," she said, her excitement growing. And then she filled him in on what Drynan had told her.

"And he just came right out and told you everything?" Joe asked skeptically.

"Yes. But I'll guarantee he hasn't a clue what really happens to those drums once they leave here."

"Um," Joe said.

"And this Tolliver, he's the one who handles picking the stuff up. I'll just bet . . ."

"We'll see," Joe said. "It's another piece of the puzzle, anyway."

"It sure is," she agreed, leaning her head on the back of the seat, letting out a breath. "Joe, let's get the heck out of here and plan the next step."

He started the car and drove out to the highway. Laurel sighed when they were clear of the chain link fences and gates. "God, I was nervous," she admitted.

"Ah, another chink in your armor."

"You can bet Drynan didn't know, though. I was good, Joe."

"Congratulations, but we don't have proof yet. Nothing we could go to court with. Now we have to find the connection between Blackwell and those drums on the reservation."

Laurel felt her high deflate. "We're getting there, though," she said. "It was you who told me Rocky Plains was the only logical source for those drums."

"And so it is," he said pensively.

The afternoon was advancing. They stopped in Golden for a snack, and Laurel used the pay phone to set up an appointment with Blackwell. While Joe drank black coffee at a nearby table, she stood impatiently tapping her foot, her eyes on him, waiting on the line. After three or four minutes on hold she shrugged and gestured to Joe—nothing happening. Finally the secretary came back on the line. "Mr. Huddy, in our public relations department, will be free tomorrow morning at ten," she said. "He can grant you an interview, but he wishes to have the questions in advance."

"Oh, sure." Laurel thought quickly and threw out a few queries: What is the future of the aerospace industry? How is the lack of military spending affecting Blackwell? And so on. Innocuous questions. She'd feel him out and spring the big one on him when they were face-to-face. God, she hoped this worked!

"Thank you so much," she said. "I appreciate your help." She hesitated then threw caution to the wind. "By the way, is Mr. Jack Tolliver in today?"

"Mr. Tolliver? I'm not sure. I'd have to call field operations to find out. Would you care to hold?"

"Uh, no, that's all right. I'll try him tomorrow. Thanks."

"Well?" Joe said when she slid back into the booth.

"Well, what?" Laurel said.

"Don't be cute. Did you get an appointment?"

"Sure did. I tell you," she said, a smile playing on her lips, "I think I've got a real knack for this."

"Right."

"Don't be a sourpuss, Joe Buck," she said. "Without me you'd be up the creek without the proverbial paddle." And then she laughed at his scowl.

"Real delighted with yourself, aren't you?" he said.

"I sure am. I'm having a ball proving to you that your boss is right, you can't always go it alone. No one can. Now, why not come out and admit it?" She leaned forward and held his dark gaze, challenging him, and after a very long moment she saw his expression soften, and slowly he nodded.

"Okay," he said finally, "but it was my idea to bring you along, remember? I never said I could handle this interviewing business by myself."

"You just can't say 'uncle,' can you?"

After they ate it was Joe's idea to look up Jack Tolliver in the Denver Metro phone book. There were several Tollivers, but only one John T. Tolliver—in Lakewood.

Standing next to Joe, Laurel breathed, "Mountain Construction is in Lakewood...."

"Sure is," Joe said.

They drove to the address, which was only a short distance from the vacant lot they'd scouted out yesterday, and Laurel was convinced there was a connection.

"Do you think we dare look in the garage?" she asked Joe while they sat in the Taurus across from Tolliver's split-level brick house.

"For what?"

"God," she said. "For that pickup that chased you! We have the license number."

"Go look," Joe said, shrugging.

"I don't get it."

"I'll guarantee you that if this Tolliver's the man we want he's still in Cortez, looking for *me*."

"Um," Laurel said, "you're probably right," but nevertheless she did get out of the car and peek into the two-car garage. There was only a compact station wagon parked there. "Oh, well," she said, getting back into the passenger seat, "it never hurts to try."

Joe started up the car. "If we can connect this Tolliver to that pickup truck, then we can connect Blackwell to the operation on the reservation," he mused out loud. "And then we've just about nailed them."

"Just about?" Laurel asked, fastening her seat belt. "Joe, it's more than enough to take to the authorities."

"Maybe," he said, checking the road before he pulled away from the curb. "What I'd like to do is catch them in the act."

"And get yourself shot at again?" Laurel looked at him askance. "I won't let you do it. Not alone. And I'll be darned if I'm going out there again and get my butt shot at.''

''No one's asking you to.''

''I'm thinking about you, Joe. If anything happened . . .'' But she couldn't finish. She knew she'd already said too much. Oh, God, she thought, how had she let herself come to care so damn much? It was Holly she needed to concentrate on, her daughter. She looked up carefully from her lap and saw the sidelong glance he gave her. Her stomach twisted.

Joe headed back toward their motel in relative silence. Rush-hour traffic was heavy, the going slow. Off to the west, the line of Rocky Mountains stood behind Denver like white-helmeted sentinels. There, Laurel thought, it was cool and pure. Here it was hot and smelled of car exhaust. She pulled off her blazer and threw it into the back seat. Her stomach growled.

Not far from their motel she said, ''I'm kind of hungry. How about you?''

''You're always hungry.''

''So? I'm used to eating on the run.''

''Um,'' he said, and began searching for a spot.

They found a Mexican restaurant on Colfax Avenue, a huge place that catered to families. Laurel was glad for the crowd and the noise, but she wasn't exactly sure why. She knew only that it had to do with Joe, with being in such constant proximity to him. Something between them had shifted, although certainly neither was admitting it, but the shift was present nevertheless. Maybe it was because they'd talked, a little, anyway, bared the truth of their romantic pasts—some of it. Maybe they'd become too intimate with each other's feelings. How odd, she thought. Or maybe it was the way she'd catch him watching her from behind his sunglasses, the way he'd look away too quickly. Or maybe it was the sudden tensing of her muscles when she'd turn to speak to him and found herself staring at his strong profile or the long, corded muscles in his brown arms. Whatever it was, she felt naked and a little scared.

They ate fiery tostadas and chili *rellenos*. Joe had a nonalcoholic beer, but Laurel ordered a cool Dos Equis beer, and then another. She felt her knees go watery as she tried hard to relax.

Joe studied her. "Are you getting loaded?" he asked, surprised.

"I'm relaxing," she said lightly. "Maybe I need to let my hair down, Joe Buck. You're enough to put anyone on edge."

"I don't know what you're talking about," he said in a low voice as the waiter refilled their water glasses.

"Oh, yes you do," she said, waving off his words. "You know exactly what I mean. Male and female. Attraction."

"Look," he said, "I think we better have this conversation another time."

"Oh, no," Laurel said. "I wouldn't have the nerve."

"Look, I..."

But she only giggled. "Oh, don't worry so darn much. I'm immune to you, Joe. I'm immune to men. Sworn right off them."

"Laurel."

"Oh, just pay the bill," she said, "and stop looking so bloody terrified."

The air outside hit her like a hot fist, and it was only then that she realized she was truly a little tipsy. And on two beers. Joe took her elbow unnecessarily and steered her despite her protests, and soon she was folded into the front seat.

He got in himself and shut the door, then eyed her. "Two drinks," he said, shaking his head.

He drove and said nothing more, but as the cool air from the air conditioner fanned her face and neck, she knew she'd poked a sore spot on Joe Buck. No woman was ever going to get close to him. Once burned, twice shy.

It was barely dark by the time they stood at their doors, keys in hand. "Are you all right?" he asked, pausing.

"I'm fine now," she said. "I was just keyed up, I guess. I really am sober." She unlocked her door, and it swung inward, exposing the drab interior.

"What?" Joe asked when she hesitated.

"Nothing," she said quickly, and then they just stood there, encased in a sudden and gravid silence.

"Listen," he said after a long, awkward moment, "I really meant to tell you... You were good today. You didn't have to do all that. You really helped."

"My, that was hard to get out, wasn't it, Joe? A compliment, my goodness."

"Oh, for God's sake, Laurel, do you always have to be so damn smart-mouthed?"

She drew back. "I guess so. It's my defense."

"Against what?"

"Life," she said. "Just, well... life."

"It keeps everyone at a distance, I guess," he said pensively.

"Yes," she admitted.

"Me, too, I suppose."

"Sure, you, too."

"And that's what you want, Laurel, always being apart from everyone?"

"It's easier that way," she breathed. "You should know that."

"I see what you mean," he said, but she didn't have the nerve to glance up at his face, to see if he were being sarcastic.

They were still alone in the dim, moldy-smelling corridor, facing each other. It was very quiet. Laurel could almost hear the beating of her pulse; she was sure she could hear the beating of Joe's. His strong brown neck rose from the white shirt he wore, and her eyes fixed on a vein that leapt beneath his smooth skin. Her gaze rose, drawn as if by a magnet, up to his face. He was looking at her, frowning a little, and she felt a terrible swelling in her breasts. *No,* she thought, *no.*

Laurel would always wonder just how it had happened, who had made that first minuscule motion toward the other. But at the time it seemed as if Joe had, and her defenses crashed as somehow she was in his arms, crushed to his chest. It felt the way she'd always known it would. Deep in her heart she'd known it would be warm and secure, sweet and wild.

"Oh, my God," Laurel whispered, but his mouth silenced her again, and in moments her door was snicking shut behind them. In the darkness she reached up and felt his face, her hands needing to memorize all of him. He kissed her yet again, hard and hot, his big hands on her back, holding her to him.

She pulled his shirt out of his pants and touched the silky skin, caressing it. She drew in his scent and felt his lips, his tongue, invading her. Her belly ached, and she moaned out loud.

Joe drew back then and held her at arm's length. "You want to do this?" His voice was husky, beautiful and deep.

"Yes," she whispered ardently.

"No smart-ass remarks?"

"No, damn it, Joe."

He drew her close again, kissing her neck, her upturned face, the tender spot where her pulse beat madly against her skin. He unbuttoned her blouse, bent to kiss the top of her breast above her bra. Unhooked her skirt so that it fell and she stepped out of it.

He was tall; she had to stand on tiptoe even though she wasn't short herself. His body was long and lean, satin over steel. She undid his belt buckle and slid her hands underneath.

Abruptly he lifted her off her feet and carried her to the bed. She thrilled at his strength. His hands caressed her everywhere, and she arched against him, her body burning inside, aching.

Laurel had never known or allowed such abandonment of her senses. She was helpless, swept to tremulous heights, making small sounds of pleasure. Time was suspended, an infinity of sensation. She was demented with a kind of unbearable joy as their bodies joined and writhed to reach the crest. Joe lay still then, trembling, holding her with all his being, moaning with the effort to control, not releasing too soon, not letting go of this burning beauty.

Laurel's body twisted against his. She could feel the oneness with him, the wild, glorious moment, every nerve in her body receiving messages from him, a drunken bliss of feeling, so much that her senses were overwhelmed. And then he moved again, and they went on together, frantic, quivering, until they reached delirious oblivion, absolute fulfillment, and hung there, pinioned by it, dying a small death.

Awareness returned in faint snatches—traffic sounds, a line of light under the door, the bedclothes twisted under her. Joe drew away gently and lay beside her. She moved languidly, her whole body touching his, needing his closeness. They lay in a kind of drugged stupor, voluptuously sated.

He raised himself on an elbow finally, bent to kiss her and ran his hand across the skin of her belly. "Laurel," he began, "I . . ."

"No, don't say it. You'll spoil everything."

"You don't know what I was going to say."

"It doesn't matter," she breathed, putting her hand on his, "not tonight it doesn't."

"What about tomorrow?"

"To hell with tomorrow, Joe Buck."

CHAPTER THIRTEEN

JACK TOLLIVER WAS FEELING a whole lot better as he dialed Tyler Grant's home number in Denver. This morning had been the turning point, that small but significant shift in his luck, and it had taken place by accident in a local café as he'd been eating breakfast.

Jack still didn't know that the big Indian woman behind the counter was the policeman's sister—he'd never have made the connection—but the conversation he overheard had made the blood heat in his veins.

"Hey, Rose," the man sitting next to Jack had said, "I hear Joe Buck got himself in hot water with his boss, then took up with some blond chick from California. That true?"

"Joe's not dumb enough to take up with that kind of woman," Rose said. "She's some writer or something, and Joe's just helping her with research."

"Sure," the guy said. "I hear she's a real looker, too."

"This town's too small," Rose muttered and then disappeared into the kitchen.

It had taken Jack Tolliver the rest of the day to track down the writer from California. It hadn't been easy, either. He'd checked every hotel and motel in town, pretending to be a mechanic who'd fixed the lady's car, a white Honda with California plates. But, darn, he'd lost her name, and did they have a blond lady from California registered?

No one did. Then he got the brilliant idea of trying the real estate companies who handled local rentals. Maybe she'd rented a place, seeing as she was staying awhile. And maybe, goddamn it, that was why he'd never been able to locate her car, because she had the thing parked in a garage!

He'd hit pay dirt at the third place. "Oh, yes, we rented the house on Cottonwood to her," the young lady at Southwest Realty said. "Miss Laurel Velarde from Berkeley, California."

"What was the address again?" Jack asked, keeping his smile in place. "She must be going nuts 'cause I haven't gotten that part for her car yet."

"It's 531 Cottonwood," the lady had said. "That's off Pecos."

Grant's home telephone in Denver rang in Jack's ear, once, twice, and then it was answered by a maid.

"I'm sure Mr. Grant's busy with his guests," Jack said, "but you just tell him it's Jack Tolliver calling from Cortez. He'll take the call."

And sure enough Tyler did. Clad in a white dinner jacket, he entered his library, closed the door and picked up the extension. "Tolliver?" he said.

"Yes, Mr. Grant. Sorry I haven't gotten in touch sooner. I tried your office, but..."

"Yes, yes, go on," Tyler said impatiently, forty of his dinner guests awaiting him. "Is everything taken care of?"

"I know where to find the Indian now," Jack said.

"You mean you haven't..."

"Not yet. But it shouldn't be long now." What Jack didn't mention was Miss Laurel Velarde, magazine writer, driver of the Honda. No point getting his boss stirred up about that little glitch.

"You'll take care of this neatly? No trail, Tolliver?"

"Absolutely, sir."

"Well, then, do it," Grand snapped. "And do it quick."

"Yes, sir," Jack said, but the line had gone dead.

THE FIRST PANGS OF GUILT twisted inside Laurel when she awakened in the Denver motel room to find Joe's arm casually lying across her naked hip. Her eyes flew open and her heart gave a squeeze as she thought, Oh, no.

She slid out of bed and felt the flush of realization sear her. In the shower she tried to convince herself it was the two beers she'd had at the Mexican restaurant, but that wouldn't wash—she'd been as sober as a judge when they'd made love. Every time they'd made love, she remembered, her cheeks on fire in the steamy bathroom.

She dressed in the bathroom, too, positive he'd been awake when she'd risen, lying still but faking it. And then, when she was ready, she opened the door again only to hear him snoring softly, not a care in the world. And that made her feel, well, somehow cheap. The least he could have done was wake up, say something, help her out of this mess they'd created.

"Joe," she said, standing over the bed, "come on, wake up. We have an appointment, Joe." Carefully she shook his shoulder, trying to ignore the satin-smooth feel of him.

He did awaken. He rolled onto his back and stretched, yawning, his long body only half covered by the sheet. Laurel looked away.

"Whoa," he said, his voice scratchy, "what time is it?"

"Late. We have to get going."

He sat up. "Do I have time for a shower?" he asked, and he reached down for his pants, exposing the paler flesh of his buttocks.

"Yes, about twenty minutes," she said, and busied herself with packing her suitcase.

With little ceremony Joe left for his room and took his shower, meeting her at the car with his duffel bag. He had the keys, of course, and so she'd stood there, for a full five minutes, torn between impatience and total embarrassment that she had to face him again. *Stupid,* she thought. *Never looking before I leap. Sure, it's easy to say to hell with tomorrow ... until tomorrow actually arrives.*

Joe tossed their bags into the trunk and slammed it shut, then unlocked her door for her. "Another hot day," he said.

And that was when she came apart. "Let's not do this, Joe," she said, facing him squarely.

"Do what?"

"Pretend, that's what. It happened. It happens all the time between men and women."

"Go on," he said, still standing there holding her door open.

"That's all I wanted to say. I don't want to make a monumental scene over this. It was good, but it's over. I have a future planned, Joe, and it doesn't include a ... well, a man right now. Do you know what I'm saying?'' she asked, safely hidden behind her big sun-glasses.

"Absolutely," he said evenly. But he was so close, standing so close.

"Look, I was burned once in the past, and it hurt. I don't want to go that route again," she went on.

"I agree," he said.

"And you were hurt, too. You said as much."

"I'm a confirmed bachelor, you're absolutely right."

"So can we put this all in its proper perspective?"

"I've got no problem with that." He nodded for her to get in. When he was behind the steering wheel he said, "Ready?"

"Yes," she said, and they drove away in silence.

Blackwell International was located in the down-town core of Denver in the Petroleum Building, the towering glass-and-steel monolith that was the city's pride and joy. With Joe alongside her, Laurel looked up and squinted.

"Impressive," she said.

"I prefer a cozy little hogan," Joe replied. "You aren't nervous?"

"Not really," she said. "I've just got to get in the right frame of mind, that's all."

"If you want, I could sit in with you, play the pho-tographer."

"Without a camera?"

"Um."

"Exactly. And besides, you'd make me nervous," she said as they entered the dim, cool lobby.

Joe waited in the coffee shop on the street level while Laurel rode the hushed elevator to the top floor, well, not quite the top; the executive dining room and gym were there. She stood in the swiftly rising car and wondered if the man who'd shot Joe had ridden this same car. It could be Jack Tolliver. Or maybe it wasn't. Maybe the pickup truck belonging to Mountain Construction was not connected to Blackwell at all. If not, she thought, they were most certainly dead in the water.

Drew Huddy, with whom Laurel had the appointment, was no slouch. For the first ten minutes of their interview he grilled her on what articles she'd sold to what magazines.

Laurel faked it as best she could, remembering always to meet his eyes full on. She told him how she'd broken into the business after journalism school with pieces on unusual outdoor sports, and then she lied through her teeth and said she'd sold an article on the failing airline industry in the U.S. to *Business Today* magazine.

"Really?" the sharply dressed blond man said.

"I'm actually very interested in the airline industry," she said. "My father was a pilot."

"Oh, which airline?"

"Eastern," she said easily. "And we all know what happened to them."

"Um. And so now you're bringing that interest to the aerospace industry. I see."

"Look, Mr. Huddy," Laurel said, feeling uncomfortably warm in the cool office, "I appreciate your interest in me, but there are a lot of questions I'd like to put to you, and I'm sure your time is valuable."

"Quite so," he said, and she went on with the interview, fudging her questions.

After another ten minutes, scribbling notes, Laurel glanced up casually and asked, "I understand the aerospace industry is taking on government contracts in the toxic waste disposal area."

"Why, yes, we are. Interesting that you'd know that," he said, his clear blue eyes meeting hers.

"I've done my research," Laurel said. "It must be very lucrative. I understand you contract with Rocky Plains, in fact, and handle their waste disposal."

"I believe that's correct," he said, "though that isn't my area of expertise."

Laurel cocked her head.

"You see," he explained, "Blackwell is just breaking into this up-and-coming industry."

"I was under the impression that Blackwell had been handling the Rocky Plains account for several years," she said.

"I believe we have," he said. "But please understand that this is still a developing industry. It involves new technology, working with the Department of Energy, the Environmental Protection Agency and the military, too. It's a very complicated process."

"I should imagine," she said. "And where is Blackwell's disposal site?"

Drew Huddy smiled affably. "Oh, there's more than one. As I said, there's new technology being developed every day, burning techniques that are cheaper and more efficient than we've had in the past, leases on unusable land where steel and concrete bunkers are being built...."

Obviously he wasn't going to tell her specifics, if he even knew them. She backed away from that subject and tried another tack. "Um, does Blackwell do the disposal work, or do you hire subcontractors to do it?"

Drew Huddy fixed her with a hard blue gaze that contradicted the smile on his lips. "We do both, depending on the job."

Laurel's heart beat against her ribs. Now was the time to ask the one question that would tie Blackwell to those drums in the desert. "I'd like to mention the name of some of these subcontractors in my article. Could you...?" She sat, pencil poised.

"I'm afraid that's just not something I'd know. I don't oversee that department, you understand. You'd have to talk to the head of our field division for that information."

"I see. And who is that?"

"A Mr. Jack Tolliver, I believe."

"That's T-o-l-l-i-v-e-r?"

"Correct."

Laurel felt dampness break out on her upper lip. "Does Mr. Tolliver work with any of your subcontractors?"

"I really don't have all those details," Huddy said.

"Could I talk to Mr. Tolliver, then?" she pressed. If she could just link this Jack Tolliver to the truck out on the dumping site in the desert, link Tolliver to Mountain Construction...

"Mr. Tolliver is out in the field. He'd be very difficult to reach."

Laurel almost asked if he was in Cortez, but she was already pushing too hard and, besides, even if Drew Huddy knew where he was, he probably wouldn't tell her.

Huddy glanced at his watch.

"I'll be done in a minute," Laurel said, giving him a bright smile. "Just one more question," she said then, playing her last card, her only card. "Would Mr.

Tolliver be associated with a company called Mountain Construction?"

"I really don't know, Miss Velarde."

Laurel flipped her notepad shut and felt disappointment settle over her. Damn, she thought. "Well," she said aloud, "thank you, Mr. Huddy. I really appreciate your time."

"I hope I've been of help," he said, rising, too.

"Oh, yes, certainly," Laurel mumbled, "a lot of help." And she let the man escort her out.

Drew Huddy steepled his fingers beneath his chin and decided that was the oddest interview he'd ever given. No sooner had Miss Laurel Velarde begun one tack than she'd switched to another. If she thought she was going to put together a comprehensive article with that, she was sadly mistaken. And she hadn't even asked about layoffs in the industry or cutbacks in military orders, not a word, and that was the main concern of the aerospace industry at present, the desperate struggle in a very uncertain economy.

Drew checked his watch and stood, gazing out the window toward the line of the Rocky Mountains that rose to the west. He then opened a closet door and took out his gym bag. It was eleven-thirty. He'd work out and then have a light lunch. He left his office, checked for messages with his secretary and then used the stairs to head up to the top floor. It was while he was working out on a Nautilus machine that Tyler Grant walked into the gym and tossed a towel on the bench near Drew.

"Morning," Tyler said.

"Good morning, sir," Drew said to the CEO of Blackwell.

Tyler climbed onto a stationary bike and set the timer. "That was quite an attractive woman I saw going into your office." He winked at Drew Huddy.

"Yes, very attractive," Drew concurred. "But basically an airhead."

"Too bad. What was she? A prospective employee in PR?"

Drew shook his head and smiled. "No. She's a fledgling magazine reporter, not very good at her job, either."

Tyler pedaled more slowly. "Well, how did she get an interview? Don't you screen those people?"

"Oh, we screened her. But there wasn't a lot of time to check her credentials. She's only in Denver for a day or so."

"Um," Tyler said. "And what's the gist of her article?"

"That's the problem, sir. Her questions bounced all over the place. She spent a lot of time asking about our contract with Rocky Plains."

"Is that so."

"Yes, sir. She even seemed curious about our waste disposal unit. Jack Tolliver, for instance."

Abruptly Tyler stopped pedaling. Five minutes later he was dialing Tolliver's motel in Cortez, his towel around his neck, sweat pouring from his temples.

"DAMN," JOE SAID as he drove out of downtown Denver.

"I know. I was so close," Laurel replied. "Either he doesn't know about Mountain Construction, or he knows and wild horses couldn't drag it out of him."

"So, it's a dead end here in Denver, anyway."

"I'm so frustrated," Laurel said.

"Hey, it happens. Investigations aren't usually easy. Sometimes they take months."

"This one couldn't . . . ?" she asked, alarmed.

"I'm not letting it go that long. I've got an idea."

"I have an idea, too. Mainly to go to the FBI. We're right here in Denver. Joe, we could go with what we have. . . ."

"No," he said curtly. "Not until we have the link between Mountain Construction and Blackwell."

"Terminally stubborn," she muttered.

"There's one more thing to try," he said.

"What?"

"I'm going to flush out that guy, the one who shot me, the one who's still in Cortez," he said doggedly.

Laurel let out an exasperated breath. "I don't believe this," she fumed. "I suppose you're going to do it all by yourself. Oh, I can just see it. What do you BIA cops do to get someone to talk? Stake him out in the sun with honey spread all over him so the ants will . . ."

Joe laughed. "You really have seen a lot of cowboy and Indian movies. Well, rest assured, Laurel, we don't do that anymore. And besides, I think you're referring to the Apaches."

"Whatever. But I want to know what you've got planned."

He was still amused at her theory about the white-eyes and the ants. "I'm going to catch the guy, but not here. This end didn't work. I'll do it at the other end, on the reservation, where you can bet your boots he's still looking for me."

"Do you think it's this Jack Tolliver?"

He shrugged, driving through the traffic easily. "Maybe, maybe not."

"Go to Charlie Redmoon," she said, then, reluctantly, "please."

"I'm so close," Joe said. "I could have this whole thing wrapped up in a day or two. To turn it over to Charlie now..."

He hesitated and Laurel couldn't help saying, "It wouldn't be the vindication you're hoping for, would it? You got your hand slapped and now your pride won't let you see the danger."

"Hey," he said as they turned onto Interstate 25, "you're partly right. I admit it. It's a major flaw in me, pride."

"So do something to remedy it, tell Charlie..."

"Not yet."

They stopped for lunch in Pueblo, a sprawling front-range enclave of Mexican-Americans, military types, blue-collar workers. She couldn't help starting in again. "I wish I knew exactly what you're planning. I just know it's got to be risky," she said, dipping a french fry in a puddle of ketchup.

"I didn't know you cared," he said, his gaze lifting to hers over the brim of his coffee cup.

Laurel felt her cheeks grow hot; this wasn't a subject she wanted to get into. It was bad enough being so close to him after they'd...made love. And that's what it had been, she realized as she played with her food: love, not lust or even affection. What they'd shared last night had been very special. And because of that she had to be careful. In a few hours they'd be back in Cortez, and Holly was there. Holly. Yes. All of Laurel's concentration was going to be focused on her child. Period.

"Cat got your tongue?" he was saying.

She forced herself back to the moment. "I care, okay, that's true, Joe. I don't want to see you get hurt. But don't read anything else into it."

"Wouldn't dream of it," he said smoothly.

As they passed through Alamosa, the subject reared its head yet again. "Joe, I've been giving this a lot of thought all afternoon. If you don't go to your boss, I will."

"No, you won't."

"You can't stop me."

"Maybe I can't," he allowed. "But by the time you go to Charlie and he gets his act in gear, I'll have the guy behind bars, anyway."

"You think it's going to be that easy?"

"Sure," he said. "You've forgotten, this dude is looking for me. All I have to do is start driving around in my old Scout and he'll surface."

"If he's in Cortez."

"Oh, he's there, all right. I'm the one snag in this operation of Blackwell's. There's got to be millions of dollars at stake. He'll still be there. You can take that to the bank."

In Pagosa Springs, Laurel, who was driving now, pulled into a shaded rest area. "I'm really worried," she said, and got out of the car, walking toward an overview where she stood and stared out across a green valley that was bracketed on three sides by jutting, snow-capped mountains.

Joe came up behind her. "Hey," he said, his voice uncharacteristically gentle, "I'm a cop, remember? I can handle this guy."

"Like you handled him the night he put a bullet in your arm?" She hugged herself, taking a step away from him.

"Come on," he said, "I'll be fine. And I won't do anything dumb. Strictly procedure."

"Oh, right. Joe Buck who got himself suspended for being a total maverick is suddenly going to mend his ways." She heard him laugh softly then, and her knees betrayed her, instantly turning to water. She felt utterly helpless, out of control because, damn it, she did care.

Her back still to him, Laurel sensed rather than felt him move toward her, and then his hand was on her arm, warm and big and tender, and he was carefully forcing her around, slowly, and her pulse began to race.

"Hey," he said again, his eyes hidden by his sunglasses, "where's my anything-goes trooper? This isn't like you."

She stared at his chest and realized her eyes were moist. "Guess I'm slipping," she said, and then his hand was beneath her chin, lifting it while with his other hand he took off his sunglasses. She tried to twist her head away, but the effort was halfhearted. And when his lips met hers with a feather-light touch, she knew it was futile to fight.

The kiss began slowly, tenderly, and then the hot ember between them began to ignite, sending flames into the embrace until they were clinging and touching and moaning, their bodies pressed together in a desperate attempt to fuse despite the impossibility of it.

Laurel never knew how long they stood there clinging and tasting. It seemed as if everything contrived to make the moment perfect—birds singing, the scent of fresh pine needles, the hot summer breeze mingling with his hands as they moved up and down her sides, across her back, her buttocks, as she tried to press herself even closer to him.

It was the car that stopped them. It pulled into the rest area kicking up gravel, and it was Joe who reacted first, lifting his head, his breath coming quickly, putting his glasses back on.

And then Laurel forced herself back to reality. Slowly she opened her eyes to find his gaze behind the dark lenses fixed on her mouth. She took in a deep, quivering breath and let it out slowly. "Don't ever do that again," she murmured.

"What if I said okay, I won't?" he asked in a lazy voice.

"Say it," she whispered.

But he only smiled.

CHAPTER FOURTEEN

FRAN SCHULTZ GAVE her daughter a disparaging look before sitting her down for a chat, and Holly knew trouble was brewing.

"What went on at Miss Velarde's, Holly?" Fran asked. "I thought the woman was going to give you more work this week."

"She was. She is," Holly replied defensively.

"Well, it seems to me she would have called. Are you sure everything went all right? You did a good job for her?" Fran began picking socks out of the laundry basket and folding them at the kitchen table.

"Yes, I did do a good job, Mom. It isn't my fault she had to leave town."

"Don't just sit there sulking," Fran said. "Help me fold some of this."

"Holly do this, Holly do that," the teenager muttered. "You're always accusing me of never doing anything right," she said. "I swear I did a good job for Miss... for Laurel. She was supernice to me, too. Like she appreciated the help."

"You got paid. I just thought it was odd she hasn't called again. You don't have to get sassy with me, young lady. And you can't blame your father and me for wondering. Your behavior this summer has been..."

"So why don't you, like, ground me for the whole year!" Holly cried.

Fran only shook her head slowly. "It was your choice to go out and get yourself drunk and leave your father worried and waiting half the evening in that parking lot."

"Big deal," Holly said under her breath, but her mom heard it.

"Maybe we will just ground you till Christmas, maybe we just will. And don't you ever use that tone with me...."

Holly snapped. Leaping to her feet and knocking her chair over backward, she came unglued. "I hate you!" she yelled, her face red-splotched. "I hate you and I'm leaving!" And with that she raced up the stairs and yanked her bag out of the closet, stuffed in some clothes and went bolting out the front door, still crying. "I'm never coming back! You can't make me ever come back!"

Holly decided to hitchhike into Cortez. With Fran standing on the porch of the old white farmhouse wringing her hands, Holly ran across the cattle-dotted field, climbed over the fence and stood on the highway, thumb stuck out.

She made it to Josh's within the hour. At least she'd stopped crying. But the doors were locked and only a note hung there: "Gone to the store, be back soon, Mom," it read, and Holly knew his folks were home from the camping trip.

She considered her other friends, but discounted every one because of the same problem—parents. They'd call Fran and Earl immediately.

She considered a motel room but she hadn't a dime. She thought about hitchhiking straight out of town, maybe to Durango or Colorado Springs or even to Denver, but without any money...

It hit her then. Laurel's place. Miss Velarde was out of town, but Holly knew where she hid the key, and what harm would it do to spend the night on the couch? Laurel wouldn't mind.

Holly walked the five blocks over to Cottonwood, dragging her bag, her face tight, her jaw locked. She felt miserable, and she felt suddenly very alone and insecure, though the feelings were all jumbled up inside her. And then when she got to Laurel's and slid aside a flowerpot to get the key, she was swept by guilt. What if Laurel got back and was mad that she'd let herself in? Wasn't this kind of like breaking and entering?

For a long time she stood at the kitchen door and stared at the lock, and then finally she put the key in it and she realized what she'd said to her mom for the first time in her fifteen years and was crushed with fear and guilt. "I hate you!" she'd yelled. Maybe they hated her now, too, and she really never could go home! God, she felt so alone, so frightened. What if she called her mom? But Fran would still be so mad. She just couldn't.

Holly opened the door and peered into the empty house and felt that her life was over.

IT WAS AFTER 5:00 P.M. by the time Laurel and Joe let themselves in her kitchen door. Dog, whom they'd already picked up, slunk behind them.

"Well," Laurel said as she opened the windows in the kitchen, her gaze purposefully averted from where Joe leaned casually against the wall. "Well," she breathed again.

And then his voice, deep-timbred and beckoning. "Come here, Laurel."

She knew she shouldn't, it was no good between them and would bring only heartbreak, and yet his summons made her belly quiver. "Don't do this to us," she managed to say, "please, Joe. I'm not as strong as you."

"Come here," he repeated.

She did. Her legs carried her across the room despite the denial inside her. And then they were together, lips crushed to lips, Joe's warm hand pushing up her blouse, cupping her breasts as she clung to him, pressing her hips to his, feeling the urgency of his desire.

They moaned and kissed and touched with a terrible need that had lain just below the surface for hours now. "Oh, Joe," she breathed, her head arching back as his mouth trailed a hot path across the swell above her bra. She put a leg behind his knee, her skirt hitching up, and he responded with a hoarse groan, his hands beneath her buttocks, lifting her as her fingers fumbled with the buttons on his jeans.

The phone rang.

At first it was ignored, as Laurel's mind and senses reeled, but on the fifth ring she picked it up.

"I hope I'm not interrupting anything," came Fran Schultz's voice after Laurel's shaky hello.

"Oh, no," Laurel said, trying to focus. She cleared her throat. "No, Mrs. Schultz, Fran, I, ah, just dashed in the door," she said, which wasn't entirely wrong.

"I was wondering," Fran went on, "would Holly be there?" And Laurel could hear the strain in her voice.

She put the phone to her other ear. "Holly wasn't supposed to be here today," Laurel said carefully. "Is something wrong?"

And the woman's voice broke. "We're just so worried," she said. "We've tried every other place we can think of. I thought... Well, Holly seemed to like you so much, and..."

"She's run away?" Laurel asked, and she could feel Joe's eyes on her. She ignored him, turning away. "Mrs. Schultz, I know how difficult this must be for you, but has Holly run away?"

There was a long pause, and Laurel could feel the woman's pain as if it were her own. Finally Fran said in a small voice, "Yes. We had a spat and she left. She's a good girl, she really is, but for the past few months she's been, well, difficult. And those kids she runs with..." Her voice trailed off.

"I understand," Laurel said, wondering where in God's name Holly was, her child, her child. "It's not easy growing up."

"Earl and I never had these problems. It's very hard for us to understand. And Holly won't communicate. Oh, listen to me," she said with a strained laugh, "here I am pouring out my soul to you. You must think I'm dreadful."

"No," Laurel said quickly, "I don't think that at all. I appreciate your confiding in me," she added. "I'm very... fond of Holly, and I know what she's going through. I'm sure she'll cool off and come home."

"Oh, do you really think so?"

"*I* always did," Laurel said with a little laugh. "She's just letting off steam."

"I hope you're right, I really do. This was all my fault."

"I'm sure Holly contributed," Laurel said, and then she wondered why she was being so darn nice to Fran Schultz.

"Earl and I talked all afternoon," Fran was saying, "and as soon as we find Holly we're all going to sit down with a counselor. We love Holly so much, Miss...Laurel. You can't possibly know what a blessing she's been to us. Without her... Well, here I go again."

"Yes," Laurel said in a small voice, her heart squeezing, "Holly would be a blessing to..." And that was when she felt Joe nudging her arm. She turned, the phone still to her ear, and saw what he was staring at: Holly standing in the doorway.

Laurel swallowed, trying to collect herself. Fran was saying, "...You've been so nice, Laurel, and as soon as we can I'd like to meet you."

"Ah, yes, sure, I'd like that," Laurel managed to say.

"I'm sure you're right. Holly will be home soon. And thank you for your encouragement. Really."

"Ah, my pleasure," she replied, holding Holly's eyes.

When Laurel finally got off the phone, Joe said, "Well, hello, Holly, good to see you again," and he glanced from one female to the other, and then back again.

"Miss Velarde," Holly said, finding her voice, her cheeks scarlet, "I'm so sorry. I only meant..."

But Joe was straightening, clearing his voice. "Listen," he said, "I think I'm kind of a fifth wheel around here. I, ah, think I'll head out to Towaoc and pick up my paycheck." And then he gave Laurel a pointed look. "Could I, ah, talk to you outside for a sec?"

She followed him out to the drive after giving Holly a reassuring smile, but Joe could see the troubled lines on her face nonetheless. "Hey," he began, standing there, his hands on her shoulders, "it's going to be okay. Stop acting as if the world's about to end. The kid's just mixed up."

"You don't know what you're talking about," Laurel began.

But he did. "I think I do know," he said slowly, tilting her face up to his. "You move to Cortez out of the blue, then you hire this girl to do yard work that would take you two minutes a day to accomplish. And you don't just hire any kid, either."

"Joe," she whispered, trying to avert her gaze. "Don't."

But he was going to say it. "Let me finish. So you hire Holly, and suddenly you're too busy to make a trip to Denver...."

"Please," Laurel said softly.

"Okay," he said, "I won't go into it. But I'm not a cop for nothing, Laurel, and a blind man couldn't miss the resemblance."

"So you figured it out," she said. "You want a medal?"

Joe laughed quietly. "No, but I want you to tell me about it sometime."

"It's not a real pretty story," she said.

But Joe carefully pulled her to his chest. "We'll talk later," he said gently, and he tipped her face to his and kissed her. When he drew back he brushed a stray lock of hair from her brow and put on his sunglasses, all business again. "You better call the Schultzes," he said, "let them know Holly showed up. Okay?"

"I will," she said.

"And I'll leave Dog here with you."

"Our guard dog."

"Right. Well, I'd better get going," he said. "You'll be all right? No taking the car out of the garage?"

"I won't, I promise."

"The shotgun's in the closet...."

Laurel shuddered. "I wouldn't touch it, but don't worry, we'll be fine."

He dropped his hands from her shoulders and strode to the car, then he paused. "She's an okay kid, Laurel," he said. "She'll grow out of this."

She gave him a half smile. "We all grow up," she said. "Some of us just do it a little harder than others."

THE SUN WAS THROWING longer shadows across the high desert as Joe drove back to Towaoc, where he'd just been to pick up Dog. He drove along and thought about getting his old Scout back in the morning and flushing out that dude in the pickup. He'd sure like to have his handgun back, though—maybe Redmoon could be persuaded to let him have it if Joe came up with a story.

And he thought about Laurel and even laughed out loud to think that they'd almost made love right in her kitchen with Holly only a room away. Holy cow.

He considered Holly, Laurel's child, for God's sake. A real troubled kid. And he wondered just what Laurel was planning. Surely she wasn't thinking about getting custody. The Schultzes would dry up and blow away without that kid. After all, they'd always had her. She was theirs.

Joe did some arithmetic in his head. Laurel was thirty-three, Holly fifteen. So right around her senior year in high school Laurel had gotten pregnant.

He steered along the arrow-straight highway and thought about that and felt an alien surge of protectiveness for Laurel that rocked him. The aloneness, the hurt she must have suffered... It flashed through his mind then, before he could stop it, that he'd like to give Laurel a baby, a dozen babies, if that's what she wanted. Yeah, he mused, but then caught himself. Hell, Joe thought, he was losing it. In the first place, what would Laurel want with a maverick like him? And besides, he needed to get involved like a hole in the head. He was a loner. What he was feeling for Laurel was pure lust.

The road made a long smooth arc around the base of the Sleeping Ute Mountain before heading on into Towaoc. Joe draped his wrist over the steering wheel and shook his head in amusement. For a minute there he'd almost slipped. Lust, he mused again, that's all it was.

"I GUESS I MUST HAVE fallen asleep on the couch," Holly told Laurel. "I'm real sorry, I shouldn't have come here."

Laurel was searching the fridge for some food, anything, but there was only a gooey brown head of lettuce and a stale loaf of bread. "I don't mind your coming here," she said. "At least you knew you'd be welcome." Was that ever an understatement, she thought as she rummaged.

"But I knew you were out of town," the girl said.

"It's okay," Laurel replied, and, sighing, she closed the refrigerator door. "Are you hungry?" she asked.

Holly nodded.

"Well, we can walk into town and get a pizza or something. But we really do need to call your folks, Holly."

Holly began crying at that, and Laurel's heart went out to her. Oh, Lord, she knew those feelings!

"Okay," she said, "I'll call them, but you've got to promise me we'll talk about this afterward."

Holly nodded, gulping back tears while Laurel dialed the Schultzes' number. It was putting her in an awkward spot, and she hoped Fran and Earl would be reasonable. It was hard, but that's what you did, Laurel figured, for your daughter. She'd done her best to persuade Holly to go home—this was hardly the best time for her to stay here—but Holly was adamant, and Joe seemed to have things under control. That left the Schultzes.

She needn't have worried. Fran and Earl were so relieved that Holly was safe they didn't even think of getting angry. Laurel tried to be businesslike and reassuring; she told them that Holly was very sorry for worrying them and very upset—here she caught Holly's eye—and she wanted to get a little distance from her problems before she came home. Yes, Laurel was glad to have her. She'd be perfectly safe here, and when Holly had calmed down Laurel would drive her home, probably in a day or two.

"And, really, Fran, I know what Holly's going through. I did the same things when I was her age. She'll be fine. Sometimes families just need a little time apart. Can Holly come to the phone? Oh, let me see . . ." Laurel looked at Holly questioningly, but the teenager shook her head fearfully. "Oh, gosh, she just got into the shower. She's fine, though, really she is."

And then Fran said something that wrenched at Laurel's heart. "Please, Laurel, just tell her we love her, we'll always love her."

Laurel had to swallow a lump before she answered. "I'll tell her," she said.

After the call she and Holly locked up the house and walked toward town. Holly was singularly quiet, and Laurel felt bad for her despite her secret bud of exultation because Holly had come to Laurel, had *chosen* her. Amazing, she thought as she strode along, surreptitiously glancing at her child. And then guilt smote her, just as it did every time she thought of the Schultzes and how they must be suffering. She hoped she'd put their minds at rest for now, not added to their anguish.

Laurel and Holly had pizza at a small stand with outside tables beneath brightly striped umbrellas. Laurel watched her eat. She watched her and studied her: the child's mouth and nose and eyes. Her beautiful hair. Her perfectly shaped ears and the graceful arc of her neck. The fine blond hairs on her sun-browned forearms. Yes, watching Holly was pure joy, and Laurel knew she'd never tire of it. They'd lost fifteen years, but maybe they could make up for some of it eventually.

It occurred to her that she could tell Holly right then and there, right over the shared pizza. How would she react? It would be such a shock. Maybe Holly would be angry with her, furious. Maybe she wouldn't believe Laurel. She sat there and watched the girl, and abruptly she knew she couldn't tell her. Not now. She hadn't either the courage or the right.

Holly liked her. She knew that. They could be—were—friends. But a parent... That was a horse of a different color. And Fran and Earl, those good people, had been Holly's parents since she was born. Fran and Earl had gone through childhood illnesses, fights, school, the pain and joy of every moment of Holly's life. That's what counted, Laurel knew, not a random biological accident.

Was there a way they could all share Holly? A child could never have too much love. Laurel looked at her daughter and remembered the old tale of King Solomon's advice to the two women who claimed the same child: Tear the baby in half, and call it justice.

No! Laurel cried inwardly. Not that way.

And then it occurred to her to wonder why the Schultzes had never told Holly she was adopted—most parents did, she'd thought. But it was the most obvious thing on earth that Holly didn't have an inkling that she wasn't their natural child. And it rankled a little, she had to admit. The Schultzes had been living under false pretenses for fifteen years. If they had told her, it sure would make Laurel's choices easier. Or would it?

"You're awfully quiet tonight," Laurel said when they'd finished eating. "Feeling bad?"

"I guess," Holly said.

"Have you ever left home before?"

The girl shook her head.

"You know," Laurel said, "I must have run away from my mom a dozen times."

"You did?"

Laurel nodded. "I was pretty out of control for a while."

"You were?"

"Uh-huh, you bet. I tried all kinds of things, too. You know, booze, whatever," she said carefully. "It was immature and dumb. The only person I hurt worse than my mother was myself. And it got me nowhere. It wasn't till I woke up one day and saw how self-destructive I was..." Laurel frowned. "The worst thing you can do is hurt yourself, Holly. It may look cool, it may feel new and exciting, but it isn't. Your folks are right to want you to stop hanging around with kids who drink and do drugs."

"But they're my *friends.*"

"Maybe. If they're really your friends, they wouldn't want you to hurt yourself. Or at least they'd respect you for not going along with the crowd."

"But then I'd be such a dork."

"No, you wouldn't. And if they think so, they aren't really your friends."

"But we have so much fun," Holly said.

"*Fun.* Hey, there're a million ways to have fun. Sports, music, work. There's not just one way. Holly," Laurel said, "do you think I'm a dork?"

"Oh, no."

"Well, see?" Laurel smiled.

"Did you fight with your parents?" Holly asked then.

"My mother and father were divorced, and he wasn't around. But I sure did fight with my mother. It never got me very far," Laurel reflected. If only Holly knew how lucky she was to have Fran and Earl! Parents who really cared.

"God, parents can be such bummers," Holly was saying.

Laurel shrugged. "Every teenager has to break away from their parents. It's just your age. You're growing up. You're maturing. You're getting ready to set up a new life with a husband, I suppose, but that's not the

way it works in our society. So there's a lot of pulling
back and forth—your parents pulling at you to stay
their little girl. You pulling away for dear life, because
something inside you knows you have to leave soon.''

"How come you know all this stuff?"

Laurel smiled. "I lived through it. I felt exactly like
you do. Which doesn't mean it's right. It wasn't all my
mom's fault, believe me."

"But how come my parents don't understand?
Didn't they go through it, too?"

Laurel hesitated. Because they aren't your real parents! she wanted to say, but that would be unconscionable. "Well, lots of grown-ups forget. And then
others, well, they never go through the rebellious stage
for some reason. They're just different. You have to
respect their differences just as they should respect
yours. That's being mature," she said instead. "One
day you'll find that you can be friends anyway."

"I feel so mixed up sometimes. I love them, but I
hate being trapped on the ranch."

Laurel gave a little laugh. "Oh, I remember. All I
ever dreamed about was an apartment of my own."

"Yeah," the girl said, "me, too. Did you, like, get a
place?"

"In college. Sure. Everyone does."

"But I've got three more years of high school."

"It seems like an eternity, I know. But it's not. And
besides," she said, "maybe something will...change."

Holly cocked her head. "What do you mean?"

"Oh," Laurel said, "I only meant that you never
know what the future might hold."

"Oh," Holly said.

They walked home, ambling along, and they talked
more, a lot more. Holly seemed to open up, trusting

Laurel, even admitting she was thinking about boys
and sex a whole lot of late.

Laurel laughed. "Yeah, that's all a part of it," she
said. "But you've got to be so careful."

"You mean like not getting pregnant or anything."

"That and other things," Laurel said. "And you
have to remember that sometimes a guy will say and do
anything to get you to have sex with him. It's just the
way it is."

"Some of my girlfriends have, you know, done it."

"I'm sure they have," Laurel said as they turned
onto the far end of Cottonwood Street. "Do you have
a boyfriend, Holly?"

"Kind of. Well, not really, I guess."

"Um," Laurel said.

"But you do," Holly piped up.

"Oh," Laurel said, "right." And she felt herself
blush. Just how much had Holly seen of that little ep-
isode in the kitchen with Joe? How... embarrassing!

"Sergeant Buck," Holly went on. "I guess for an
older guy he's pretty handsome."

"An older guy..." Laurel said. "Well, he is a nice-
looking man, Holly, but we're really just... friends."

"You are?"

"Yes, we are. We met by accident, and I sort of got
into helping him with some research. That's about it."

"It is?"

"Yes," Laurel said firmly. "Let's just say we both
have a different agenda." Which was certainly true,
Laurel mused as she unlocked the kitchen door. True,
but somehow the man had invaded her peace of mind.
It was as if he was always there with her, just at the
edge of every thought and movement. She didn't know
what she was going to do about that, either. And here

he was, ready to set himself out as bait for some homicidal maniac. If anything happened to Joe...

"You know," Holly was saying, "this is so cool of you to let me stay here."

"I'm glad to have you," Laurel said. "I really am."

"It would be so neat if you were, you know, like my mom or something."

Laurel felt a flash of warmth in her belly and she was certain she flushed. "Wouldn't it?" was all she could manage to say.

Across the street the dusty white pickup truck pulled to a stop, and the driver shut the engine off.

He stared at the house, at the light in the kitchen, and thought he saw the silhouettes of two women—Laurel Velarde and the kid he'd seen let herself in with a hidden key earlier.

The kid's presence was an annoyance, but that could be handled. The trouble was, the big Indian was nowhere to be seen, and that *was* a problem.

Jack drummed his fingers on the seat next to him and thought about that.

CHAPTER FIFTEEN

"BLAST IT ALL," Joe muttered when he pulled into police headquarters and saw Redmoon's car still there. So he waited, and waited. But old Charlie never came out and finally it got late, and Joe knew Nancy Bearcross was going to go home soon. Then he'd never get his paycheck. Not tonight, anyway.

With a sigh he got out and stood on the hot asphalt for a moment, then shook his head. If he ran into Redmoon, so what? There was no law against Joe picking up his check.

"Hi there, big guy," Nancy said, looking up when he came in. "Long time no see."

"I've been busy," he replied.

"So I hear," she said knowingly.

"What in hell is that supposed to mean?"

"The new girlfriend, the writer."

"She's not my girlfriend," he said. "And how do you know about her, anyway?"

"Charlie met her, Clara met her. So did Rose and everybody."

"Yeah, that's right," he was forced to admit.

Nancy grinned. "Small-town life is grand, isn't it?"

Resentment flared briefly in Joe and died, then a small flame of alarm ignited. Everyone knew about Laurel? That was too damn many people when he'd hoped to keep her out of the picture.

But Nancy was only referring to the tribe. No one except tribal members and their guests were allowed to attend the Sun Dance. The man Joe was looking for would never have been there, not in a million years. Nor would he have any contact with tribal members. "Everybody" certainly did not include *him*.

Still, he felt a sudden, irrational urge to race back to Cortez and stand guard at Laurel's house, but he couldn't. Holly was there, and he'd already made a fool of himself bursting in once before. No, he'd call her, though, and tell her to be careful, to lock up. He was glad he'd left Dog with her.

"Busybodies," he muttered under his breath.

"So, to what do we owe this honor?" Nancy was asking, and Joe told her. She began rummaging through her desk, through the in-and-out files, taking her sweet time while she looked for his check.

"Will you hurry it up?" Joe finally asked as he inadvertently glanced toward Charlie's office.

"I know it's around here somewhere." Nancy hefted herself out of her chair and started looking through a pile of papers on top of the filing cabinet. "I just saw it today." And then she came up with it and dangled it loosely between two fingers. "Must be nice to get a check when you don't have to work for it," she said coyly.

"Yeah, I'm really enjoying myself," Joe said, taking it from her.

And then Nancy looked surprised and snapped her fingers. "Oh," she said. "Charlie said that if you stopped in he wants to see you."

"He wants to see me? What for?" Damn! he thought.

Nancy shrugged.

"Okay. Is he in there now?"

"Yes, he's in his office."

"No time like the present," Joe muttered. "Thanks, Nancy."

"Anytime, handsome," she said in her vamp voice.

He knocked on the doorframe of Charlie's office, as the door was open.

"Come in."

"Captain Redmoon," he said neutrally, carefully wiping the frown off his face.

"Sit down, Joe."

Joe sat. He regarded Charlie, who was leaning back in his chair, studying him. "You wanted to see me," Joe said.

"Clara's been after me about you. She wants you to come to dinner. She doesn't approve of the way I've handled things."

"Yes, sir."

"Now, I know Clara doesn't run the police force, but she may have a point. I could have been a bit hasty."

"About what, sir?" Joe wasn't going to make it any easier for the old man, not after the embarrassment Charlie had made him suffer.

"About your suspension, Joe."

"Uh-huh."

"Come on, Joe, give me a break. I was only trying to save your life. And, goddamn it, you deserved that suspension."

"It's my life, sir," Joe said carefully.

"And Clara doesn't want to see you throw it away."

"Aunt Clara is a sweet person. I appreciate her concern."

"Come over tonight, Joe. She'd be pleased."

"And you, sir?"

Charlie looked annoyed. "Me, too, Joe. Wasn't I your father's friend? Didn't I give the blessing when you were born?"

"Maybe that's the trouble, sir. You're too emotionally involved," Joe ventured.

"I can still do my job, young man."

"Yes, sir."

Charlie sighed in exasperation. "Come tonight. I'll call Clara."

Joe thought for a second. It had taken a lot for Charlie to relent. And he was an elder and a medicine man, besides being Joe's boss. Then, too, Joe adored Aunt Clara. "Yeah, I'll come," he said. "What time?"

Charlie was already reaching for the phone. "Seven. That all right?"

"That's just fine, sir. I'll be there." Laurel needed time on her own right now, and so did he. They'd been together too much, way too much. That had probably been why they'd... He felt the heat in his groin at the thought; it made him unaccountably angry.

"Hey, Nancy, can I use your phone for a quick call?" he asked when he was again in the outer office.

"Anything, lover. Just don't call Paris."

But as soon as Laurel answered he knew he'd made a mistake. He should have found a pay phone, because Nancy was unabashedly listening to every word. He turned his back and lowered his voice.

"That's right," he said, "at the office still... I'm not whispering." Then he added, "You called her folks? Good. Uh-huh... Pizza? You didn't drive... Good." And then in a low voice he told her to keep the place locked up tight. He'd be there in a few hours. "That's right, dinner at the Redmoons'... I'll behave," he mumbled, "sure. Now, remember to keep the doors locked. I'll use the key outside... No," he said. "Everything's fine, I just want to be cautious." Then he asked, "Hey, would you feed Dog...? Okay, see you later." He replaced the receiver in the cradle and turned to Nancy to face the music.

"So, she's not a girlfriend, huh?" Nancy said. "Well, you never talk like that to me."

"Sure I do. All the time."

"Get outta here, Joe Buck. I'm hurt, I really am. Mortally wounded."

"I'm leaving. I'll be at Charlie's for dinner in case anyone needs me."

"Anyone?"

"Yeah, you know, Rose or Lawrence or somebody."

But Nancy only folded her arms across her formidable bosom. "And you left your mutt with her. You must be in love, Joe."

"For God's sake, Nancy," he said in disgust as he left.

HE DID GO TO HIS HOUSE, though, depositing his dirty clothes in the hamper, showering, very well aware that there could be someone outside even now, waiting till night fell, stalking him, hiding in those stunted piñon trees to the east, or maybe right in the dusty backyard, crouched in the sagebrush.

Joe hadn't asked Charlie for his gun. He'd thought about it, but Charlie would have asked him why he needed it. He had the shotgun at Laurel's, but he couldn't lug that around with him. Right now he'd like the feel of the revolver on his hip, he thought. Familiar and heavy and close at hand. Maybe he'd think up some excuse and ask Charlie for it tonight.

He left his house quietly, standing for a moment in the growing dusk, his senses keen. Somewhere nearby a squirrel chattered, not a warning, just a call to a mate. That was good. He made his way to the car then, taking in the scent of nightfall. It was a hot summer evening, too, bone dry, with red clouds streaking the western sky. In the near distance, the Sleeping Ute rested on his back, his profile staring endlessly up, his arms endlessly folded. On the far side of Towaoc the mesas would soon turn to shades of orange and burnt sienna as the light quickened and died.

And out there in the desolation of Indian country those fifty-five-gallon drums still lay buried, Joe thought as he drove to the Redmoons'; maybe some of them had been there for years. Leaking deadly poison, slowly, almost imperceptibly killing the land and its inhabitants. He set his jaw and decided: tomorrow he'd fire the old Scout up, drive around Cortez. And sooner or later they'd make a try for him. Of course, Laurel would be out of it. He couldn't go near her place with the Scout, nor could he stay there after tonight. He'd have to move back into his own house. Yes, that's what he'd have to do. Him and Dog, the way it had always been.

It crossed Joe's mind while he drove the familiar road that he could tell Charlie the whole thing tonight. He could. But Charlie would be on the phone to the feds instantly. And that wouldn't do. The link between that white pickup's license number and Blackwell International had to be made first.

No, Joe thought, he couldn't let Redmoon in on this yet—Joe had taken it this far, he'd go all the way now.

To Joe's surprise, Charlie had driven home and prepared a sweat bath. "Would you join me before din-

ner?'' he asked Joe, who felt a sudden warming toward
the old man.

"Thank you," Joe said. "I'd like that."

The sweat lodge was a small domed tent, no metal
allowed in its structure. Inside was a pit in the center
with a wood fire and twenty-four volcanic rocks.
Twenty-four was the minimum number, although if
there had been more men, Charlie would have used
additional rocks. Still, it was hot and close inside the
lodge, the way it should be, and more stifling still when
Charlie threw water on the rocks and the very air hissed
and steamed.

A neat pile of chokecherry branches lay there, for the
men to fan themselves with, and Joe held one, breathing in the heavy air, relaxing into the correct frame of
mind. He was genuinely honored by Charlie's
thoughtful gesture. It meant he wished Joe to travel the
spiritual path with him, to be on his side against their
common enemy of disharmony. It was, in other words,
a genuine offer of friendship and forgiving.

Charlie began the prayers in a low, deep voice, asking the Creator to bless them. He threw more water on
the rocks and steam billowed. Joe closed his eyes and
breathed slowly, rhythmically, feeling his earthly worries recede to distant ghosts.

Charlie began to speak, in English, as Joe did not
speak the old language well enough. "The sweat lodge
is a tool, Joe. We can use it to walk the path to enlightenment if our minds are ready." He threw more
water on the rocks, and Joe felt sweat burst out of his
pores, slick on his naked skin. "Is your mind ready?"

"I don't know," Joe answered honestly.

"You have to be willing to let go of the world. There is no separation between the spiritual life and the physical one, so it is an easy thing to do."

"It isn't easy for me, Charlie Redmoon."

Charlie sighed, his round belly shiny with sweat. "This is good, then, Joe Buck. Let it work on you. Practice. You need the peace it will bring to your mind."

"That's true."

"Arrogance of spirit leads to tragedy. We are all members of the tribe. Even the Christians teach that. We have to work together, cooperate. Evil comes from a man working on his own without regard to his brothers." Charlie fanned himself with a branch. "I don't want to lecture you, Joe."

Joe smiled. "But you can't help it."

"I'm your elder. You're supposed to learn from my wisdom, not repeat the mistakes I've made. That's what makes us human, Joe. Learning what went wrong in the past."

Charlie was right, of course. And Joe did respect his elder's wisdom in most areas. He set his mind to empty, then to accept. In respect for Charlie he put aside rebellious thought.

Charlie prayed again, this time in the old tongue. The cadence was mesmerizing, the man's voice very strong. Joe got the feeling he always did in the sweat bath, of being in touch with something elemental.

He could understand most of the words of the chant. It was about the Creator, who was the god of all people, a bisexual and infinitely understanding god. There was no hell, no guilt in this god's domain. When you died you went to a happy place in the sun to live with this Creator. Charlie asked for guidance from the Creator, from the sun, moon, stars, from plants and animals. He rocked back and forth, deep in his chant song. Joe closed his eyes, felt the sweat gather and roll down his skin, and let the words enter his mind.

Finally Charlie ended his song.

They would talk now, and Joe would be expected to bare his soul, to go along the path to truth and enlightenment with the elder of the tribe. Abruptly Joe was flung back into the physical world. There was a thing he could not divulge, which would interfere with the quest he and the old man were on, but he had to keep it secret. There was too much at stake. He wondered if Charlie suspected something, but decided it was impossible.

As his mind raced he hardly heard Charlie's words.

"I've been having dreams lately, dreams of red, bloodred. People, animals, the sun itself, all red. It's a very bad sign."

"Yes," Joe replied, knowing the old belief but not paying it much heed. He had to force his attention to Charlie's words and keep his mouth shut.

"There is an imbalance," Charlie was saying, "in the land. People are sick. Animals are dying."

"I know that. I have heard."

"At the Sun Dance the young men danced very hard. Their minds were clear, their hearts were pure. They didn't eat or drink. It rained, and I thought the Creator had blessed us, but there are still people getting sick and my visions of red are with me. I'm concerned."

Joe looked down, felt sweat trickle around his neck, down his chest to drip viscously off his bare nipples. His silence was stony.

"I tell you this so that you are aware. I have told everyone, but we must be on the watch for signs in the animals and plants. Sooner or later the source of this imbalance will be revealed to me. We have to work together on this."

"I understand."

"Good. You have a sharp eye, Joe Buck, like your father, so I will depend on you."

"Thank you," Joe said, his insides twisting, and he knew he'd have to tell Charlie soon. He just wanted a few days to flush them out, maybe only a day or two. Was it so wrong, if the result was good?

"Clara's waiting," Charlie said then, and he gave a short laugh. "Now that I've nourished your mind, she'll nourish your body."

Clara had fixed roasted lamb and fry bread, corn and squash from her garden. They drank water and strong coffee. It was dark, and they ate outside on the back porch, where they could see the stars and feel the refreshing breeze. Joe was unusually quiet, but Charlie was in an expansive mood from the sweat bath, and took up the slack, recounting some of the old stories, every one with a lesson to be learned.

"You've heard the story about how the Colorado River canyon was formed," Charlie said. "You've forgotten it? It went this way. The chief of all the Utes lost his wife and mourned for her without end. The spirits showed him the way to where she was so that he'd be able to see that she was happy. They rolled their magic ball before him to the beautiful spirit land, making a trail, and the chief saw that his wife was indeed happy. The spirits then warned the chief and all his people never to walk that road again, but the spirits were afraid he would, anyway, so they rolled a mad, raging river into the trail, which would overwhelm anyone who would go there.''

"My mother told me that one," Joe said. "And she described the spirit land."

"The whites called it the Happy Hunting Ground. Silly name, but our name doesn't translate," Charlie said. "Still, it's a nice place." He drained a cup of coffee. "Then there's the one about Old Coyote and Porcupine. Porcupine learned to ride a buffalo by holding its horns, and Old Coyote made so much fun of him for wanting to ride the beast that Porcupine got mad. They had a race, with Old Coyote on a horse and Porcupine on his buffalo. Porcupine won. Never underestimate your opponent."

"The tortoise and the hare," Joe said, half to himself.

"Sure, same story."

"Someone should write all these stories down, Charlie," Clara said. "I've said it before."

"I might someday."

"Don't wait too long, old man," she said playfully.

"When I retire," Charlie said.

Joe looked at him. This was the first time Charlie had ever mentioned retirement.

"Oh, no, not yet," Charlie said, smiling. "I'm not that old."

"But soon," Clara urged, catching his eye.

"Maybe," Charlie grunted.

They sat there in comfortable companionship, Joe pushing away thoughts of those drums out in the desert whenever they tried to intrude. Not yet, he told himself. He'd know when the time was right.

"This is good," he told the Redmoons instead, tilting his chair onto its two back legs. "I've forgotten a lot of the stories. It was good of you to have me."

"It's been too long since you visited," Clara said. "Come again soon, and bring that pretty girl with you. The magazine writer."

"Laurel?" He was embarrassed. "Well, I don't think... I mean, we're not exactly that close."

"You're friends. She's welcome here."

"Did she like the Sun Dance?" Charlie asked.

"Uh, yes, she was very impressed."

"Good." Charlie held Joe's gaze. "She wasn't patronizing, I hope, like so many whites are."

Joe thought for a moment. "No, she wasn't." And he tried to suppress the spurt of defensiveness he felt at Charlie's implied criticism. What did Joe care what anyone thought of Laurel Velarde?

It was getting late. The moon was high in the sky, nearly full. Only one slim curve remained to be filled out in order to make a perfect silver globe. Maybe, as Laurel had said, the night sky *was* closer here.

"I'd better go," Joe said, rising. "It's late."

"I'm so glad you came." Clara rose and walked around the table to kiss his cheek, rising on her toes to reach him.

"Thank you, Aunt Clara."

"I'll walk you to your car," Charlie said.

In front of their neat bungalow the moon flung light over everything, making sharp black shadows on the silvery landscape. Charlie followed Joe to the Taurus.

"What happened to your Scout?" Charlie asked.

"Oh, it needed some repairs. It's in Cortez," Joe lied, feeling the discomfort return. He could tell Charlie here, now, when they were alone.

"Joe, I wanted to talk to you. I've been thinking."

"Yes, sir."

"Stop that 'sir' business."

"Okay. What's on your mind?"

"I'm getting older. Not too old. But I have so many other things I could do. This sickness in the land, it worries me, and I wonder if I shouldn't devote more of my time to it."

Joe's skin tightened all over his body. Outwardly he listened politely.

"I may just retire soon. Within a year or so. Clara's been after me, and maybe she's right. I used to feel like I was doing some good on the reservation, but now with this casino, it isn't the same."

"Everything changes," Joe said.

"Yes, it does. The Creator teaches that, but maybe I haven't changed enough with it. I go to work nowadays as if it's a burden. I used to look forward to every day as a new challenge. Maybe it's me."

"It is harder. Even I can see the changes. All the tourists."

"And money. There's money now, and I don't even want to think of how it'll be spent. Whatever it does, it certainly won't get us closer to the harmony within, I know that."

"I'm afraid you're right. It'll take some adjustment," Joe said.

"Well, maybe I don't want to adjust. I'm too old to change now, but you're not too old."

Joe peered through the dusky light, trying to read Charlie's face.

"What I mean is, you could take over my job."

Joe was silent for a minute. His mind whirled. Charlie offering him the job as captain? After suspending him?

"All right, you're surprised, I understand that. Think about it. You're well qualified. You're a fine officer. You could be the one who makes it work."

"Well, sir, I..."

Charlie held a hand up. "As I said, think about it. There's no hurry. I'd recommend you to Superintendent Thomas. This...uh, this suspension...well, there's no official letter of reprimand in your file. I saw to that."

"Thank you, sir."

"You'd have to learn to curb that reckless streak, though. Discipline. It would take discipline. You can't keep trying to solve every case, take care of every problem on your own, Joe."

His gut twisted. "You may have a point there," he mumbled.

"I hope this suspension taught you something. I'm only sorry it had to be me who did it."

"Well, thank you for everything," Joe said, wanting to get away from this generous old man. "I'll think about that offer," he said as he reached for the door handle of his car, and that was when Charlie dropped the bombshell.

"Oh, did your army friend ever find you?" he asked Joe.

"My...?"

"Nice fella, bit older than you."

"Charlie, I don't..." he began, but suddenly his throat constricted.

"Now, what the devil was his name?" Charlie wondered aloud. "John," he said. "No. It was...Jack."

Charlie smiled, proud to have remembered. "Jack Tolliver. That was it. Did he..."

But Joe never heard what he said.

TOLLIVER LOOKED at his watch and swore. It had been hours since it had got dark, and that Velarde woman and the girl—obviously her daughter—had been asleep for at least one of those hours, but the damn Indian still hadn't shown up. Jack had sat there in his truck, tired, hungry, cramped, his gut killing him, waiting and waiting, but Joe Buck hadn't shown his face.

Maybe he wasn't coming back. Maybe he was. But Jack was sick of waiting. And that call yesterday from Tyler Grant. The woman had been to Blackwell, pretending to do an interview, asking questions! Grant had been frothing-at-the-mouth mad, Jack apologetic. Tonight was it—tonight he had to take care of it. Except that the Indian hadn't shown up. And maybe he wasn't going to.

The plan had been forming in Jack's mind for the past hour, and now he tested it mentally, looking at all the angles. Yes, it was good. It would work. In fact, it was better than the original plan of doing it in the house. Cleaner, safer. It'd look like an accident, and no one would find them out there for days, weeks maybe.

Okay, he'd waited long enough. This was it. Jack took a gun from the glove box, checked it, opened his car door and headed toward the dark and silent house.

CHAPTER SIXTEEN

LAUREL AWAKENED so suddenly she couldn't discern between the noise in her dream and the snarl that came from Dog. She sat bolt upright in bed, not really knowing what was happening but reacting to a shot of adrenaline so strong that her heart knocked against her ribs.

It was dark, but the moon lay a broad silvered strip across the floor. She was aware of Dog's growl, rising in pitch, aware of a body, someone, in her room, someone moving through the silver.

"Joe?" she asked. Then Dog's snarl rose to a hideous crescendo, and she saw the swift leap of his shadow, then heard a man curse and stumble, thrashing, knocking against a dresser.

She flew out of bed, her brain scrambling, her body ready for flight. *The lights!* her mind screamed. *No! He'll see me!*

The struggle going on a few feet away was a bewildering tangle of grunts and snarls and thumps, and she couldn't tell what was happening. Dog, she prayed, get him, get him! But then there was a yelp and a thump and a terrible silence.

She held her breath, the blood pounding furiously in her veins. She heard it then, a kind of rasping, slow and even, and then abruptly there was a blinding light and she saw him, a man, near the light switch by the door.

A shortish, heavyset man with rumpled clothes and a baseball cap. He was holding his arm, blood seeping through his fingers, his shirt tattered, a gun hanging from his hand. He's hurt, she thought in a reflex reaction, and what had happened to Dog? She began backing away until the wall stopped her.

"Who are you?" she whispered. "What do you want?"

"Never mind who I am," he said gruffly. "We're going for a ride, you, me and that kid in the other room."

"No, I won't go..."

"Just shut up, lady, and get the kid up and get dressed, fast."

Not Holly, no! "Take me," she said. "Leave Holly."

"Both of you. Get going."

"You want money? I don't have much, but I..."

He laughed harshly. "This is no robbery," he said. "Now move."

She went toward him slowly, because he was next to the bedroom door. Plans flicked through her head like old film, jerky and splotched. Run, scream, grab the phone, get Holly out a window. The back door, the front door, the... The gun. The shotgun in the coat closet! If she could get to it. But she had no idea how to use it or even if it was loaded.

"Move, lady."

She was close to him now, and she saw Dog's spotted body crumpled on the floor, blood on his head. Her heart sank. She sidled by the man, then, just as she was abreast of him, she made a desperate lunge for his bleeding hand and the gun. She almost got it, but he jerked back and grabbed her with the other arm, crooking her neck in his elbow and holding her thrashing body with the bloody hand.

"Goddamn you!" he said viciously, tightening his arm until Laurel was seeing spots of light. He let her go finally, and she slumped to the floor, coughing and gasping. *Holly*, she thought through the red haze. *Holly*.

It turned into a waking nightmare after that. The man made Laurel get dressed right in front of him, and then he made her go into the other room and wake Holly.

It broke Laurel's heart to see the fear in her daughter's eyes when the situation became clear to her. Oh, God, it was her fault, all her fault.

"Laurel?" Holly said, "what's he going to do? What does he want?"

All the man said was "Shut the hell up and move it."

When they were both dressed, he herded them into the kitchen with a wave of his gun, and then he tore through the drawers until he found a notepad. "Sit down and write what I tell you," he said to Laurel.

"I will not," she began, but he grabbed Holly's arm until she cried out, and Laurel dropped into the chair like a stone, writing exactly what he told her. When she was done, she looked up and glared at him. "So you're Tolliver."

She left the note on the table and got to her feet, going to Holly. "You can leave all the notes you want," she said to him, "Joe's not that dumb. He'll never fall for this."

"Shut up," he said mildly, dangerously, and Laurel did.

Hugging Holly to her side, she watched the man in horrified fascination. This was him, the one who'd shot Joe, the one who'd eluded them all this time. Tolliver of Blackwell. The man who had supposedly been out of town on a job. Some job.

"They know all about you," she bluffed. "We told the FBI. They're on their way, so it won't do any good to..."

"Shut up," he repeated. "Let's go. One at a time. Outside. Leave the light on so he'll find the note. And don't try anything. I'm a damn good shot."

Holly's hand tightened on hers convulsively. "Don't worry," Laurel said, trying to keep up the girl's courage. "Joe will find us, Holly. We'll be okay."

"Yeah, he'll find you, all right," Tolliver said. "That's exactly what I'm counting on." He gestured with the gun. "Get going. Now. Out to the truck. Lady, you drive. Quick, now." And the three of them went out into the night and got into the dusty white pickup with the license plates EMC-451.

JOE BURST INTO LAUREL'S house. He stood stock-still just inside the door and assessed the scene. The old lock on the door had been forced. No Dog came to greet him, and the lights were on in the kitchen and Laurel's bedroom.

"Laurel?" he called softly, but he knew there would be no answer. His pulse began thudding slowly, heavily in his ears. He moved to the open door of her room—her bed had been slept in, and her nightgown had been flung hastily onto the floor. He went over to the nightgown and picked it up and his heart stopped in midbeat—there was blood smeared on the silky material that still held Laurel's scent. Whose blood? He looked around the room desperately, seeking answers.

It was then that he saw Dog, sprawled on the floor against a wall. He felt an instant pang and knelt by him. The animal's heart was going, but he had a nasty cut on his head that was still oozing blood.

He ran his hand over Dog's spotted fur. "Good boy, you were trying to protect Laurel, weren't you?" And then he swore under his breath, hating himself for leaving two defenseless women and a dog alone. He should have been there!

He rose and went into the other room. No Holly. Of course not. The kitchen. The light in the small yellow room was pitiless. It shone on a hastily scrawled note on the chrome-and-Formica table. He read it, head bent as if braced for a blow.

The note wasn't signed, but it didn't matter. He knew who had forced Laurel to write it—Jack Tolliver or one of his flunkies. What mattered was that Laurel and her daughter were in deadly danger. The man who'd broken in here had taken them far out into the Ute Tribal Park. Joe knew the place only vaguely, an Anasazi ruin called the Night Cliffs, but he knew he could find it. And that was exactly what the man wanted, for Joe to be lured out there, and then he'd kill all three. No witnesses.

The shotgun. Joe went to the closet and opened it. There it was, untouched. Useless. As useless a protection as he'd been.

He clenched his teeth so hard it hurt, and told himself the women were safe as long as they were useful in luring him. They wouldn't be harmed. Not yet. And then he shut down the fear that could make his judgment go bad. Trying to see this as a hostage problem, a common police problem, he ran through the possibilities.

Okay, so it wasn't the best situation, but it wasn't hopeless, either. It looked like one man, only one, had done this. He'd have a gun, maybe several, but apparently he was alone. Sooner or later he'd need sleep, his vigilance would relax. And Joe would have to bank on that, because there wasn't a whole lot else he *could* bank on. The man's weaknesses and Joe's own strengths.

But he knew suddenly and irretrievably he couldn't do it alone. For the first time in his life he needed help; he had to have backup.

He went into Laurel's bedroom and squatted on his haunches next to Dog. He sighed heavily, picked up the limp animal and carried him outside to the Taurus, bundling him into the passenger seat. He got behind the wheel, took a deep, cleansing breath, and looked up at the brilliant orb of the moon. Then he shot out of the driveway and headed back toward Towaoc, speeding, knowing what had to be done.

THE MAN MADE LAUREL DRIVE the whole way, Holly next to her and on the outside the man with the gun always trained on one of them. For a brief second she recalled with ironic detachment the night Joe had made her drive through the reservation, but it had been so different that night, different from the first moment. With Joe, despite the time and place and his bloody arm, she'd never felt that she'd been in danger. But this man, this ordinary-looking, middle-aged man with the hard round belly and sweat-stained baseball cap, this man was like a visitation from evil.

She was afraid, mostly for Holly, for her little girl, whom she'd embroiled in this awful mess because of her own selfishness, her own utterly thoughtless craving to see the flesh of her flesh. She never should have let Holly near her until this case was over. Maybe she'd asked too many questions in Denver, alerted someone. It didn't matter now, though, because it was too late.

On she drove. They'd passed Towaoc and were on the long, straight road through the reservation. She'd tried surreptitiously to speed up right in front of police headquarters in Towaoc in case there was a policeman around, but the man had tapped her on the arm with the barrel of the gun. "Uh-uh," he'd said warningly, and that had been enough.

Joe. She thought of his phone call that evening. He'd been concerned. Lock up, he'd said. And she had, but the man had gotten in, anyway. Antiquated locks had never stopped a determined housebreaker, she guessed. And Dog, lying hurt, maybe dead... Oh, God, Joe would never forgive her—or himself.

"Where exactly is this Anasazi ruin?" she finally asked.

"Never mind."

"If it's far we'll run out of gas. It's only half full," she said.

"There's enough."

"We'll need water and food. Is there some where we're going?"

"Shut up."

She drove, silent for a time, then she tried again. "Joe Buck will get you. He won't give up. You don't have a chance."

"Lady, I told you..."

"You shot Joe that night. It was you, wasn't it?"

"Laurel, don't..." Holly whispered.

"It's okay, honey. He won't be able to do anything. Joe already knows. He'll get the whole police force after us, the FBI, everyone. We already told them all about it in Denver," she lied. "We even know the license number of this truck. It's EMC-451. We told them that, too. They'll all be looking for him." Then she gave the man a sidelong glance, feeling an illicit thrill when she saw she'd got a rise from him.

"Goddamn it," the man said. "Keep your mouth shut."

"They can prove now that Blackwell's been using you to bury those drums. You know that, Tolliver, don't you?"

He said nothing this time, his face set in granite, and Laurel couldn't resist one more jab.

"Do you know what this man does for a living? He buries nuclear waste illegally on Indian land. And it's leaking and contaminating the reservation," Laurel said.

Then the man leaned past the child and backhanded Laurel across the face, sharp and hard. The truck swerved to the left and Laurel fought for control as a spurt of hot anger gushed through her veins.

"That was real smart," she hissed even as she put a hand on Holly's shaking knee.

"Drive," Tolliver said, "just drive," and by the tone of his voice, Laurel knew she'd really got to him this time.

She licked the corner of her lip and tasted blood and tried to picture Joe's reaction when he got to the house that night. The forced-in door, the note, Dog. He'd be scared for her and Holly, angry with that grim, silent fury she'd seen all too often etched on his face.

They'd both miscalculated badly, though. This man was more desperate and cunning than they'd thought. He'd tracked her down and neatly trapped Joe into following them. She drove, her body wired with fear and anger, her nerves leaping under her skin. She never noticed her split lip again. The land slipped away on either side of the truck; brush and rock and gullies. The moon was lower in the sky now, the stars so brilliant it hurt. Laurel drove and felt her daughter's leg alongside hers, the girl's shoulder touching her own as Holly cringed away from the man. And one thing became clear in Laurel's mind: Holly had to be kept safe. No matter what she had to do, no matter what she had to sacrifice, Holly would be safe.

"Turn up ahead. Left," the man said finally.

It was an unmarked dirt road that followed a shallow valley. Laurel tried very hard to note landmarks, to locate herself in case she needed to return the same way. A dark line of a butte in the distance, a gnarled tree to the right. But otherwise to her the land was featureless.

He seemed to know exactly where they were going, though. It occurred to Laurel that he could do anything he wanted to them out here: no one would ever know. They were, she figured, in the middle of the Ute Tribal Park now, somewhere in that huge area that was empty but for ancient Anasazi ruins, coyotes and jackrabbits. It was not known to tourists the way neighboring Mesa Verde was, and few people visited this part of the park.

It seemed as if they had been driving forever along the dusty dirt road, rising a little. They'd crossed a river on a rickety bridge, the Mancos River, Laurel thought. Ahead was the dark smudge of an escarpment, a flat-topped mesa, the moon coating it with silver. They drove straight toward it until the road ended in a jumble of rock, and Laurel sat there in the idling truck, waiting.

"Turn it off. Give me the keys," he said. "We're walking. Get out, kid, and don't try anything cute. Then you." And the ugly eye of the gun pointed the way.

It was light enough to walk with ease, although the shadows cast by the setting moon were elongated and eerie. The man took a flashlight from the glove box and turned it on. Just like Joe had that night. She almost laughed at the irony of it, but she shivered instead.

"Get going. You two first. Just remember I'm right behind you with the gun," he said.

Laurel went ahead, following a path. There'd been a weathered wooden sign at the start of the trail, a very old sign. All the other signs and trails Laurel had seen on the reservation had been kept in good repair. She shuddered. No one used this path any longer. Tolliver must know that. They were utterly alone in the black vastness. Laurel fought her fears, then tried to give Holly a reassuring glance.

They were definitely walking up now, winding through sculpted spires of rock that jutted from the ground. The moon glinted off the tops of the monoliths, and it was even darker on the path now; sometimes she stumbled. She felt short of breath all the time, her leaping heart using up all the oxygen she needed for walking.

"You okay, Holly?" she asked over her shoulder.

"I guess so," Holly replied, and Laurel's heart squeezed at her forlorn tone.

Still, despite all her fears, her concern for Holly, Laurel was waiting for the time to do something, a quick duck into the rocks, a place to dart into the shadows, a lapse of the man's watchfulness. But she couldn't, not here, not without Holly, and she couldn't communicate her plans to the girl fast enough. She'd only get one of them hurt. But sometime there'd be a chance and she'd grab it. The man couldn't stay awake forever, and there were two of them.

They were approaching the cliff face that Laurel had seen from afar. They must have been walking for an hour or so; she couldn't see her watch, so she wasn't sure. The face loomed closer and closer above them. Finally they stopped at its base, amid loose rock and thick brush. The trail had ended.

Laurel turned questioningly. "What now?" she asked.

The man pointed with his gun. "Up there," he said.

Laurel looked, craned her neck. My God, yes, she saw it. A ladder like one of the old Anasazi ladders that led to their cliff dwellings. She looked harder, and there, eighty, maybe a hundred feet above them, she could see a shadowed recess in the cliff.

"An Anasazi ruin," she breathed. "You really want us to...?"

"Get going."

"But will the ladder hold us?" she asked.

"It was put here for tourists."

"Tourists, here?"

Then the man grinned. "Yeah, they come here about once every five years or so. Maybe." Then he stopped grinning. "Go on. You first, then the kid. And don't worry, I can shoot and hold on with one hand."

She started up. Behind her Holly was crying, scared. "Just hang on, honey," Laurel said. "Follow me. One rung at a time. It's easy."

It wasn't so easy. She got tired quickly, her hands aching, her calf muscles screaming from the unaccustomed exertion. She went very slowly, afraid to look down. Behind her she could hear Holly sniffling, and then, further down, the man's heavy breathing. He wasn't in great shape. This was hard for him. Maybe he'd have a heart attack and fall off the ladder, she thought with a spurt of pleasure.

Finally she was at the top, holding on to the two sides of the ladder that extended beyond the rungs, stepping onto the plateau. She turned quickly, hoping maybe to grab Holly off the ladder, and together they could push it so that he'd fall. But no, he was crowding Holly, clambering right behind her onto the mesa, the gun right there in his hand.

They all needed to catch their breath from the climb. Laurel could see in the moonlight how sweat glistened on the man's face and darkened his shirt. His breathing was labored. But he was managing.

She pulled Holly close to her side, putting her arm around her. "It's okay. We're fine now. Look at this place. An old ruin. Pretty neat. Don't cry now, honey."

Indeed, it was an ancient ruin wedged back under an overhang, the way the Anasazi often built their pueblos for protection from their enemies, just like the ones visited by millions in Mesa Verde. But this ruin was tumbled, only piles of stones. It hadn't been reconstructed like the more popular ones. This ruin was sad and neglected, melting back into the ground from where it had come.

She suddenly remembered Joe telling her that the Ute avoided the Anasazi ruins because there were spirits hanging around them. Unhealthy, he'd said. She looked around her at the piles of rocks, the bare outlines of square rooms, the sinister shadows that sat like dangerous beasts in the corners of this deserted dwelling of a long-dead, ancient tribe. She looked around her and she shuddered.

The man finally caught his breath. The eye of the gun waved at them. "Back there," he said.

Laurel turned to look. She saw only the shadow of the overhang.

"Go on. Back there." He shone the flashlight into the darkness.

She took Holly's hand and moved around a crumbled mass of stone, and there was a ladder there, only the top of it showing because it descended down into a dark opening.

"Get down in there," the man said.

"What?" Laurel asked, looking from the ladder to the man then back again.

"I said get down there. Now."

She approached the stone. It was utterly dark, a black pit. She shivered again. "How far is it down there?" she asked.

"Far enough."

"You can't do this," she said with false bravado. "They'll be here soon."

"Watch me." The gun gestured.

Laurel stepped onto the ladder and backed down a couple of rungs. A cold, dank smell rose up around her. A pebble she dislodged fell, hit bottom, echoed.

"Quick now or I swear I'll knock this kid around," the man said.

Above her Holly started down, too. Looking up, Laurel saw Holly silhouetted against a moonlit sky, so bright compared to the Stygian darkness into which she was descending. She felt below her carefully with each foot. The bottom wasn't really too far, maybe fifteen or twenty feet, but it was cold and black and smelled of dust and ancient things. Laurel stepped off the ladder and helped Holly down.

"It's a kiva," Holly whispered, her voice small, shaking. "I'm so scared, Laurel."

"I know, honey, but Joe'll find us, don't worry." And she held the girl in her arms, stroking her hair, feeling the talons of guilt dig into her for what she'd got Holly into. Her daughter, her only child.

They both heard the noise at the same time and raised their heads. The ladder was being pulled up; their only link to the outside world was being withdrawn, sending a shower of stones down onto them, then disappearing from their view.

They were absolutely alone in the darkness of the kiva, the ancient chamber where the spirits visited and told of happenings in the other world.

CHAPTER SEVENTEEN

CHARLIE REDMOON WIPED a hand across his face, trying to shake off sleep. Inside the bungalow Clara was attending to Joe's dog, and if it hadn't been for the gash on the side of the mutt's head, Charlie, as he listened to Joe's fantastic tale, would have thought the man had gone plum loco.

"And this all began when?" Charlie asked Joe as they stood beneath the porch light.

"I told you," Joe said impatiently. "Right after I got suspended."

"And all this time you've been tracking these men on your own?"

Joe Buck grimaced in shame. "Yes. With some help from Laurel, but mostly on my own. Don't you think I know how foolish it was? If anything happens to Laurel and that kid..." he whispered. "It's ego, Charlie, my goddamn ego."

"Yes," the older man said. "We better hope this lesson isn't too costly."

While Charlie hurriedly dressed and Clara made an Indian blanket bed for Dog, Joe stood in the living room churning with rage and worry, going over and over in his mind the terrain he and Charlie were going to have to traverse. It had been a very long time since Joe had been anywhere near the site of the Night Cliff ruins, and he wished to God he could recall the contours of the land, the gullies and washes, the actual configuration of that cliff face.

After a call to alert the tribal police, they gathered up full canteens of water and a bag of deer jerky and drove Charlie's patrol car straight into Towaoc, where they picked up climbing equipment and a veritable arsenal, tossing it all in the trunk.

"So, when we get there," Charlie asked once they were in the patrol car, "what's the plan?"

Joe frowned. "I'm not sure yet. It'll depend on the cliff. Do you know the area?"

"No. I was there as a kid once."

"It's been years since I was there, too. I thought there was a rock slide, though, off that cliff. Maybe I can get up it. Maybe I won't even need all this equipment."

"He'll hear you," Charlie said.

"Not if you cover me, keep him busy."

Charlie only grunted.

"He'll be tired," Joe said as if to himself.

"So will you. What if you can't get up that cliff?"

"I'll just have to, won't I?" Joe said grimly, and he gunned the car, turning onto the highway, leaving a cloud of dust in the night air as they headed out into the vast expanse of the reservation.

A few miles out of Towaoc, Joe gave Charlie a side-long glance and tried to gauge the man. Once Charlie Redmoon had been a real sharpshooter, one of the best elk hunters with a rifle and scope in the Four Corners region. Hell, Charlie had knocked down more than a few old bulls at five hundred yards. But could he still do it?

He thought a lot about the Night Cliff ruins, too. Obviously Tolliver was familiar with them, knew that the old foot trail leading up the arroyo to the foot of the mesa was narrow but exposed. And Tolliver was counting on Joe using that trail—alone. Of course, when Joe got to the ruins, Tolliver would expect him to try to trade his life for the lives of the two women. Tolliver would agree, and at an opportune moment, he'd kill them all.

That had to be his plan.

But Joe had a different scenario in mind. The trouble was, a helluva lot of it depended on Redmoon.

They turned into the river valley and began winding along the old road, the patrol car bottoming out when Joe took the curves too quickly.

"Slow down," Charlie told him more than once. "Your friend will wait. He has no other choice."

They talked about that as the moon set behind the mesas, and the stars on the eastern horizon began to dim. Both Joe and Charlie figured this Tolliver character would not harm either of the women, not until he'd used them as live bait to lure Joe up into that cliff dwelling.

"It's a good plan," Charlie mused. "Your enemy knows you too well, Joe Buck."

"Yeah," Joe was forced to admit. "He knows I work alone and I take chances."

"He's counting on that," Charlie said, "which is good."

"Yeah, real great," Joe muttered as his gut twisted for the hundredth time since he'd read the note. "Never again," he told Charlie. "I'll never let my damn pride endanger someone else again. I swear it."

The land began to rise now, the darkened mesas stretching away into the distance. Soon the road would end and they'd be going it on foot. The path Tolliver would have taken earlier was perhaps two miles in length, but the route Joe and Charlie planned to follow was a great deal longer. By the time they reached the foot of the mesa from the northern approach, the sun would be high overhead and the broken land as dry as bleached bones. It was going to be rough. And their plan hinged on Charlie making that brutal trek. Damn, Joe thought, but caught himself. Charlie wasn't going to let him down. He needed the man. They needed each other. And that, Joe realized, was one heck of an alien notion for him.

"It'll be light soon," Charlie said from the darkness beside Joe.

"Yes," Joe said. "And by the time we reach the dwellings of the Ancient Ones you'll be able to see this Tolliver clearly in the scope. At least we have that going for us."

"It's been a while since I've hunted the big game," Charlie said, thinking aloud. "But I'll ask for a steady hand." And Joe knew he meant to ask the old spirits for guidance. He liked that notion—he trusted Charlie's covenant with the spirit world.

They left the car where the road ended, left it parked right alongside Tolliver's pickup truck. Joe sneered at the man's gall, thinking he was going to kill three people and then simply drive away. No doubt he didn't even care if it looked like an accident. The secret of the buried drums would still be safe, and who would ever link the engineer from Lakewood—hundreds of miles away—to three deaths in the desert?

Fingers of gray dawn began to reach across the twisted land as Joe and Charlie set out, making their own trail to the north. If Joe correctly recalled the terrain they were soon to traverse, it was going to be a very long, hot morning.

With Joe bearing the bulk of the weight—water canteens, two handguns, a nylon climbing rope and grappling hook—all in a backpack, and Charlie carrying the rifle and scope over his shoulder, they navigated the awakening desert, approaching the mesa from the north. The going was even rougher than either Joe or Charlie had anticipated. Frequently they had to climb down into the deep, dry washes and then scramble up the far sides. Giant boulders often blocked the most direct route, and never was the footing even.

Charlie stopped at the top of a wash and caught his breath. "I am ashamed," he panted. "I am ashamed in front of the Ancient Ones, who are surely looking down on me now in disgust."

"How's that?" Joe asked, scanning the terrain, choosing their route.

"I'm in terrible shape," the old man admitted. "I live in that patrol car."

"I'm sure the Ancient Ones understand," Joe said. "What they probably don't understand is the poison buried on our land."

"The sickness," Charlie muttered. "Now we know."

"Yeah," Joe said, "we sure do."

Overhead a pair of golden eagles circled lazily in the gathering light, their occasional whistles echoing across the land. Here and there a rabbit darted, and prairie dogs poked their heads up out of the hard earth. Joe saw a small herd of deer feeding in the sage ahead of them, pricking up their ears, ever vigilant. The two men inched across the desert floor, mere specks on this cauterized terrain, and the dry, cruel land teemed with life as the first rays of sun touched the crown of the mesa before them and spilled like blood onto the ancient rock.

JACK SQUINTED IN the harsh morning light and looked at his watch. 10:00 a.m. That goddamned Indian had had hours to get here—hours. So where in the hell was he?

He stood and peered over the rim of a crumbling wall. He could see for miles, practically all the way down the foot trail to where they'd parked the truck. The Indian had to be somewhere on that damn trail! If only he'd thought to bring along his binoculars!

Jack remembered the last time he'd been to the ruins. He'd had binoculars with him then, and tents and sleeping bags and three days' worth of food and water. It had been almost fifteen years ago, and the whole family had been there. God, what a good time that had been, the kids still small and bursting with innocent excitement, his wife trim and all sunburned with that white zinc stuff on her nose and the silly old army hat she'd always worn camping.

Jack sat back down and sighed, remembering. Those had been real good times, before money had got so tight, before his wife's operation, the bankruptcy, college tuition and never-ending home mortgages. But things were easing up. The handsome bonuses Tyler Grant always bestowed on Jack after a successful unloading in the desert were sure helping. There was bound to have been a snag, too. Jack had always known that, and he guessed it could be worse—the Indian really could have called the feds, and they would have been crawling all over the place by now. He'd never believed that woman, anyway. So now there were still only three people who knew, well, two and the kid.

It was too bad about the girl. But Jack couldn't dwell on that. The whole operation, his own family, was far too important to let go down the drain over one person. No. He wouldn't let that bother him.

His stomach growled and he wet his lips, which were beginning to crack as the sun arced higher in the sky. He should have thought about food—at least water—but the plan had only come to him last night while he was sitting outside the woman's house. And besides, it wouldn't be too much longer before Jack was back at the truck, this frustrating business over and done with, and wasn't there an unopened can of soda under the front seat?

He rose again and pulled a handkerchief out of his back pocket and wiped the oily sweat from his neck while gazing out across the land. What a helluva vantage point, he thought. The cliff commanded a view of the entire valley. No one was going to come up that trail without Jack spotting him. Yeah, he mused, the damn Indians had at least got one thing right, the place was virtually impregnable.

IT WAS COLD IN THE KIVA, bone-chilling cold, and Laurel hugged Holly close to her as the child slept on fitfully.

Sun spilled in from the narrow opening in the top of the kiva and formed a dusty column of light that afforded no warmth. She wondered what time it was, and how long it would take Joe to get there. If he was coming; if he'd gotten the note.

She felt like crying. Not for herself, not even for crazy, wonderful Joe, who surely was going to put himself in terrible danger to rescue them. No. The tears that kept forming in her eyes were for Holly, who could have, *should* have been safely at home with the Schultzes if it weren't for her own selfishness.

She carefully ran a finger along the girl's dirt-smudged cheek, and finally she did weep. What right did she have to barge into people's lives and turn them upside down? If she had never come to Cortez, Holly would be safe, doing the things that teenagers did, good or bad—but safe.

With her free hand, Laurel wiped her tears away. Crying wasn't going to get her anywhere. What she had to do was think. There had to be a way out of this. *Dear God,* she thought, *there has to be a way to save Holly's life.*

THE RATTLESNAKE was curled on a flat rock right in their path, warming himself. He raised his blunt head, and Joe heard the warning rattle. He held up a hand and sensed Charlie's plodding footsteps halt behind him.

Above them the sun was a burning orb that sapped the desert dry and sucked the fluid from a man's flesh. All the animals had gone to ground for the day, all but the birds of prey, soaring high on thermal currents, and the snake, who drew his strength from the heat of the sun.

They went around the rattler, respecting his dominance. This was his home, not theirs. On they trudged, drinking water sparingly and resting for short periods—much more often than Joe would have liked. Worry sat on his shoulder like a Skinwalker, an evil presence, but he bore the necessity stoically, with an impassive expression that cloaked his anxiety.

He knew that Tolliver wasn't going to wait forever up there on that baking cliff. Sooner or later—and probably sooner—the man was going to get frustrated. At the very least, he'd realize Joe was up to something. And that was going to make Jack Tolliver all the more dangerous.

"I'm sorry," Charlie was saying, "I need only a minute more to rest."

"You want more water, some jerky?"

But Charlie waved a hand. "No, I'm fine, really. It's just the heat."

And it *was* hot. Even Joe felt the scorching sun begin to sap his strength, and he wondered if Charlie was really going to make it.

"How much farther do you think we have to go?" Charlie asked as he got to his feet.

"Two, two and a half miles, maybe. Not far. You sure you can...?"

"I'll make it. If I have to crawl," Charlie vowed, "I'll make it. And I can still shoot, Joe. These eyes may be old, but the spirit of the eagle has always guided my aim."

"I know that," Joe said, walking beside him. Just hold on, my friend, he thought, call on the spirits, use all your power, but hold on.

CHAPTER EIGHTEEN

BY NOON JACK TOLLIVER was certain Joe Buck wasn't coming. Either he never went back to the house to find the note or he'd decided the woman wasn't worth it. Then Jack caught himself; of course Buck was coming. He was just being careful. Maybe he was out there right now, hiding behind a hillock or a rock or a clump of sage, watching the cliff face. Maybe he was out there sweating in the effing sun, broiling, dry as dust.

Jack licked his cracked lips. He'd sure like some water. Forgetting it had been dumb, but it'd be over soon. He could hold out.

The Indian would have water, he supposed, but he'd be alone. Yeah, he was a maverick, he'd heard around the res. Liked to get all the credit by his lonesome. And that was what Jack was banking on. But it was hard to think straight. Jack was tired, real tired, and so thirsty. Too parched to even be hungry. Strange notions popped into his mind, weird, disconnected images. His wife, Tyler Grant, those damn drums buried miles away across this godawful hot desert. Cool water trickling, running over mossy stones, sparkling. He could smell the wetness, he really could.

He lifted his baseball cap off and wiped his forehead with the back of his wrist. Staring out across the land, he blinked, trying to focus. Everything danced and shimmered in the sun-drenched, washed-out light.

God, he realized in a moment of lucidity, the Indian was planning it this way! Waiting patiently, waiting until Jack's brain was fried by the sun and he was exhausted, and then he'd somehow surprise him.

No, no, impossible. Jack's plan was foolproof. No one could approach the cliff in daylight without Jack seeing him. He felt the heft of his gun lying across his knees as he sat on a collapsed wall and smiled. He was okay, sure he was.

It wasn't a minute later that the woman began calling from down in the kiva again. Caterwauling like a banshee, demanding food and water. She'd been driving him crazy for hours.

"Shut up!" he hollered down into the dark. At least they were cool down there, he thought, sweat trickling down his neck, the heat encasing him like a too-tight wet suit. God, he was tired.

Laurel was thinking the same thing. She and Holly had dozed off for a little while, but the man must have stayed awake, watching and waiting. He must be exhausted.

"He didn't bring any water," Laurel told Holly. "He's got to be dying of thirst up there in the sun."

"What if he leaves us here?" Holly asked. "What if no one ever finds us?"

"Joe will come. He's probably out there right now, waiting until it's dark maybe. He'll have a plan, though. He's smart, Holly. And he'll have water and food and equipment. He's a professional. Now, don't worry."

"I'm so thirsty," Holly said, "and my parents..."

"They won't even start worrying yet. They think you're with me, at my house. We'll be out of here and back before they even hear about it," she said with forced cheer.

"They'll kill me."

"No, they won't. This isn't your fault. If anything, it's mine. Now, stop worrying. It'll be fine," Laurel said, though the truth was that Joe was probably going it alone, as usual, blaming himself for this predicament, unwilling, too proud, to get help. *Oh, Joe,* she prayed, just ask for help this once!

Her mind had been spinning for hours, trying to figure out how to get out of the kiva. If she could get out, she knew she could do something to make sure Holly was safe. And, too, she kept trying to rattle the man, not wanting to push him into violent behavior, but trying to irritate him, distract his attention.

She stood in the pillar of sunlight under the entrance hole of the kiva and started again. "Mr. Tolliver! Please let us up. We need food and water! Come on, let us up!"

"Goddamn it, shut up!" he yelled back, in what had become his usual litany.

She hated him. She wanted to scream, to sob out her fear, but she couldn't, not in front of Holly. She had to keep control, to think. "Please, we can't stay here anymore. Can we come up? We can't stand it any longer. Mr. Tolliver? Let us up!"

No reply.

"Okay, let us up one at a time. You know one of us won't do anything when the other's still down in the hole. Please! Just for a little while. I promise we won't try to get away or anything. Just for a few minutes. It's horrible down here. Come on, Mr. Tolliver."

Nothing.

She kept it up, though, her voice growing hoarse as she got drier and drier. She stopped for a time, trying to gather some saliva into the cotton-dryness of her mouth.

"He'll shoot us," Holly said, tear tracks dried in funnels of dirt down her cheeks.

"No, he won't, not yet. He needs us. Joe won't get near if he doesn't see us alive, and the man knows it. We're his ace in the hole."

"I want to go home," Holly whispered brokenly, and Laurel's heart clenched in anguish and guilt.

She started up again, calling to the man, begging, promising, bargaining. Even using his first name now, over and over until she couldn't stand the sound of her own voice. Her throat hurt, her tongue felt fuzzy and swollen. She stopped and took a breath, and it was then that Tolliver's face appeared over the edge of the hole above her.

She gaped in surprise and stepped back into the shadows. "Please," she rasped.

"Okay, okay," he said. "Just shut up! One at a time. No funny business, though."

Laurel's heart leapt. "I promise, I swear. Please, put the ladder down."

"You'll shut up then? No more of your yelling?"

"I promise. Please, let me up."

His face disappeared, then she saw the ladder sliding down toward her, and she closed her eyes and thanked God. "I'm going first," she whispered to Holly.

"No, don't leave me here alone!" Holly cried.

"Only a few minutes, Holly." She didn't dare say a word about trying to do something when she was up there. Besides, she hadn't any idea of what to do. Only that she had to somehow get Holly out of there, whatever it took.

The ladder thumped down, raising a cloud of dust. The man's face appeared again and his hand, holding the gun on her. "Slow, now," he said.

Laurel climbed up, rung by rung, slowly, carefully. The man pulled the ladder up with one hand as she stepped out onto the floor of the cliff dwelling, but he still held the gun on her with the other hand. She squinted in the brightness and felt the force of the sun hit her.

The man looked awful. His eyes were sunken, his lips cracked. His sleeve was black with dried blood where Dog had bitten him.

"Water," Laurel said. "We're so thirsty."

"Don't have any. Guess you'll have to wait for your boyfriend to show up." And he grinned a death's-head grin.

"He's out there, you know," she said. "He'll get you. You can't last forever. He only has to be patient."

"You've got two minutes," the man said tonelessly.

She moved out toward the edge of the cliff, away from him. Maybe, maybe if Joe were out there, he was only waiting to see somebody. Maybe he had a rifle and was waiting for the man to show himself. Maybe he had an army of snipers out there, their fingers twitching on their triggers, just biding their time.

No, she thought for the hundredth time, Joe would do it alone. He'd never ask for help, not Joe Buck. In the end, she knew, it was largely up to her.

Tolliver was standing back under the overhang, behind a fallen wall where no sharpshooter could see him. She had to get him out into the open where he'd be a target. She stood on the very edge of the cliff, staring out over the cracked brown scenery, a hand shading her eyes. *Joe,* she thought, *I'll do what I can, but you've got to help me.*

"One minute," the man said.

She had to act fast. What should she do? If she were a man, she'd try to wrestle him down and get his gun or try to trick him into getting too close to the edge. She had to try something, and quickly, but what? In a minute she'd be back down in that dark hole, and he'd never let her up again. This was her only chance.

She flung herself down close to the cliff edge, sprawling, crying out, "Oh! My ankle! Oh!" She moaned, lying there, holding her ankle, making awful noises.

"Time's up," the man said.

"I can't move! I think it's broken. Oh, oh! It hurts. Oh, my ankle," Laurel cried. How long could she keep this up?

"Goddamn stupid bitch," Tolliver said, moving toward her. He crouched, though, staying low, snatched her back toward the kiva. She struggled, still moaning and crying, trying to delay him or throw him off balance, anything. But he was strong, too strong.

She felt the sharp stones and gravel rake her skin as she was hauled across the ground, breathing in choking dust. "Stop!" she cried, "please, let me go!" Then she gathered her strength, doubled up her legs and flung her whole body weight against him so that he was pulled forward, upright. He yanked at her and swore, and then something whined by her ear and hit the wall behind her, sending a shower of rock splinters flying. She couldn't figure out what it was, her mind slow and stupid, and then, a terribly long time afterward, there was a flat cracking sound that echoed and echoed across the desert.

"What?" the man said, frozen in his crouch now.

And then Laurel knew what it had been—a bullet! Joe was out there, and he'd shot at the man! She edged away from him now, crawling across the rough ground. If she could lure him out into the open again, this time Joe would get him!

The man whirled then, crying out at something Laurel couldn't see. He fired his gun, the sound reverberating against the cliff, and then Laurel saw a body lunging toward the man. Joe! Oh, my God! The man was aiming his gun again, and without thinking, Laurel threw herself across the space at Tolliver, shouting, grabbing at him, her fingers merely brushing his arm as he pulled the trigger. She landed hard, winded, her heart pounding so wildly she wasn't sure if it was the gunshot or the adrenaline exploding in her veins. But there were two men on the edge of the cliff now, struggling. They were locked in a fight over the gun, grunting with effort, swaying, faces set.

Laurel threw herself at the man, snatching at his leg. He kicked at her, but she never felt it. She got some cloth and hung on, yanking. Then Tolliver was off balance, teetering. Time stopped for one horrible, gut-wrenching moment as the man flailed wildly, and then he was falling, screaming, grabbing at the ladder, which held him for an instant, then his momentum broke his hold, and he dropped to the earth far below.

IT WAS A VERY LONG afternoon. Laurel, Holly and Charlie waited at the base of the cliff while Joe trekked out to where they'd left Charlie's patrol car to radio in for a helicopter from Cortez. Not far from where the three rested in the shade, Tolliver's body lay inert, covered by Joe's police windbreaker, flies buzzing around it in the hot sun. No one looked in its direction.

"It was your shot that distracted him," Laurel said to Charlie.

Charlie shook his head. "It was a lousy shot. I missed."

"But it got his attention away from Joe long enough for him to get onto the ledge."

"No, no, it was you pulling that stunt."

"Falling, you mean? I really don't think so. He was dragging me back to the kiva."

"I could see you in my sight rolling around. I couldn't figure out what you were doing," Charlie said, "because I couldn't hear you."

"You were so far away," Laurel breathed. "I can't imagine..."

Charlie grunted. "I missed my target. You gave me the chance and I missed."

"Well, it was a good miss."

He only shook his head.

Laurel sat with her back against a rock, Holly sleeping with her head on Laurel's lap. Her legs were going numb, but she wouldn't have moved for love nor money. She stroked Holly's hair off her sweaty forehead and loved the feel of her daughter's smooth young skin.

"So Joe asked you to help," Laurel said. "I can't believe it. I figured he'd go it alone."

"I guess he was smart enough this time," Charlie said. "He knew he needed help, but I'm not sure he picked the right person."

"Of course he did. It's all over, isn't it? The good guys won."

"It was too close. I don't like that. I'm getting old. The spirits have left me."

The hours ticked by slowly. They knew Joe had to walk all the way back to the car, and then the helicopter had to be readied. He'd left all his food and water with them and told them it might be three or four hours. There was water in Charlie's patrol car, so Joe would be fine.

"You won't get lost," Laurel had said, looking into Joe's eyes, "and leave us here?"

He'd smiled at her. "Remember? Indians don't get lost. Besides, Clara knows where you are."

"Okay," she said, "you be careful, though." And she'd watched him walk away, back down the shallow, rocky gully, his back straight, his long legs eating up the distance effortlessly. She sighed and then turned back to Holly.

That had been at least three hours ago. She and Charlie kept watching the sky and listening for the unmistakable beat of a helicopter's rotors, but there was only hot, empty, blue silence.

Laurel shifted her position carefully, trying not to wake Holly, but the teenager opened her eyes and lifted her head.

"It isn't here yet?" she asked.

"No, but it will be soon."

Holly sat up and hugged her knees, staring out across the parched landscape. "It's hot," she said.

"Want some water?" Laurel asked.

"A little, maybe." She took the canteen from Laurel and swallowed some, then made a face. "It's warm."

"Charlie, want some?" Laurel asked, holding out the canteen, but he only waved it away.

"Come on, Charlie, you've been enough of a hero today. Have some water," Laurel urged. She knew he and Joe had been going for more than twelve hours. Dehydration was a real danger.

"Later" was all Charlie said.

Holly got up and wandered around, kicking at stones. She was restless with the impatience of youth, and she was apprehensive about facing her folks, Laurel knew. Poor kid.

"This has taught me something," Charlie was saying. "I can see now why I was chosen for this operation. The spirits guided Joe, even if he doesn't believe in them."

"Why?" Laurel asked.

"It taught me that it's time to retire. Clara was right. I'm getting too damn old. A good leader knows when it's time to make room for the young warriors."

"Things have a way of working out, don't they?"

"The Creator sees to it," Charlie said.

"What will you do when you retire?"

"I've had a couple offers from the casino to handle their security. But I think I'll do what Clara's been after me to do for a long time." He nodded to himself. "Yes, this was a sign. I will write those stories down."

"What stories?"

"The Ute myths, the ones I learned from my father and he from his, all the way back. The ones my sons didn't care to learn."

Laurel leaned forward. "That's a wonderful idea! There's so much interest in native American history these days."

"It's not for anyone but my tribe," Charlie said. "It's our heritage."

"One man's heritage is another man's art," Laurel said. "Get your stories published and they'll be immortal."

"Maybe," Charlie said.

"What will Clara think about getting them published?"

"I don't know, but I'm sure she'll make a good decision."

"And you'll listen to her?"

"I always do what Clara says," Charlie said, deadpan.

It was nearly five by the time the thud of rotors filled the air. Holly jumped up and yelled, waving her arms. But the chopper already knew where they were from Joe's directions.

It landed fifty yards away amid a maelstrom of grit and dust, and the medic on board jumped down and ran to them.

"You can all make it to the helicopter?" he asked. "We thought someone might be hurt."

"Only him," Charlie said, pointing. "One deceased white male. Jack Tolliver. Cause of death, a fall."

The medic craned his neck to look at the cliff. "From up there?"

"That's right. I'll be filing a report," Charlie said.

The three of them went toward the helicopter, ducking under the rotors, climbing in.

"You folks okay, then?" the pilot asked, having to yell over the noise.

"We are now," Laurel said.

"Joe Buck got out okay?" Charlie asked.

"He radioed from a patrol car, and he said he'd drive out. He'll meet you in Cortez, oh, in about an hour or so. 'Course, it'll only take us twenty minutes." The pilot grinned, proud of his machine.

Indeed, they were landing on the helipad in Cortez in twenty minutes. It seemed too fast, Laurel thought. Her mind had no time to switch from survival mode back to everyday life. The helicopter lowered, vibrating, until it was centered, then it dropped gently onto the ground. There were some people waiting there, a medical team with a gurney, a couple of Cortez policemen, a few others. Laurel searched the crowd, hoping to see Joe, even though she knew he couldn't possibly have gotten there yet. She needed to talk to him now, to go home and relax and just talk it all out.

Then she noticed that Holly was still sitting in her seat, not looking out the window, biting her lips. Unshed tears shone in her eyes.

Laurel patted her hand. "It'll be fine, Holly. They'll be so glad to see you."

"They'll kill me," she whispered.

"No, they won't. I'll tell them what happened," Laurel repeated. "I promise."

"Oh, Laurel," Holly said brokenly, "you've been so brave and everything, and you saved me and I did everything wrong! If I hadn't run away, if I hadn't gone to your house..." And she clung to Laurel.

"Shh, stop. Try to smile. You'll only upset everybody," Laurel said, stroking Holly's hair. "Come on, now. We'll face them together, okay? You and me together."

Holly looked up and tried to smile. "Okay, but you stay by me. You will, won't you?"

"I promise."

The medic slid back the door of the helicopter, and Charlie Redmoon got out and went straight to the policemen. Laurel held her daughter's hand tightly, and they climbed out together. She only had time to say, "You okay now?" when Holly gave a cry and started sobbing, pulling her hand from Laurel's and rushing to an older couple, a couple Laurel knew without asking must be the Schultzes. The girl threw herself into their arms, and they held her, enfolded her, hugged her fiercely.

"Miss Velarde?" someone was saying, but Laurel didn't hear. She stood there in the late-afternoon sun, the tarmac hot under her feet, her hand still tingling with the phantom touch of Holly's fingers, and suddenly, despite all her best intentions, a tear rolled down her dirty cheek.

CHAPTER NINETEEN

IT WAS GOING TO BE an early winter. Everyone in the Mile High City of Denver said so when they awakened on that August morning to see the dusting of snow on the sentinel peaks to the west.

But in the high plains city it was sunny, an idyllic, crisp summer day that saw the sports-minded population take to the jogging and biking trails early, filling the tennis courts and golf courses. Heck, tomorrow it might start to sizzle again, better to take advantage of the perfect weather today.

Tyler Grant IV was no exception. Despite a dozen federal agencies trying to link Blackwell to Mountain Construction, trying to tie Tyler into it all, he awakened in a good mood, had sex with his young wife and called the Cherry Hills Country Club for an early tee-time on the exclusive golf course.

At eight-thirty his three golfing partners awaited him at the first tee, already making their bets. "Hey, Tyler," one of the partners called, "I want three strokes from you today."

Tyler parked his golf cart next to the tee box and pulled his graphite driver out of his two-thousand-dollar leather bag. "I'll give you two shots," he called back amiably. "I should give you only one, but I'm feeling generous this morning."

Indeed he was. True, there was the threat of a lengthy and messy investigation hanging over his head, but Glen Cohen—his golf partner and lawyer—had told him in the locker room not ten minutes ago that it was all a formality. The dead Jack Tolliver was going to take the rap, and the government would never get close to a federal grand jury indictment, not with Blackwell or Tyler. "They've got zilch, buddy. Without Tolliver alive to answer questions, they've got nothing."

"What about Mountain Construction?" Tyler had asked. "Can it be traced to Blackwell?"

Cohen laughed. "Not in a million years."

And Tyler believed him. There'd be a lot of speculation and a big flap over Blackwell's role in the whole affair, but essentially it was Tolliver who'd contracted to dispose of the waste, and Jack Tolliver who'd take the fall, albeit posthumously. "By the time the government gets done passing out blame," Glen had said, "you'll look like a saint."

Tyler teed up his ball, took two practice swings and then drove it onto the emerald green fairway.

"God," one of his opponents mumbled, "what was that? A career shot?"

The sun glinted off Tyler's thick, silver hair, and he let a grin slide across his lips. "Sure is," he said.

It was a little past twelve noon. Three men stood near the green on the eighteenth fairway at Cherry Hills, looking terribly official and out of place. One man was clearly a government type dressed in a dark, summer-weight suit and wearing sunglasses. He *was* government, the FBI bureau chief in Denver.

The other two men were attired officially also, in blue police shirts, pants and western boots. Both were native Americans.

"That looks like Grant's party coming up the fairway now," the FBI man said.

The older Indian nodded; the tall, younger one with the long ponytail and sunglasses merely set his jaw.

"I think our man's going to be pretty surprised," the bureau chief went on, patting his pocket where the arrest warrant rested. "I'll bet not even that fancy lawyer of his knows we made the Blackwell-Mountain Construction connection."

The younger Indian shifted his gaze to the government man. "That was a nice piece of police work," he was forced to admit. "I've gotta really hand it to the FBI on that one."

"Well, thanks," the bureau chief said. "We do try."

It was Tyler's turn to make his approach shot to the eighteenth green. He took a seven iron out of his bag and lined up the shot. With the ease and grace of a pro, he stroked the ball, sending it into a smooth arc in the sun. When it landed, it bounced just off the green, taking a fortuitous roll to within six feet of the hole.

"Um," the older Indian said, "he'll like that one."

The younger Indian snorted.

Tyler did like his shot. In fact, he was so absorbed in his near-perfect game he failed to see the three men standing between the clubhouse and the green. He parked his cart, got out with his partner and awaited his turn to putt, already mentally counting his winnings. When it was his turn, he lined his shot up from all angles, and with the confidence for which he was noted, Tyler made his stroke, sinking the ball.

"Nice putt," his lawyer said.

"Thanks," Tyler replied graciously, while the other two men could only shake their heads, and that was when he spotted the official types standing nearby. He looked over to his partner quickly, and the lawyer gave him a reassuring smile. But it wasn't two minutes later that the smile was wiped from Cohen's lips and the color drained from Tyler's face.

"You have the right to remain silent," the FBI chief was saying, "you have the right to have an attorney present..." and he began to fasten handcuffs onto Tyler Grant's wrists.

"This is an outrage," Cohen said, rapidly scanning the arrest warrant. "You have absolutely overstepped the boundaries of..." And then he saw it on the paper, the link, the paragraph stating that Tyler Grant IV and Mountain Construction were one and the same.

"What the hell is it?" Tyler barked as he watched his lawyer's expression.

"Impossible," Cohen was saying.

"What...?" Tyler said again, automatically struggling to free his wrists.

But it was the younger Indian who spoke. "You see," Joe Buck said, stepping forward, "your pal Tolliver wasn't so dumb after all. He left a little something with his wife, a little insurance, a paper, in fact, telling us just how to make the connection."

"You're lying!" Tyler growled.

"Remember the bank account on Grand Cayman Island?" Joe said coolly. "Well, it seems Tolliver set it up in two names. Yours and Mountain Construction's. Too bad, huh?"

It was then Tyler felt his knees buckle. "Oh, shit," he said.

LAUREL POURED A SECOND cup of coffee and opened the newspaper to page two, where she finished reading the lead article. There was a full column on the cleanup operation and a quarter-page color picture of the dumping site. So far, the Environmental Protection Agency had unearthed 230 fifty-five gallon drums of nuclear waste on the reservation. They had no idea how many more drums there were or how many had leaked.

She scanned the rest of the column, which described the isolated site. She already knew all about that. What interested her was the part about Joe and Charlie and yesterday's arrest of Tyler Grant IV.

"...Accompanying the FBI were two representatives from the Bureau of Indian Affairs, Chief Charles Redmoon and Sergeant Joseph Buck, both police officers stationed in Towaoc on the Ute Reservation near Cortez...."

She knew all that, too. She scanned some more. "...Redmoon would not comment at this time on the length of his investigation or for how long the BIA has been aware of the existence of the illegal dumping site...."

I'll bet, Laurel thought, smiling to herself. At least Charlie was sticking up for his maverick cop.

She read on. "...A grand jury will be convened to decide on the charges that have been brought against Tyler Grant IV, whose name appears in conjunction with Mountain Construction Company, traced through a bank account in Grand Cayman Island. Sergeant Joseph Buck was evidently the first to make this link through a pickup truck driven by the late John [Jack] Tolliver of Lakewood, an employee of Blackwell...."

"Yeah, yeah." Laurel sighed. But the rest of the article interested her. After all, when she did her feature article—already *Time* and several other newsmagazines were interested in it—she'd need a lot of background.

"...Blackwell International is not the only aerospace giant to be contracting with producers of nuclear and other toxic waste materials. However, there are virtually no viable plans for waste disposal on the drawing boards, and it is estimated that Rocky Plains Munitions alone has stockpiled in warehouses over forty years' worth of waste.

"...Senator Wirtz of Colorado stated at a press conference Wednesday evening that 'the problem of waste disposal will follow this nation well into the twenty-first century.' When asked if Blackwell will receive a hand slap, the senator said, 'We intend to prosecute to the fullest extent of the law. If these charges are proved to be valid, what Blackwell's perpetrated is unconscionable.'"

Sure is, Laurel thought as she rose and poured some bagged food into Dog's bowl, which he wouldn't touch. "That's it, you mutt," she said, "no more people food, not while I'm baby-sitting."

She'd had Dog for two weeks now. First there'd been the whole long mess in Denver with the FBI, the EPA, the DOE, and Joe and Charlie stuck there. And then it had been back to the reservation for the beginning of the cleanup. Then up to Denver again when the FBI had discovered the so-called—and now infamous—"insurance papers" Tolliver had left with his wife, the papers that had nailed Tyler Grant to the wall.

But Joe was due back tonight.

She stood looking at the living room floor that was littered with cardboard boxes—packing boxes. And she felt suddenly drained. Ten weeks ago, when Laurel had first arrived in Cortez, she'd been full of energy and goals and ready to take the bull by the horns. But now...

It seemed unfair. There was Joe, bopping back and forth to Denver, his whole life on track now, positive he'd learned his lesson. He was ready, willing and able to take over Charlie's job; in fact, so ready, that was about all they'd discussed during his phone calls. Oh, Joe had plans all right, plans to improve the police force, to modernize equipment, take on more trainees, everything. He had plans, too, to fund a new tourist information center that would coordinate such things as weather reports and fire danger in the backcountry with the police force. Joe had telephoned just last night and told her all about it—not about arresting Grant or anything mundane like that, but about the information center.

Well, she thought, at least Joe knew where he was headed. She sure wished she could say the same about herself.

She glanced at her watch. Joe's flight was due into Durango at six-forty that evening. She had the rest of the day to finish packing up the house, work on her article and then drive to pick him up, but there was something else she needed to do, something that was going to rip her heart out, but it had to be done. Someday, she thought, in a few years, she'd return to Cortez, and Holly, an adult, would sit down with her and she'd tell all. They'd have those years then, years in which they'd truly get to know each other. But not yet. Now it was still Fran and Earl's time. Nevertheless, Laurel was not going to leave in the morning without saying goodbye. No matter how much it hurt, she needed to see Holly one last time.

With Dog getting hair all over the back seat of her Honda, Laurel drove out at noon to the Schultzes' ranch. She'd driven by before. When she'd first gotten to Cortez, Laurel had driven out this way at least three times in hopes of catching a glimpse of her daughter. She hadn't. But then—an eternity ago—she hadn't known Holly. Now she did, and it was even harder.

Now she wondered. Just seeing the green fields, the cattle and grazing horses, the sturdy white farmhouse, brought tears to her eyes. It was Holly's home and she couldn't share any of it.

Apron tied around her waist, Fran met Laurel at the door and graciously invited her in. It was lunchtime, and obviously they'd all been having a sandwich. "I'm sorry," Laurel said right away, "I didn't realize..."

But Fran soon had her sitting with Earl and Holly, a sandwich in front of her. "I just had to stop by before I left," Laurel told them. "I couldn't go without telling you again how bad I feel about that whole mess with that creep, Tolliver."

And then they went into it all over again, how it wasn't Laurel's fault. But there was something new going on now, something quite fantastic. It was Earl who said, "We got our little girl back. The incident made us all realize how short life really is."

"How precious it is," Fran added. "It's terrible that something awful has to happen to wake everyone up, but almost losing Holly..."

Holly was shaking her head and turning the color of a beet, but it was as plain as the nose on her face to Laurel that this was a family again. She couldn't stop tears from showing in her eyes. "Well," she said, "anytime I can help," and they all laughed.

They talked for a time about the on-going investigation and Joe's role in it, and Holly even teased Laurel. "You know, like, Sergeant Buck and Laurel are real close. I'll bet Laurel gets to write his whole story."

"I hadn't thought of that," Fran said with interest. "You'll have quite a story to write now."

"I was working on it this morning," Laurel admitted.

"Do you have any offers?" Earl asked.

And Laurel told them about *Time* magazine's offer and they all said "wow" at the same time.

When lunch was over and they stood on the porch, it was Fran who ventured, "So, you're going back to Berkeley now?"

"Yes," Laurel said.

"I thought you might have decided to stay here."

Laurel looked at her for a second. "Oh," she said, "you mean because of...Joe. Well, I..."

"No," Fran interrupted, "I didn't exactly mean that." And she gave Laurel a curious glance before they all walked to her car. Earl said goodbye, he was off to the barn, and then Holly was there, patting Dog through the car window. It was at that moment, when Holly was preoccupied, that Fran caught Laurel's eye and whispered, "Thank you," and Laurel knew. She bit her lip. She'd thought endlessly about telling the Schultzes who she really was but had decided against it—it was just too selfish of her at this stage of Holly's life. But now, Laurel guessed, the cat was out of the bag, anyway. Fran took her hand then again said in a whisper, "Thank you, Laurel, she's a gift. If you do decide to stay here, Earl and I would be very happy."

Laurel had to swallow hard. She squeezed Fran's hand and fought for control. "Someday," she finally said, "someday when she's all grown."

"Yes," Fran said, but Holly interrupted them.

"Why do you have to go?" she was asking. "I thought you liked it here. I mean, you and Sergeant Buck and all."

"Sergeant...Joe, that is, has a life of his own, Holly, and so do I. Sometimes... Well, sometimes people are like ships passing in the night. You know."

But she didn't. And when Fran gave Laurel a hug and disappeared, Holly lingered by the car. "You could stay, if you wanted, you could," she said.

"Oh, Holly, I wish it were that easy." They finally hugged, and when Laurel had to let her go, it was the hardest thing she'd ever done.

"You could come back next summer," Holly said when Laurel was in the car, fighting for control. "You could do more articles on the mountains and stuff."

"Maybe," Laurel allowed, and she gave her child one last painful look before putting the car in gear. "I'll try," she said, then she reached out to give Holly's hand a last squeeze. She drove away shortly, her heart sinking.

At three o'clock, while Laurel was sitting lethargically on her couch, staring at the half-packed boxes, her phone rang. She picked it up, speaking woodenly.

"Hey" came Joe's voice, "you sound...awful."

"Thanks," she said, unable to bear the deep, familiar timbre of his voice. My God, she thought, how much was a person supposed to take?

"I mean it," he was saying. "Did something...?"

"I saw Holly," Laurel got out. "I saw Fran and Earl, too, and they know, Joe, they know who I am."

"I'm not real surprised," he said carefully. "I mean, there's a helluva resemblance, Laurel. And they got the baby in California."

"Yes," she said, "of course."

"Does Holly know?"

"No. She doesn't even suspect."

"Um," he said. "It's too bad you're leaving. I mean, you could see her. You know."

"Yes, I know," Laurel said. Then she asked, "Where are you?"

"Denver. My flight's not for a couple of hours. I just wanted to touch base."

"Everything's fine here," she said dully. "And don't worry, I'll be at the airport. I'll even bring Dog."

"Ah, good," he said, "I appreciate all you've done."

"No problem," she said. "I saw today's paper, about the arrest and all."

"It was a real pleasure."

"I bet. And on the golf course. He must have been humiliated."

"He didn't have time for it," Joe said. "He was too shocked."

"Um," she said.

"Well . . ."

"Well, I'll see you in a few hours."

There was a pause on Joe's end. "Laurel," he began, but nothing came of it and soon they both hung up.

She drove to Durango as the sun was turning the mountains to gold. She drove and she thought. If only Joe had given her a sign, anything, but he hadn't. And they'd both been honest, too, admitting that neither of them wanted a relationship. Joe had his life. She had . . . Holly. But now that had changed. At least she had changed. Her beliefs, her values, everything. And she wanted to tell him that. She desperately wanted to tell Joe Buck that she'd been so wrong. You *could* trust people. The Schultzes, Joe himself. She didn't want to be alone any longer. What if she'd died up in that cliff house and never had anyone? What did a magazine article matter when there was no one to share any of it with? Her life-style had lost its appeal, and now there was a new empty place in her heart that couldn't be filled with travel and adventure.

Oh, God, Laurel thought, she'd been so wrong about everything.

His plane arrived on time and he stepped out into that gilded light and crossed the tarmac looking so handsome and self-assured she wanted to cry. Dog, who waited out by the fence with her, wagged his tail and looked so happy that Laurel was jealous. At least *he* wasn't afraid to show his feelings. And then Joe was there and they were all piling into her car and she was driving again, gripping the steering wheel tightly, her emotions whirling miserably inside her.

Joe was awfully quiet. He sat in the passenger seat and merely stared at her. "What?" she finally said.

"You," he said. "You're a mess."

"Why, thank you." She knew it showed. She couldn't go through saying goodbye to both her child and Joe in a single day and not have it show.

"Want to talk about it?"

"No," she said, her knuckles turning white.

"Well, I do." He hesitated a moment and then said, "Pull off up there." Joe pointed.

"Why?"

"We need to talk is why."

And so she did, and he had her drive for a time up a long, steep road that came out on top of a piñon-dotted ridge that overlooked the entrance to Mesa Verde, the distant mesas crimson in the last light.

They got out, and while Dog sniffed the territory, Laurel and Joe walked to the cliff edge. "So?" she said, folding her arms stiffly, ready for some kind of a lecture about Holly.

"Pretty country," he said, standing very close to her side.

"That's it?" she asked. "You made me drive all the way up here for the view?"

"No," he said. "I made you drive up here to see what you're leaving. That's the eastern edge of the reservation." He pointed out across the desert. "It's never going to change. There's never going to be a city or airports or interstates. In a hundred years, three hundred, it will look the same."

Laurel was silent. She felt her nerves begin to leap under her skin.

"I want my children to be raised here," he said. "And their children. And I want them to know about Coyote and the spirit world of their ancestors. I want them to walk on this land and leave no footprint. Can you understand that?"

She nodded slowly.

"I've been thinking a lot about this," he told her, and she turned a little to catch the dying light on his strong profile. "This whole thing with those drums being buried on our land and with Charlie retiring..." He paused and carefully organized his thoughts. "It's taught me a lesson. I don't want to go it alone anymore. I've been too proud and too selfish, and a man who can't live in his circle of family only brings harm to his people, to the land." And then he was turning to her and his big hands were on her shoulders. Her insides gave away.

"I don't want you to leave me," Joe said in a whisper. "I want you to stay here on this land with me. You can write, you can travel, I don't care as long as you always come back here. Come back to me."

Again, wide-eyed with disbelief, Laurel only nodded.

"I think I've loved you since the minute I first hopped into your car," he went on. "I want you to marry me and have my children."

A nod.

And then Joe Buck cocked his head. "Well? Aren't you going to say something? You always have *something* to say."

She tried to swallow the bubble of joy that welled inside her. "Just give me a minute," she got out.

"I'll do better than that, Laurel, I'll give you a lifetime," he said.

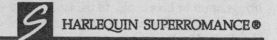
HARLEQUIN SUPERROMANCE®

COMING NEXT MONTH

#618 MEG & THE MYSTERY MAN • Elise Title (*Class of '78*)
Meg Delgado goes undercover as a wealthy socialite on the
cruise ship Galileo. Her mission: to catch a thief. Her suspect:
Noah Danforth, who's got the looks, the charm and the wit of a
Cary Grant. But if Meg isn't who she seems to be, neither is Noah.
And together they discover that deception and disguise lead to
danger…and to romance!

#619 THE COWBOY'S LOVER • Ada Steward
Lexi Conley kidnaps rodeo cowboy Jake Thorn because she
needs him to manage her family's ranch while her father's in the
hospital. It doesn't help that Jake, her sister's ex-husband, may be
the father of Lexi's adopted son—or that he's still the only man
she's ever loved.

#620 SAFEKEEPING • Peg Sutherland (*Women Who Dare*)
An unexpected snowstorm traps Quinn Santori and her two young
companions in an isolated mountain cabin. A cabin that's already
inhabited—by a man toting a gun. They make an odd foursome—
Quinn, the two little girls in her charge and ex-con Whit Sloane.
And chances are their number will increase to five before the snow
melts. *Quinn's about to have a baby!*

#621 THE LOCKET • Brenna Todd
Transported back through time, Erin Sawyer is mistaken for her
double, the adulterous Della Munro, whose husband is a powerful
and dangerous man. But Erin finds herself attracted to his partner,
Waite MacKinnon, a man whose compelling eyes have been
haunting her dreams for what seems like forever.

AVAILABLE NOW:

#614 LAUREL & THE LAWMAN
Lynn Erickson

#615 GONE WITH THE WEST
Dawn Stewardson

#616 PERFECTLY MATCHED
Candice Adams

#617 JAKE'S PROMISE
Helen Conrad

HARLEQUIN SUPERROMANCE®

WHERE ARE THEY NOW?

It's sixteen years since the CLASS OF '78 graduated from Berkeley School for Girls. On that day, four young women, four close friends, stood on the brink of adulthood and dreamed about the directions their lives might take. None could know what lay ahead....

Now it's time to catch up with Sandra, Laurel, Meg and Kim. Each woman's story is told in Harlequin Superromance's new miniseries, THE CLASS OF '78.

ALESSANDRA & THE ARCHANGEL
by Judith Arnold (Sept. 1994)
LAUREL & THE LAWMAN
by Lynn Erickson (Oct. 1994)
MEG & THE MYSTERY MAN
by Elise Title (Nov. 1994)
KIM & THE COWBOY
by Margot Dalton (Dec. 1994)

Look for these titles by some of
Harlequin Superromance's favorite authors,
wherever Harlequin books are sold.

CLASS

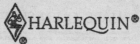

HARLEQUIN®

Don't miss these Harlequin favorites by some of our most distinguished authors!
And now you can receive a discount by ordering two or more titles!

HT#25483	BABYCAKES by Glenda Sanders	$2.99	☐
HT#25559	JUST ANOTHER PRETTY FACE by Candace Schuler	$2.99	☐
HP#11608	SUMMER STORMS by Emma Goldrick	$2.99	☐
HP#11632	THE SHINING OF LOVE by Emma Darcy	$2.99	☐
HR#03265	HERO ON THE LOOSE by Rebecca Winters	$2.89	☐
HR#03268	THE BAD PENNY by Susan Fox	$2.99	☐
HS#70532	TOUCH THE DAWN by Karen Young	$3.39	☐
HS#70576	ANGELS IN THE LIGHT by Margot Dalton	$3.50	☐
HI#22249	MUSIC OF THE MIST by Laura Pender	$2.99	☐
HI#22267	CUTTING EDGE by Caroline Burnes	$2.99	☐
HAR#16489	DADDY'S LITTLE DIVIDEND by Elda Minger	$3.50	☐
HAR#16525	CINDERMAN by Anne Stuart	$3.50	☐
HH#28801	PROVIDENCE by Miranda Jarrett	$3.99	☐
HH#28775	A WARRIOR'S QUEST by Margaret Moore	$3.99	☐
(limited quantities available on certain titles)			

TOTAL AMOUNT	$	
DEDUCT: 10% DISCOUNT FOR 2+ BOOKS	$	
POSTAGE & HANDLING	$	
($1.00 for one book, 50¢ for each additional)		
APPLICABLE TAXES*	$	
TOTAL PAYABLE	$	
(check or money order—please do not send cash)		

To order, complete this form and send it, along with a check or money order for the total above, payable to Harlequin Books, to: **In the U.S.:** 3010 Walden Avenue, P.O. Box 9047, Buffalo, NY 14269-9047; **In Canada:** P.O. Box 613, Fort Erie, Ontario, L2A 5X3.

Name: _____

Address: _____ City: _____

State/Prov.: _____ Zip/Postal Code: _____

*New York residents remit applicable sales taxes.
 Canadian residents remit applicable GST and provincial taxes.

HBACK-OD

"HOORAY FOR HOLLYWOOD" SWEEPSTAKES

HERE'S HOW THE SWEEPSTAKES WORKS

OFFICIAL RULES — NO PURCHASE NECESSARY

To enter, complete an Official Entry Form or hand print on a 3" x 5" card the words "HOORAY FOR HOLLYWOOD", your name and address and mail your entry in the pre-addressed envelope (if provided) or to: "Hooray for Hollywood" Sweepstakes, P.O. Box 9076, Buffalo, NY 14269-9076 or "Hooray for Hollywood" Sweepstakes, P.O. Box 637, Fort Erie, Ontario L2A 5X3. Entries must be sent via First Class Mail and be received no later than 12/31/94. No liability is assumed for lost, late or misdirected mail.

Winners will be selected in random drawings to be conducted no later than January 31, 1995 from all eligible entries received.

Grand Prize: A 7-day/6-night trip for 2 to Los Angeles, CA including round trip air transportation from commercial airport nearest winner's residence, accommodations at the Regent Beverly Wilshire Hotel, free rental car, and $1,000 spending money. (Approximate prize value which will vary dependent upon winner's residence: $5,400.00 U.S.); 500 Second Prizes: A pair of "Hollywood Star" sunglasses (prize value: $9.95 U.S. each). Winner selection is under the supervision of D.L. Blair, Inc., an independent judging organization, whose decisions are final. Grand Prize travelers must sign and return a release of liability prior to traveling. Trip must be taken by 2/1/96 and is subject to airline schedules and accommodations availability.

Sweepstakes offer is open to residents of the U.S. (except Puerto Rico) and Canada who are 18 years of age or older, except employees and immediate family members of Harlequin Enterprises, Ltd., its affiliates, subsidiaries, and all agencies, entities or persons connected with the use, marketing or conduct of this sweepstakes. All federal, state, provincial, municipal and local laws apply. Offer void wherever prohibited by law. Taxes and/or duties are the sole responsibility of the winners. Any litigation within the province of Quebec respecting the conduct and awarding of prizes may be submitted to the Regie des loteries et courses du Quebec. All prizes will be awarded; winners will be notified by mail. No substitution of prizes are permitted. Odds of winning are dependent upon the number of eligible entries received.

Potential grand prize winner must sign and return an Affidavit of Eligibility within 30 days of notification. In the event of non-compliance within this time period, prize may be awarded to an alternate winner. Prize notification returned as undeliverable may result in the awarding of prize to an alternate winner. By acceptance of their prize, winners consent to use of their names, photographs, or likenesses for purpose of advertising, trade and promotion on behalf of Harlequin Enterprises, Ltd., without further compensation unless prohibited by law. A Canadian winner must correctly answer an arithmetical skill-testing question in order to be awarded the prize.

For a list of winners (available after 2/28/95), send a separate stamped, self-addressed envelope to: Hooray for Hollywood Sweepstakes 3252 Winners, P.O. Box 4200, Blair, NE 68009.

CBSRLS

OFFICIAL ENTRY COUPON

"Hooray for Hollywood"
SWEEPSTAKES!

Yes, I'd love to win the Grand Prize — a vacation in Hollywood —
or one of 500 pairs of "sunglasses of the stars"! Please enter me
in the sweepstakes!

This entry must be received by December 31, 1994.
Winners will be notified by January 31, 1995.

Name _____

Address _____ Apt. _____

City _____

State/Prov. _____ Zip/Postal Code _____

Daytime phone number _____
(area code)

Account # _____

Return entries with invoice in envelope provided. Each book
in this shipment has two entry coupons — and the more
coupons you enter, the better your chances of winning!

DIRCBS

OFFICIAL ENTRY COUPON

"Hooray for Hollywood"
SWEEPSTAKES!

Yes, I'd love to win the Grand Prize — a vacation in Hollywood —
or one of 500 pairs of "sunglasses of the stars"! Please enter me
in the sweepstakes!

This entry must be received by December 31, 1994.
Winners will be notified by January 31, 1995.

Name _____

Address _____ Apt. _____

City _____

State/Prov. _____ Zip/Postal Code _____

Daytime phone number _____
(area code)

Account # _____

Return entries with invoice in envelope provided. Each book
in this shipment has two entry coupons — and the more
coupons you enter, the better your chances of winning!

DIRCBS